Dangerous, Deceptive Webs

A Psychosexual Thriller-Erotic-Romance Novel with
Explicit Graphic Sex to Show the Destructive Power of
Inappropriate Sex, Stalking, Sex Addiction, and Incest.

Steven W. Pollard, Ph.D.

iUniverse, Inc.
Bloomington

Dangerous, Deceptive Webs

A Psychosexual Thriller-Erotic-Romance Novel with Explicit Graphic Sex to Show the Destructive Power of Inappropriate Sex, Stalking, Sex Addiction, and Incest.

iUniverse books may be ordered through booksellers or by contacting:

iUniverse
1663 Liberty Drive
Bloomington, IN 47403
www.iuniverse.com
1-800-Authors (1-800-288-4677)

Because of the dynamic nature of the Internet, any web addresses or links contained in this book may have changed since publication and may no longer be valid. The views expressed in this work are solely those of the author and do not necessarily reflect the views of the publisher, and the publisher hereby disclaims any responsibility for them.

Any people depicted in stock imagery provided by Thinkstock are models, and such images are being used for illustrative purposes only.
Certain stock imagery © Thinkstock.

ISBN: 978-1-4620-7210-1 (sc)
ISBN: 978-1-4620-7211-8 (ebk)

Library of Congress Control Number: 2011962177

Printed in the United States of America

iUniverse rev. date:02/10/2012

To my daughter Joy and former wife, Jerry for giving me help and inspiration.
To Polly Wolf for making it a better book.
To Rosemary for excellent help with the final edit.

"Who knows what evil lurks in the hearts of men? The Shadow knows."

Prologue

I hate prologues. It's a novel. Enjoy it.

PART ONE

Chapter 1

Randy Age Eleven

"Come on guys it's a quarter each if you want to see," I told the boys gathered around me on the playground when the after-school program had ended. The grass was all dead and brown with lots of mud spots where the water hadn't all dried up. The boys were all about the same age eleven or twelve. There was a soft breeze blowing and it scattered the dried up parts of dirt from the playground in a circle around the boys next to me as if selecting them.

I couldn't remember when I'd started or how long I'd been doing it. I sensed that the kids weren't my friends and didn't really like me, but I didn't want to care. *At least this way I felt like I had some friends.* I wore old-fashioned coverall pants, held up with a safety pin and old worn-out muddy work boots.

I remembered one of my teachers saying, "You're going to end up in a mental ward." I didn't fit in with the other boys who wore khaki pants, pressed short sleeve shirts, and penny loafers.

I collected the quarters from the kids. "You in, Butch?" I asked a bigger boy, who just shook his head and ran away. "You'd better not tell!" I yelled after him. The rest of the kids began to drift off too. They all knew what the other kids and I were going to do.

"Okay, let's go. And remember you have to keep quiet, or you can't come back," I told them as I led them into the gathering dusk that was fast becoming night.

There was a feeling of excitement and anticipation as the boys play-punched each other as they tripped over tree roots in the path or stepped on twigs that snapped.

"You guys have got to be quieter!" I hissed out in a low whisper.

I led them single file through some woods behind the school, across the railroad tracks, to the "bad side" of town. There was some nervous laughter from the boys, with the ones who had gone before joking and teasing the new guys.

Jerry, one of the new guys, asked me, "Do you get to see them doing it, I mean you know," he stammered, "Are they naked?"

"Can you see her tits?" another one asked excitedly.

"Hey, you can see her tits and they really do it just like dogs. You can see his big dick going in her. And she moans and says she's cuming," one of the old timers said with that self-satisfaction that comes from knowing something the others don't and that made him feel more important, as an insider.

"What's that mean?" asked Erin.

"You'll see," I said. "We're almost there. Quiet or they'll bust us."

As they got to the edge of the woods they looked out on a campsite that was only twenty feet from the line of trees and dense brush that hid the boys. A Coleman lantern on the other side of the couple gave a warm glow of yellow light so that the naked couple was clearly visible.

I had the boys spread out and told them to keep their heads low. They could hear the sounds from the couple on the sleeping bag. The boys raised their heads up and peeked over and through the bushes. The woman was on her hands and knees parallel to the line of trees. The man behind her was doing it. They could see it all.

The boys, especially the new ones, were awe-struck, their eyes wide in disbelief, wonder, and excitement. Some of them were stroking their own hard dicks.

"Oh! god, I'm cumming!"

"Holy cow!" Erin shouted out loud.

The woman's head snapped around and she looked at the tree line, her long, dirty blond hair hanging down and blocking her view. She couldn't see them, couldn't even focus her eyes due to the drugs and alcohol she had been taking, but she shouted at them, "Randy, you get the hell out of here! And you'd better not come back. I'll get you!" The man banged into her with a growing sense of urgency.

Chapter 2

"Let's go guys," I yelled and ran for the trail with the others right behind me. We ran stumbling over roots and rocks until we got to my hiding place in the woods.

"Shit, Erin, why'd you have to yell out?" I gasped, bending over.

"Yeah," Jerry said also gasping for breath, "We didn't even get to see them finish."

"I couldn't help it. I've never seen a naked woman before and they were . . . were really doing it. And that was your mother, Randy," Erin sputtered excitedly.

"Well it was worth the quarter weren't it?" I asked in an irritated voice. *Besides she's just my foster mother*, I thought. The other boys all nodded and most of them were rubbing themselves through their pockets.

None of them thought that what they had been doing was peeping or where it might lead them.

"Shit. Now I can't go home for a couple of hours. I'll have to wait until she's passed out," I said; my anger still covering up my deep hurt I always had towards my foster mother. That was part of my reason for taking kids to spy on her, to get even and hurt her.

"I'll bet you get a whooping," Jerry said.

"Nah, probably not this time. That was a new guy with her and she was pretty drunk. She may not remember it," I said in a more relaxed tone as the boys all lapsed into silence.

Chapter 3

Lisa Age 8

The few walks my biological father had taken with me when I was a child were my best memories of my real father. When I was about age five or six my dad died in a car accident, but being a child, no one ever told me the details. My mother, Elisabeth, told me the same stories over and over, "It would take you and your father over an hour to walk a half a block as you were always stopping and looking at little things on the ground, like ants, leaves, small rocks, odd pieces of trash, and you'd ask your dad, 'Papa, what's this?' You'd bend down, and squat the way only young kids can, and you'd point and put your face a few inches from the object of your interest."

I loved to hear the stories about my dad and myself. I know it made me feel lonely and vulnerable to anyone who paid attention to me. I felt bad that I didn't really remember him. I had fiery red hair and alabaster skin. My parents didn't know where the hair or skin came from as they both had brown hair and were olive skinned.

My mother was a young and very attractive woman but was voraciously bitter after my father's sudden death. She would often complain to me "Now I don't have anyone." It was like she had forgotten about me, as though I didn't count. *I'll try to fill the void but I can't possibly take over my father's role.* My father's estate was large enough so that we could live comfortably.

About two years after my father's death, my mother told me, "I've started dating an older man, Thomas Bancroft. He is 15 years older than me and has plenty of old family wealth."

Mr. Bancroft had his own manufacturing company and pursued my mother with passion. They were married when I was eight and I got to be the flower girl in the wedding. "You're a nice young lady," Mr. Bancroft told me and he treated me politely but was very distant, like he didn't really know how to treat me. *Things will be better now that my mother is married again.* Things were better for my mother, she wasn't depressed anymore and we had moved into Mr. Bancroft's huge mansion in the richest neighborhood of Deerfield just outside of Cleveland Ohio.

For me, although I had any of the material things I wanted, things got worse. My mother spent all her time with Thomas and was always going on trips with him. I was left with the snooty live-in maid and an even stodgier butler, neither of whom provided any love or emotional support. They weren't mean to me but I was just another person to be looked after.

I spent most of my time alone in my room, playing computer role-playing games and drawing. I made up fantastic stories of princes who conquered the world and beat back the bad kings. I spent most of my time in my head making up my own world where I'm loved and happy. I liked it there and was happy and could laugh. It was as though I had a real life.

Chapter 4

Randy Age Eleven

After getting back with the boys to my hiding spot in the woods, I thought, *I need something to get their attention.* "Want to have some fun?" I asked, looking around with a crooked smile. The boys nodded and laughed, as they were still high from the sex they'd seen. We were in the deep woods with many tall older trees and several large boulders in a clearing down the trail from my camp. I pulled two glass pop bottles from behind a tree. They were about a quarter filled with gasoline and some oil with the tops covered by tinfoil. I pulled off the top off one and stuffed a rag halfway inside. "You guys ever seen a 'Molotov cocktail?'" *I remember how excited I was when I found out how to make them.*

They shook their heads, not sure what I was going to do. "Watch this," I said as I pulled a lighter from my pocket. I lit the rag and held the bottle in my right hand. "Watch that big rock over there," I said, pointing to a boulder about 15 yards down the hill from them. I threw the pop bottle hard, in a high arc. I was thin but wiry and pretty strong.

The bottle shattered on the rock and was followed by a large boom and a ball of flame as the gas fumes exploded.

"Holy cow!" Erin exclaimed again for the second time that night.

I could feel my dick getting hard and wanted to keep my friends excited. I stuffed a rag in the second bottle, lit it and threw. The second explosion wasn't as exciting as the first one to the other boys, but I still had a woody.

The other boys, though excited, were nervous and talked about having to get home. They couldn't wait to get home to jerk-off. Masturbating in front of each other wasn't something they had tried yet.

"Ah, come on," I whined, "You guys can stay a little longer." The other boys were talking excitedly as they began to wander off. It wasn't long before I was left alone in the woods. I jerked off to thoughts of the fire and the image of my foster mother's tits swinging back and forth.

Later, I reached into the hiding place where I kept my quart-sized money jars, pulled one out, unscrewed the lid, and dropped in the quarters. The jar was almost full and I had two others that were full. I knew I'd have to take them to the store to change them for dollar bills. However, I hadn't thought of a good excuse to tell the clerk if she asked where I'd gotten all the quarters. Anyway, I enjoyed just having them, like a security blanket. *There isn't anything I want to buy; if there were something I wanted I'd just figure out how to steal it from somebody.*

I didn't even think about getting some new clothes. *I didn't think that stealing was wrong; it was just something you did. That's what Bobby, my stepfather said.*

Sometimes Randy wondered where his life was going. The few times he did think about it and looked back at his life, he saw mostly major problems in the future. He just didn't know what they would be.

Chapter 5

Lisa Age Ten-Twelve

About twice a year Mr. Bancroft would take my mother and me to visit his half-brother, my Uncle Vincent, in Northern Italy. Mr. Bancroft told me, "I have some business with Uncle Vincent. And then your mother and I are going traveling for a few weeks. But you'll have Uncle Vincent to keep you company."

That was fine with me because I really love my Uncle, as he was always very kind to me. We took long walks together and he read books to me and he talked to me like I was an adult. He listened to me and took me seriously but not so seriously that we couldn't have fun.

He paid lots of attention to me. We would play board games and he would tickle me and bathe me and helped me make up elaborate games. He told me, "We have to keep these games secret from your mommy and daddy." *Well he's not my real dad anyway,* I thought. He taught me the basics of cooking and how to appreciate music, fine wine, and art.

I loved my Uncle Vincent. He gave me lots of hugs. My mother almost never gave me any hugs since my father died and Mr. Bancroft never touched me except to occasionally, absent mindedly, pat me on my head.

I craved and loved the attention and hugs I got from Uncle Vincent. I loved the visits to Italy to see him and about twice a year he'd come to Deerfield to visit. We always found time to be alone. He seemed to be the only adult who understood me and accepted me. When he wasn't around I spent most of my time in my make-believe world in my head.

I can tell Uncle Vincent anything and he understands and listens; I feel very close to and loved by him yet I somehow feel something about our relationship is wrong.

Unfortunately my Uncle died shortly before I entered the sixth grade. The loss of his compassionate understanding was severe.

I miss him, but part of me is glad he is gone but I don't know why and I try to not let myself think about the secret games we played. It was after his loss that I became much more private about things like bathing and wouldn't even let my mother in the bathroom with me. My mother just thought it was puberty and so forced me to listen to the "talk" about boys etc. Both my mother and I were so uncomfortable about the subject that it was never discussed again.

School had been the same for as long as I could remember. My mother, until she remarried, and then the butler would drive me and drop me off in front of the school.

I would lug my bulky black book bag and walk over to the low brick wall that surrounded the flagpole. I'd sit or stand by myself waiting for the bell to ring. I never hung out with any friends. I didn't really have any. While the other kids waited for the school doors to open they gathered in groups, the jocks, the preppies, the druggies, the geeks, the Goths, and even those who didn't have a group hung out together. I knew I didn't fit in and had quit trying.

I look more like a Goth than anything. I wore almost exclusively black, black jeans, black T-shirts, black scarves and black wristbands and lived my hidden life in my head.

Sometimes, just so my mother couldn't say I wore nothing but black, I varied my costume to dark grey or purples. I felt like an outcast but I wasn't lonely. It's just the way I am, I told myself. My white skin was a sharp contrast to my dark clothes and bright red hair. I wanted to wear dark eye shadow but my mother wouldn't let me. It hadn't been until high school that I'd been able to talk my mother into letting me get my ears pierced. I wanted a tongue ring and an eyebrow ring but knew I'd never be able to get them.

My red hair was the only spot of color about me. One time I tried dying it black with blue streaks. "Far out!" some of the kids said to me. They weren't mean to me. Most of the time they just ignored me and I returned the same. My mother was mortified by my hair dye, and that secretly pleased me.

Chapter 6

Randy Age Eleven

About a year after coming to live with my current foster parents, the Canfields, I had found a cave hidden in a gulley deep in the woods. I'd stumbled into it, falling down a jagged crack that was covered by twigs and leaves. Lucky not to have broken anything, I looked around and found that the crack I had fallen into slanted down and then widened out into a large open area. At first I'd been shaken from my fall and then scared there might be a bear or other animal in the cave. It smelled moldy but there weren't any animal smells. Water dripped from parts of the ceiling; there was just enough light from the crack I'd fallen through to see the outlines of the cave. There were some large dry areas and some small holes at the top of the cave and what looked like some light coming from the far side of the cave.

I rushed home and got a flashlight to explore the cave some more. There was a small pool of fresh water that flowed up from a spring somewhere below, and another very small opening to the cave on the far side of the hill.

It had been filled with rocks, but with some work, I was able to open a hole big enough to crawl through and found myself on a hillside covered with scrub trees and weeds.

About fifty yards away was an old, once red, barn and about one hundred yards from that, an old farmhouse. The wood on both was silvered with age and both had some broken windows that looked like no one had been in them for quite some time. I watched the farmhouse and barn for several days and nights but I never saw any activity at either place.

When I explored it, I found the barn covered in dust and cobwebs were everywhere. It had the feeling of abandoned property, yet when I flicked on a light switch a light came on. In what looked like a big workbox at the back of the barn I found some electrical wire, which was wound around a big wooden spool with ends that must have been thirty-six inches in diameter; beside the box was what turned out to be a live electrical outlet. There were other electrical parts in the box; plugs, sockets, pliers and other tools. I was hyped about my find and how I might be able to use it thanks to my foster father, Bobby Ray, teaching me some basics about electrical wiring.

Over the next several weeks, I gradually made myself a home in the cave. I'd broken into the local Boy Scout shed and stolen a canvas cot, blankets, a sleeping bag, an old pillow, a Coleman lantern, cook stove, a trenching tool, and fuel. I didn't see anything wrong with stealing; that's just the way life is; if you wanted something you figured out a way to steal it and not get caught. Bobby Ray also had taught me that. I set up the old army cot and my Coleman Lantern in a dry area with the cook stove nearby.

A few nights later I connected a plug to one end of the spool of wire and rolled the spool through the front of the barn and out toward the back of the barn. I made a hole in the back wall. It was easy to do as the wood near the ground was mostly rotted away; all I needed was to push a screwdriver through several times to make a hole. I pushed the plug through. I went back inside and secured the plug to the outlet but didn't plug it in yet. I rolled an old tire over the outlet to hide it in case anyone happened to come into the barn, though there was no evidence that anyone had been there in a long time. Later I'd have to go back and plug it in.

I rolled the wire spool from the back of the barn up to the trees and the crawl hole to my cave. It was a real struggle and sometimes I didn't think I'd make it, but I kept trying and did. Using my trenching tool, I went back and buried the wire several inches under the ground and covered the trench with dirt, leaves, grass and twigs so that it looked like the rest of the area. I was very happy. I'd done it all by my self and now I had power for my home.

A couple of years after I had been placed with them, Bobby Ray lost his job and started drinking every day and was home most of the time. He beat up on Ruth Ann so badly that he put her in the hospital. That time I had again been hiding in the bushes behind the house but I could still hear the yelling and cursing. Ruth Ann was knocked out the back door and Bobby Ray came out after her and hit Ruth Ann in the mouth with his fist.

I felt like I was getting the beating, like I had in the past from Bobby Ray. I wanted to stop my tears but I couldn't and I felt like a coward for not going out and stopping Bobby Ray. *I'll show you I'm no coward*, I thought; but didn't know how I'd do it.

"You bitch, you cunt, you whore," Bobby Ray kept shouting. I watched in fear from my hiding place and saw a tooth fly out of Ruth Ann's mouth and the splatters of bright red blood on her white summer dress. It was like I was feeling the blows myself. Bobby Ray hit her some more even when she was passed out.

I kept on crying silently, too scared to go out and try to help, and too scared to run away. I wanted to go out and hold my mom and comfort her but I couldn't; I was too scared. I repeated to myself that I was too much of a coward.

Eventually Bobby Ray sobered up enough to take his wife to the ER, and claimed she'd been in an accident. The hospital personnel suspected abuse but, as too often happens in abuse cases, Ruth Ann was too scared to save herself, let alone me. They couldn't get any information about it from Ruth Ann or me.

After that last beating, Ruth Ann didn't even try to protect me. She joined her husband in his drinking and in her confused and drunken state, she started hitting me too, telling me, "It's all your fault."

I began to believe it was my fault and started hiding from her also so that I wouldn't start anymore fighting. I started staying out in the woods behind their doublewide in my cave and sneaking in at night hoping to find some food. I'd then stay out all night alone and scared, waiting until they were gone for the day before I'd return to the house.

Chapter 7

Lisa Age Twelve

The first three grades had been easy for me. I made all A's without really trying, I was so smart. In the fourth and fifth grades it had been harder and harder to keep up and complete all my work. In the sixth grade, it all seemed to catch up with me. I couldn't keep up with all that stupid homework and began to give up. My grades fell to F's.

Combined with my dark colored clothes, this was too much for my mother.

"Lisa. That's enough," my mother said. "I'm taking you to see a shrink. There is something wrong with you."

"Nothing's wrong with me mother! You're the one who needs a shrink! You can't make me go!"

"Don't you use that tone of voice with me young lady. You'll be grounded if you don't cooperate." *Don't use that tone of voice. It was one of my mother's favorite sayings.*

"Oh! Mother!"

The psychologist, Dr. Laster, was very nice and gave me lots of tests and took a history from my mother and talked to my teachers. I didn't mind it.

I thought, *he's kind of goofy, using puppets and telling me "knock knock" jokes. I bet he hadn't had any friends in school either with a name like Laster. I can imagine the teasing he must have gotten with a name like that.*

Dr. Laster had scheduled a session to give the results of his evaluation to my mother. I insisted that I be allowed to listen. My mother objected but the Doctor said it was okay and that he believed it was good for me to hear the results.

The Doctor addressed most of his comments to me, though he also occasionally looked at my mother.

Smiling at me, Dr. Laster told me that I had what is called ADHD Attention Deficit Hyperactivity Disorder. He said they used to call it ADD, Attention Deficit Disorder, but they changed the name just to confuse everybody. They are both the same. You can have it with or without hyperactivity. In my case it was without hyperactivity, so it's called the Inattentive Type.

I just stared at him and seemed to be drifting off.

"Lisa," he said, grabbing my attention, "you with me? Look me in the eye. See what you just did? That is one of the symptoms, being easily distracted, having a short attention span, and getting off track easily. Lisa," he said to bring me back again.

"This doesn't mean you're retarded or stupid," Dr. Laster continued. "In fact the tests I did with you indicate that you have superior intelligence. Unfortunately, they also indicate that in addition to ADHD, you have a learning disability or LD. You're Dyslexic."

"What do you mean?" my mother asked.

"Both of these are neurologic disorders. The ADHD is primarily a problem with paying attention to things that aren't inherently interesting to Lisa."

"So that's why she can do her art and play computer games for hours but can't seem to finish her homework assignments?" my mother asked.

"Yes, that's right. But Dyslexia is different from ADHD." Dr. Laster gave me a handout that explained that Dyslexia is a broad term that encompasses the complex brain activity of encoding information from the external world and decoding it again in the brain and then putting it back out in written or verbal form.

I had drifted off again. "Lisa look at me," Dr. Laster said pleasantly but sternly, "These are real neurological, that means in the brain, disorders that . . ."

"I know what neurological means!" I snapped. I wanted to hear the results of my evaluation but I didn't like being talked down to.

"Okay, that's the bad news. You have these problems. The good news is that now both you and your parents know about it and you can get help."

"What kind of help?" my mother asked.

Dr. Laster said that we could get some family therapy to help me learn ways of coping with my symptoms of ADHD.

The handout that Dr. Laster had given me was really great in explaining that it is a matter of being super-organized, using lots of checklists, and other reminders to help me.

Dr. Laster continued saying, "This has to be done in a matter of fact way without any anger or lectures. Lisa isn't doing this because she's mad at anyone. She has some problems with the way her brain works. Medication sometimes helps, but in my experience, usually only for the hyperactive type of ADHD."

"I won't take any pills!" I snapped.

Dr. Laster said that I didn't have to take any pills and for the LD I could get tutoring and accommodations from the school. For example, I could be allowed to give oral reports since it takes me so long to write them. I could also get and use a computer to help with spelling and many other things. The key thing is to emphasize what you're good at and like, and learn to get the rest of the stuff done as best you can. You have got to train yourself to do the things that don't interest you first, and then reward yourself by doing the things you like.

"One of the other symptoms, or I should say consequences, of these disorders is that you probably don't fit in socially."

"Duh! You finally got something right, Doc," I said sullenly. Secretly I was happy to know that there was something wrong with me and that that was why I was the way I was. Somehow that made it easier.

Chapter 8

Randy Age Thirteen

Watching my mother have sex with guys wasn't very exciting to me anymore. It was just a way to make some money; pretend I had some friends, and besides, she wasn't my real mother. I didn't know what had happened to my birth mother or who my father was. I thought the name on my birth certificate, Randolf Parson Jr., must have been made up.

I had been in a series of foster homes since as early as I could remember. I'd been told that my mother had abandoned me in an alley outside a bar just after my birth.

I remember one time, it was a Thursday night and I had just finished washing the dishes and my foster mom came and took just one look, and I could tell she was mad.

"What's wrong with you Randy? Can't you do anything right?" she said in her harshest voice. "Just look at the grease you left on those dishes. You'll have to do them all over again," she said glaring at me.

"I guess I can understand how your mother just walked off and left you in the slime in the alley, at least that's what I'd do if you were mine."

I knew that she wanted to hurt me, and she always told me how worthless I was. I didn't want to believe I was worthless, but I began to feel I was. I didn't say anything back; I'd learned not to do that. I just did a slow burn. She'd just confirmed what I'd learned from all my prior foster parents. No matter how hard I tried or how I smiled and tried to be polite, I was never good enough.

I had been with my current foster mom and her husband living in Deerfield, Ohio, since I turned eight or nine. I was thin but tall for my age with short cut golden blond hair. I had a natural cheerful smile and nice blue eyes.

I didn't have any clear memories of the prior foster homes, though I did remember several broken bones and had burn scars on my arms and butt.

What wasn't visible, however, were the deep emotional scars inflicted by various other foster parents.

Even at age four I'd earned a reputation as "being likely to run away." I didn't know what else to do to get away from the pain. I had tried hard to get along with my various foster parents and to make friends. I was also very cunning and wiry; could run like the wind in my very old tennis shoes.

When I thought about my past I remembered seeing several counselors or social workers and vaguely remembered someone saying I needed love as well as discipline; well I'd gotten the discipline but very little love. At best I was just another mouth to feed and a source of income to the foster parents; they usually spent very little of the money they received for upkeep on me. I remember one shrink saying that I would end up a psychopath and in jail or a mental ward. I didn't even know what a psychopath was until I began living with Bobby Ray and even then I didn't know what the word meant but it seemed to me that he must be one.

At first, Ruth Ann, my current foster mother, had been different. She'd been loving and caring, especially when the foster care authorities came around to "inspect." We lived in a doublewide house trailer that had been mounted on cement posts. It was out in the country and there was a big yard, pasture, and woods out back.

Ruth Ann was married to Bobby Ray Canfield. He was tall at about six feet and heavily muscled. Mostly he wore various T-shirts that usually had some anti-authority theme, jeans and heavy work boots. As a stepdad he was okay until he was drinking, which was most every Friday after work and all weekend and some days during the week. Sometimes he'd take me on jobs with him and show me how to do basic carpentry and electrical wiring and how to steal stuff I needed.

When he was in one of his more philosophical moods, Bobby Ray had often talked to me about beating up his younger brother all the time. He was kind to me and at those times and it seemed like he cared for me.

Whenever he was mad, angry, or hurt Bobby Ray enjoyed watching his younger brother crying until one time he came to suddenly realize the truth in his life. It jolted him. He wanted his brother to feel as bad as he did because he felt bad. It dawned on him that everyone in life had this hurt. "Somewhere in his or her heart everybody is hurting," he told me like he was trying to teach me about life.

Bobby Ray believed that he would never get away from it nor would anyone else. His life experiences seemed to support his belief. The hurt, was always there for a variety of reasons: his being poor, being sick or alone, not being loved, not getting what he wanted, for being bad, or not good enough for other people. There was always something that was devouring him and he knew that the same types of things in other people were eating their hearts out.

I wondered why, and he said a priest had told him, "God made us this way so that we would need each other for comfort from the pain."

I didn't seem to understand much of this but I took it all in as one of life's important lessons, I just didn't know why.

When he was drunk Bobby Ray had a mean temper, like a pissed off scorpion, and was likely to hit anything that got in his way. I had gotten my share of lickings, sometimes for spilling something at the table, but most times I didn't know why.

Bobby Ray would sometimes call me over and hit me in the face and call me a "little fag" if I cried. Other times

Bobby Ray would take off his belt that had a big buckle and lash out with it, hitting me anywhere he could.

I learned to hide out behind the bushes close to the doublewide when Bobby Ray came home, until I knew if he'd been drinking. At first Ruth Ann had tried to protect me from Bobby Ray but if she got in the way Bobby Ray would just beat the shit out of her first and then go looking for me. Ruth Ann kept telling Bobby Ray not to leave any marks on "the boy" or the foster care inspectors would take me away.

They needed the money they got from caring for me. She did care for me but not as much as for the money. The little money she made as a waitress and topless dancer at a local bar was barely enough to pay the electric bill and buy gas and some food. Bobby Ray drank up and gambled away most of the money he made working for a local construction company. Ruth Ann's mother had left the lot and trailer to her so they didn't have to pay rent, but money was scarce.

He didn't know how to say it; didn't know the words for it. But despite his joy of the night sounds, and escape from abuse when he went to his cave, he was still profoundly lonely and remembered what Bobby Ray had said about anger. He'd cuddle up with his Teddy Bear and rock himself to sleep.

I could even cut school if I wanted, but I didn't do that too often as I liked the science classes, learning how things worked and how to use computers and even the acting classes.

I knew I was basically bright; had a curious mind and was a quick learner. When I did cut school, I knew how the school operated. They'd send a note through the mail asking why I hadn't been in school. It was really simple. I would go home in the early afternoon before either Ruth Ann or Bobby Ray would get home and check the mail and if there was a letter from the school I'd use my foster mom's stationary and a stamp and send a short note back saying that Randy had been sick and to please excuse his absences. And then I'd forge her signature. No one ever checked.

I had begun clicking a ballpoint pen, I had found, over and over again. In some mysterious way this seemed to help me cope.

Chapter 9

Randy Age Fourteen

Bobby Ray moved out several months after the last beating. He'd gotten drunk and announced he was leaving and not coming back, claiming he'd had enough of her whoring around.

Ruth Ann couldn't convince him she hadn't been, because in reality she had been for extra tips. He got in his truck and left. Ruth Ann started drinking more and she'd come home drunk most every Friday and Saturday night, usually with a different man. She fucked them on the living room couch or fucked them in bed with the door open. I watched my foster mother fuck in fascination as I played with myself. It was a way to take away the bad feelings, at least for a while.

She usually passed out and sometimes the men would stay and some times they'd go. If they passed out too, I would go through their pants and steal any money I found, it was just normal behavior for me.

Chapter 10

Randy Age Fifteen

As I got older I was less interested in just looking, and one time, after my foster mother passed out, after the man left, I tried to have sex with her. I put my penis in her but didn't feel anything and soon lost my woody.

I knew that I wanted something more than sex with my passed out stepmother. I was getting tired of charging the kids from school to watch my foster mother have sex. As I got older I stayed out in my cave more and more. I didn't have any real friends. I didn't fit in. If I hadn't had my foster mother to let the other kids watch, I wouldn't have had anyone to hang with. I soon needed more excitement to ward off my loneliness, and since I had nothing else to do I started taking walks at night. I felt more alive when I knew everyone was asleep in their homes.

I carried my supplies with me: lighter, knife, pliers, lighter fluid, some small rope, gloves, and my ballpoint pen. *You never knew when you'd need something, living by yourself in the woods.* Sometimes I wouldn't go home for several days at a time. I felt more at peace by myself in the woods. I'd build fires and stare into the flame and feel the warmth, clicking my pen in and out. Sometimes I'd stick my hand in the fire just to make the pain real. It was a way of dealing with my pain that gave me some control over it. The pain made it so I could jerk-off better and get release.

One time a scrawny stray cat followed me into the woods. I fed it and tied a rope around its neck and tied the rope to a tree. I was hurting, and I wanted to hurt someone else the way Bobby Ray told me he did. I took a can of lighter fluid, and without thinking about it, sprayed the fluid all over the cat.

The cat hissed and tried to get away but was held by the rope. This was the second cat I'd tied up. I hadn't tied the noose tight enough around the neck of the first cat and it was able to pull free and run off. I lit a small rag and threw it on the cat. The cat seemed to explode with flames and the screeches and yowls were like nothing I had heard before. My pain was gone and I jerked-off. It didn't take long for the cat to die. I didn't feel anything for the cat; it was just something I used to get my own needs met.

Chapter 11

Dr. Longfellow

Aroused by her last therapy session, Dr. Longfellow eagerly anticipated getting home to her husband. She was on her way out of the psychology clinic. It had been a long day and the heels of her shoes tapped rhythmically on the wooden floor as she strode quickly down the hallway. Her light blond hair brushed her shoulders. She was tall and her stride was long, causing her nipples to tingle as her breasts swayed under her silk bra and blouse. Friends said she looked like Meryl Streep. As she walked towards the back door she heard voices and laughter coming from the open door of the student carrels.

At the end of the day graduate students gathered in the carrels that were provided as a place for them to study. Instead of studying however, they usually ended up playing "Primary Process." It was a game of free association where anyone would call out a word and then someone else would reply with another word. It was fun. There weren't really any rules nor any winners or losers unless someone didn't say anything.

There wasn't supposed to be any censoring; yet they had to work at breaking social politeness—the women more than the men. In response to a word, they were supposed to say the first word that popped into their minds. It usually swung into unrestrained sexual content. They were studying subjects like Freud and the subconscious mind. Free association was also taught by the professors at the University of Cleveland's Clinical Psychology Department as both an assessment and therapy tool.

The students, most of them single, about an equal number of males and females, loved to play the game as it offered a guilt-free way to talk about sex.

Dr. Longfellow's stride slowed as she neared the door to the carrels and stopped just outside as she listened to the game.

"Eat," a female voice said.

"Pussy," a male voice replied.

"Cat," another female.

"Hair," a male.

"Pie, "another female.

Dr. Longfellow walked in with a rueful smile. Surprised to see her, several students moved from their slouched positions, dropping their feet off the tabletops to the floor, to try to appear more "studious," or at least more respectful.

"Hi Dr. Longfellow," Hart said somewhat sheepishly. A few other students echoed his words but most just nodded their heads in greeting. A chair was accidentally knocked over making a loud clang in the now silent room; conversation had stopped. No one seemed to know if they should invite her in, which might be perceived as presumptuous, or not invite her in, which might be perceived as rude. Students didn't want to irritate professors who would be grading them.

Dr. Longfellow recognized Hart and most of the other students. "It's okay. I used to play the game myself," she said. "But you might want to keep the volume down and the door closed. There might be patients walking by."

"Yeah. Okay," Hart said smiling.

"Okay. Have fun," Dr. Longfellow said as she walked out closing the door behind her. *Well, they're all going to be Doctors some day and will be making life and death decisions, saving marriages, and preventing suicides among many other tragic things that plague peoples' lives. That's why we all played that game. Life is a primary process. And to do therapy you have to be real. Thoughts are important and often lead to the feelings.* She did, however, wonder why Hart had been so reluctant to enter therapy.

In the carrels, the door now closed, the game continued.

"I'd like to longfellow her," one of the males said.

"Spread," a female said.

"Farm," said another.

"I wouldn't mind plowing her."

Ask any graduate psychology student why they want to become doctors, and they'd say to help others or if they were more honest with themselves, they'd say that they wanted to live vicariously through the intimate lives of their patients. Hart was different, he seemed to be more interested in working on understanding himself so that he could better help others. Part of my job was to teach the psychology interns that all we are is a reflection of our parents and our thoughts, and every relationship is often just a repeat of the patterns unless we learn to change them.

As therapists it is hard to separate our personal lives from our professional lives. It's a walk on a high wire without a net; if we totally separate our selves we lose the therapeutic alliance and if we give to much of ourselves we lose our purpose and it becomes more about us than the patient, Dr. Longfellow thought as she walked on.

Chapter 12

Hart Age Twenty-eight

All of the clinical graduate students had to participate in their own therapy. It was a necessary and very useful part of their training. I remember the very first time I'd gone to see a shrink when I had been an undergraduate and knew I needed help with my life. It was like the session was just yesterday; I could still taste the bitterness I'd been left with.

At that first session, years ago, Dr. Hall had said, "Come in Mr. Albertino. Please be seated."

Dr. Hall had indicated a chair in front of his desk. He had greeted me with a handshake and then walked behind his desk sat down and waited for me to speak.

When I hadn't said anything, Dr. Hall said, "Well, why don't we start by you telling my why you're here."

"Cause I'm all fucked up Doc," I had blurted out in obvious irritation. I didn't know what to say or how this was supposed to work. I was angry and frustrated.

"Well," Dr. Hall had said, leaning back in his chair with a yellow legal pad on a clip board and pen in hand, "Can you tell me about that?"

"Yeah. What do you want to know?"

"What do you want to tell me?" Dr. Hall had replied.

"How do I get un-fucked up?"

"How did you get fucked up?"

I had started to tell Dr. Hall about my brother, Jeff, dying and about all that had happened since then. I was crying and shaking as I related my history.

Periodically, Dr. Hall had said something like, "I see," or "How did you feel about that?" Or "Can you tell me more?" or "Uh-huh." He was always busily writing something on his yellow pad.

I had desperately wanted some advice about how to cope with my life. My drinking was out of control and I was passively suicidal. I drove drunk and at excessive speeds, not caring if I lived or died. I had become more and more frustrated with the "therapy" session.

Towards the end of the "45-minute hour," Dr. Hall had looked at his watch and said, "We'll talk about your parents next session."

"But what am I supposed to do!" I had exploded.

Dr. Hall had seemed to ignore my question and emotional outburst, looking at his calendar, and asked, "Will next Tuesday at 3 PM be okay?"

"Sure," I had muttered, looking at the floor.

I had left the shrink's office in a foul mood, muttering to myself, "If that's what therapy is I don't need it."

I didn't go back. *The body is made to live, but when things get too tough, some turn to suicide,* I thought to myself as I walked out.

Chapter 13

Hart Age Twenty-nine

Because of this prior experience with "therapy," even though it was several years ago, I dreaded having to go to therapy as part of my clinical training. *Each body is a person,* Hart thought, *and deserves respect. We're born; we live; we die. We put things to rest only to have them rise up and smack us again and again.*

My major professor had confronted me for the fourth time and told me I couldn't graduate until I completed a course of therapy.

"What do you mean, 'completed?'" I asked, although I knew from talking to the other students.

"When your therapist thinks you're ready to leave therapy. It won't be that bad, Hart, and we've all had to do it. It will make you a better therapist and a better person. Life is the most fragile unpredictable thing," he went on, "and constantly surprises both the therapist and patient. Only one thing about life we can be sure of is 'it ain't over till it's over.'"

Chapter 14

Hart Age Twenty Nine

Sullenness emanated from me as I walked in for my first appointment. "I guess you want to talk about my dead brother," I stated belligerently.

Dr. Longfellow looked at my chart. Johnson Hartford Albertino, or "Hart" as he was known, was in his fourth year and had completed all his course work for his Ph.D. in Clinical Psychology and was finishing his internship on the Mental Ward of the local hospital. He was of average height with a swimmer's muscular build and had a stiff bearing left over from his days in the military. His salt and pepper hair was cut close to his head.

"Please be seated Mr. Albertino," Dr. Longfellow said, indicating a comfortable leather recliner that was at an angle across from her own chair. Her desk was along one wall of her office and wasn't between them.

Wanting to put him at ease, Dr. Longfellow said, "You may call me Marge or Dr. Longfellow, whichever you're comfortable with. May I call you Hart?"

"Sure," I said, beginning to relax despite myself. I liked her easy style. She wasn't one of the regular faculty members but was a full-time clinical staff member of the training clinic. She supervised some of the practicum courses.

I had checked her out with the other graduate students before going to see her.

"She's beyond hot," one had said, "but the oven is closed to all but the baker."

"I'd like to bake her," another one said.

The consensus seemed to be that she was cool and kept the information given to her in confidence.

She was in her mid-forties, married, and had two grown children. She was attractive and stylish in her dress and very professional in her manner. Her dark blue eyes seemed to twinkle. The single black pearl at her throat accented her calf-length dark blue skirt of some kind of very soft material and a cream colored blouse. Crossing her legs, she leaned back in her chair as I checked her out.

She was sizing him up also. Again, she took notice of his bearing left over from his military training. He wore casual college dress with a short-sleeved sport shirt, grey slacks, and penny loafers. She knew from his history that he was twenty-nine years old and had never been married. "Do I pass?" she asked smiling.

"Oh yeah, sure," I replied, embarrassed. "It's just that my first time in therapy wasn't great." As I continued telling her of my experience with Dr. Hall, I found myself liking her and it felt very easy to share with her.

"I hope this time goes better," she said. "I do need to get some background information so I will be asking questions and listening, but I promise you I'll also be giving you some specific alternatives for you to consider using to cope with your problems."

"How do you know I have any problems now!" I asked bristling.

"You are human aren't you?" Marge replied with a slight smile.

"Yeah I think I am," I replied with my own slight smile. "I lost a part of my life; my whole life and just wanted to blow someone up," I continued with a repressed raw edge to my voice.

"Where would you like to start?" she asked.

"I don't know."

"Okay then, how about you tell me how your brother died?" She had known of the death from the family history questionnaire I had completed prior to my scheduled appointment.

"I don't really know. I was seventeen and he was twenty. He'd been working construction with a crew out in the country for a week. When he came home, he got sick, was hospitalized, and within a week he was dead."

"How did it happen?"

Hart got up and started pacing in the small office. "Like I said, I don't really know. I was in high school at the time. I never knew. No one ever told me and I'm not even sure the doctors knew what killed him. Some kind of meningitis.

All I knew was he was home, then hospitalized, and then dead."

I shrugged my shoulders, sat and looked down at the floor. "I remember when I went to visit him in the hospital; he seemed to be in a semi-coma. He couldn't talk or even move much. There wasn't anybody else there when I went in to see him.

"He was just lying there with an IV in his arm." I shifted my feet and waved my arms wondering what to do. "I wanted to do something to help. He seemed to indicate he needed to pee, and the nurse didn't come even though I pushed the call button over and over."

"That must have been awful for you."

"Well, yeah it was." I stopped and grabbed a Kleenex from the box by the chair to wipe my tears away.

"It wasn't so bad. I left him shortly after that as I had a student government club meeting to go to that night. I didn't make it back to visit again until two days later.

I knew something was terribly wrong when I walked down the hospital hall towards his room. My mom was walking from his room sobbing with her head down; her whole body was shaking. I asked her what was wrong but she couldn't answer and just shambled away.

A nurse came out of his room and told me he was dead. I couldn't believe it. I was in shock. I couldn't believe it.

Tears were flowing down my cheeks as I talked. "It's okay to cry," Dr. Longfellow said, handing me the box of Kleenex. "Take all the time you need."

"Don't tell me it's all right Doc. It ain't all right. Tell me what to do," I said angrily.

"Okay. First, take a deep breath, and hold it," Marge said as she demonstrated by taking a deep breath, "and then let it out slowly. Let your shoulders drop and tell yourself to relax. Okay, that's it," she said as I followed her example. "Now do it again. Can you feel it?"

"Yeah. That does help," I said with a small smile. I took the tissues, wiped my eyes, blew my nose, and threw the tissue into the small trashcan beside the chair.

"Breathing won't take away the pain of the memory but it does help somewhat. What happened next?" Dr. Longfellow asked.

"It's all a haze, jumbled images. My family fell apart completely. My dad disappeared for over a month. Nobody knew where he was. My mom was a basket case. She was crying all the time. Friends and neighbors were always coming over with covered dishes, casseroles. It was gruesome. I went to class just to get out of the house as much as anything. I don't even remember the funeral."

"How did you cope?"

"I don't know. I think I was still in shock," I said shaking my head. "I kept moving and doing all the things I was supposed to do. I graduated from High School, got a summer job. Those kinds of things. I'd been raised a Baptist and tried prayer. The church counselor tried, with all the usual platitudes, about how my brother was in a 'better place.' I didn't buy any of that bullshit. Pardon my language, Doc."

"It's okay."

"If he was in a better place, I was in Hell. We weren't that close, in fact we used to fight a lot, especially when we were younger. I still have a scar from when I tried to club him with a milk bottle and it broke and almost cut my thumb off." I showed the scar to Dr. Longfellow. She didn't say anything, just touched it briefly with her finger and I suddenly felt better. It was like she had connected with me. *Some physical touching is often helpful in establishing a therapeutic relationship.*

"You know that movie about the brothers in the boating accident and one of the brothers dies?"

"Yeah I know it. 'Ordinary People.' I recommend it to my patients."

"My family was like that, not as rich, but we were all torn apart by my brother's death and we weren't allowed to talk about it. I didn't want to start mom crying again and dad never talked about anything anyway. A man was supposed to 'suck it up and get on with things.' Nobody suggested that the family or I get therapy or counseling. And then when I did try that in college. Well I told you about that.

"I had inherited my brother's car and often had dreams that were so real. That he had come home. He wasn't dead, and I was always giving his car back to him. Those dreams seemed so real. I still have them.

"So I sucked it up and pretended that there wasn't anything wrong. My brother had died, so what? The next Fall I went to college, again pretending like nothing was wrong, except I started drinking way too much and was always angry and moody."

I paused for a few minutes. "It didn't keep me from making the Dean's List but I was fucked up and knew it."

Dr. Longfellow noted he hadn't apologized for his language this time, *Progress,* she thought. She was about to make some suggestions for coping when he continued.

"Anyway, Doc," I took a deep breath, "to make my long tale a bit shorter, I graduated from college with a BA in Psychology and was full of anger and very often drunk. This was back during the time they still had the draft. I went into grad school in studio art, to get a deferment, but I couldn't hack the academic bullshit any more.

"I knew I was about to get drafted, and didn't want to be a grunt, so I volunteered and went to OTS: Officers' Training School. And ninety days later, 'by an act of congress' I was made 'an officer and a gentleman' in the US Air Force.

"It was all a joke, Doc," I said shaking my head. "I was still drinking heavily; hell the military encouraged it back then. I volunteered to go to Nam. Instead they sent me to an isolated base in Turkey as a 'nuclear weapons custodian.' Can you believe that shit? God, the tales I could tell you about the military," I paused for a while.

"I hated it, but it was a life-changing experience for me," I said, looking thoughtfully at the floor.

"What do you mean Hart? How did it change your life?"

"Well, there were only a few dozen Americans on the base and no women and it was way out in the boon docks. Everybody was miserable and played the 'Ain't It Awful' game, the one where you complain constantly about everything. Every night, unless you were on duty, everybody went to the 'social club.' They didn't separate the officers from the enlisted and we would drink Jack Daniels, or whatever your choice was, at ten cents a shot, and complain.

"Things changed for me when a guy named Tony got in camp. He wasn't like the others. He didn't play the game. He was happy. He found things to do. I looked at myself, at the others, and at him and told myself I was tired of being tired and depressed and wanted to be like him. I started exercising and finding things to do. I didn't get better overnight. It took me several years and I'm still working on it. But that guy changed my life and he doesn't even know it."

"He didn't change your life, Hart. You changed your life."

"No, Doc, if it hadn't have been for him, I'd still be fucked up."

"He was a good example, but it was you who chose to follow him and make the changes in your life. Give yourself some credit Hart. You were full of anger and rage and didn't know how to cope with it."

"Okay, Doc," I said somewhat unwillingly. "He did help me decide about what I wanted to do with my life. I wanted to help others."

When Hart seemed to be finished I said, "You asked me to give you some coping strategies and you're already using some of my usual suggestions, like exercise and developing a menu of pleasurable activities and doing them on a regular basis. And remember to breathe. I'll give you one more," I said, handing him a rubber band. "This is a very expensive piece of psychological equipment. It's a portable negative self-stimulator."

"Yeah," I laughed taking the rubber band.

"Put it on your wrist like this," she demonstrated, putting a rubber band on her own wrist. "Now pull it back on the inside of your wrist," again she demonstrated. "More, pull it back more," she said as I was following her directions. "Now let it go." Again she demonstrated popping the inside of her wrist. "Stings doesn't it?"

I nodded. "Why would I ask you to do that?" Not waiting for Hart to reply I said, "To demonstrate to you how you hurt yourself with negative thoughts. It's human nature to think things like 'I'm no good; I'm a fuck up.' You can't keep negative thoughts from coming into you head, but what's important is to not dwell on them or to let them make a home in your mind.

"Those negative thoughts hurt just as much and more than the rubber band and it is to remind yourself to stop hurting yourself. Or, if you insist, pop the shit out of yourself."

I laughed, "Okay Doc, you're good. Not at all like my first shrink."

"Well let's stop here for today. You've been doing most of the talking today. Next time, if you want, I have a lot more coping strategies to suggest. I'd like to learn more about your parents if that's okay with you? I see you struggling Hart and I want to help you. Will you let me help you? What is real or not real gets mixed up and we can't always tell them apart. It's my job as your therapist to help you do that, but you're the one who has to actually do it," Dr. Longfellow said.

"Sure. Can we make it next week at the same time?" I asked, looking at my watch. I couldn't believe the whole hour had passed.

"Okay," Dr. Longfellow said. "Shall we make it weekly at the same time for the next several weeks, so that my calendar doesn't get filled up?"

She, like all good shrinks, never took what a patient said at face value but invariably looked for the deeper meaning hidden behind the spoken words. Sometimes it came easily to her and at others it might be days or several sessions before she sussed out the true meaning of the patient's spoken and unspoken words; the origins of their black despair or unrealized ambitions. *With Hart I wasn't sure but felt that something was missing,*

"Okay, Doc." I headed out the door with a light-hearted and yet exhausted feeling. *This wasn't so bad after all,* I thought. She seemed like the mother I'd never had; no, more than that, like the kind of shrink I wanted to become. I didn't know how or if I could, but I wanted to help others the way Dr. Longfellow helped me.

Chapter 15

Randy Age Fifteen

There was a bully, Carl, at school, who often gave me a hard time and threatened to beat me up and take the money I'd just gotten from some kids to "go for the show."

One time, when I'd let my guard down; wasn't paying attention; he'd come up behind me and said, "Hey wise ass, you gonna let me an my buddies watch your mother fuck?"

I knew I was in trouble. I didn't care if Carl and his friends watched but I'd seen Carl beat up other kids for no other reason than that he could. I had avoided Carl and his friends in the past by staying out of their way and running if they came near. I was thin but I could out run them all. This time Carl's buddies had caught me. They had formed a circle around me and the other kids watching in the background backed off knowing something was coming. Carl was the biggest and worst bully in the school. I looked to see if I could find an adult but there were none around. I tired to run but was pushed back into the circle. I was wiry and strong but I was no match for Carl, who was three years older, six inches taller and outweighed me by more than one hundred lbs. Carl was huge, even if most of it was flab.

I landed one punch and tried to kick Carl in the balls but missed and then Carl connected with a big right fist to my chin and I was down. I curled into a fetal position as Carl and his buddies kicked me for several minutes until they ran out of breath. Then they stood around me, took out their dicks, and peed on me while the other kids from the school looked on. No one moved to help me.

Finally Carl and his buddies walked away laughing and yelling jeers at me as they left me lying in a puddle of mud-soaked urine, "By pee boy, see you next time." I was so scared, humiliated, and beaten that I couldn't even move for several minutes. There was one red-headed girl who came towards me to try to offer some help but I shouted at her to go away.

Chapter 16

Randy Plots Revenge

I went to my cave in the woods behind the school rapidly clicking my pen. The clicking gave me something to do, something I could control. Humiliated, I vowed to get revenge as I built a fire to keep warm in the night and plotted. I washed the urine off in the pool in the cave.

I need to know Carl lives. It'll be easy to follow him to his house. I would stay far enough away so that Carl wouldn't never see me.

Two nights later, I snuck from the woods up the dark streets to Carl's house. As I walked I was thinking about how good it would feel to get my revenge. I was getting hard just thinking about it. The hour's walk was nothing to me and I'd brought a coke and a tuna sandwich I'd snuck from my foster home. I was ready to wait all night if I had to. There was a street light just down from Carl's house. I thought, *it might make me too visible.* So I picked up some rocks and by the fifth throw I got the light out.

A man came out of Carl's house and looked about and called, "Who's there?" I wanted to shout out that I was there to kill Carl, but I didn't; I just clicked my pen and stayed hidden in some bushes on the side of the house. When there was no response the man muttered, "Damn kids, I'll have to report it tomorrow." He turned and went back inside.

I waited in the dark behind the house until all the lights were out and then walked around it twice to make sure. I was pretty sure I knew which window was Carl's bedroom.

I was about to light and throw a "cocktail" through the window when I saw a cat emerge from a 'cat door' onto the back porch. I rummaged in my coat for a piece of the tuna sandwich and held it out to the cat.

"Here kitty, nice kitty," I coaxed the cat holding out the tuna; *strangely I do care for animals.* The cat sniffed and approached warily and finally licked the tuna. I got some more and soon was able to pick up the cat and pet it. I reached into my pocket, got a piece of rope and tied it tightly around the cat's neck and it began to hiss and struggle.

I dropped the cat, holding on to the rope and got my lighter fluid and lighter. The cat hissed more when I sprayed it with the fluid. I pulled the cat by the rope around the house and tied the rope to the front-door handle. Grinning to myself, I didn't even think about the cat's cries waking anyone.

I rang the doorbell two times and then threw a small rag I'd lit to set the cat on fire and ran to the bushes. The fire and the cat's screeches had me hard. It was all I could do to not pull out my dick and jerk-off right there. The light came on over the door and a man opened it and his cursing joined the cats yowling.

I was thrilled as I snuck back into the woods so I could jerk off to enjoy my revenge to the fullest. It just seemed like normal behavior for me.

I'll show them not to mess with me. The ballpoint pen was forgotten for now. I'd gotten something better to take its place.

The next day I was happy to go to school. I waited until I found Carl near a bunch of teachers. I walked up behind Carl, clicked my pen a few times, and as he passed I said in a low voice, "How's your cat?" Carl started to grab me but I'd started talking to a big male teacher who didn't tolerate any fighting. "Just wait," Carl hissed softly to me.

I was surprised that Carl hadn't learned his lesson, so I avoided him the rest of the day and snuck into the woods before Carl could get to me. I wasn't scared but I felt angry that I hadn't gotten the message to Carl to not fuck with me.

It just ain't fair. That night I went back to Carl's house and waited again. I was glad I hadn't tried to throw the "cocktail" through Carl's window as when I checked this time I noticed that there was a screen over the window which would probably have kept the "cocktail" out of the house.

I paused and used my box-cutting knife to open a large hole through the screen. Then I threw my lit cocktail straight through Carl's bedroom window easily breaking the glass. I stood for several seconds transfixed by the blaze. I could see the fire and hear the screams before I ran back to the woods with a satisfied smirk on my face. I'd show them that I wasn't somebody to fuck with.

At school the next day I heard that there had been a fire at Carl's house and that Carl had been so badly burned that he was in intensive care. It would take years, one of the teachers had said, and many painful operations, before Carl would be back to school.

I was smiling inside and also worried that one of Carl's buddies would rat me out, but I kept a blank face as I clicked my pen. When I saw some of Carl's buddies, I whispered in a low voice, so only they could hear me, "Some people just don't learn. Wouldn't want to burn up like a rat." The threat was real and it worked. No one ratted me out and I didn't have any more troubles with any bullies at school. It gave me a strange new feeling of power but it didn't seem to last very long and the few kids who tried to make friends with me, kinda like joining forces since I had taken out the meanest kid in the school, soon dropped me as I guess I smelled so bad from living in my cave. No one told me about it, they just quit hanging around with me.

Chapter 17

Lisa Age Fourteen

Things did get somewhat better at school. My mother talked to the teachers and they made accommodations to help me get my work done.

I began to excel at my art and I took to using my "new" Macintosh laptop computer like it was an extension of my brain. Of course I'd been using an older table model at home for years. Somehow I just knew how to figure things out on the computer. It didn't argue with me or get mad at me. I learned to use it as a tool that helped to change my life. I even learned how to do digital art and design. Of course there was some ridicule and some vicious teasing from some of the other students now that I was getting "Special Ed" help.

I still didn't fit in but I didn't mind so much or at least that's what I told myself. But some kids sought me out to get help with computer stuff. I had a few people I could talk to now and some even did role-playing games with me. My mother had taken notice of me talking to some kids and asked me who they were.

I reluctantly said, "Oh that's just Sally, Pete, and James, and a few others."

"That's so nice," my mother said. "What are there last names? Maybe we can invite them over or something."

"Oh mother," I said in exasperation, "That's so lame."

"What? Tell me their names and I'll look them up in the book and call their mothers."

"Never mind mother," I shrugged, and walked off to my room. Aside from the fact that my mother was trying to commit me to social suicide, I didn't want to admit that I didn't know their last names.

Chapter 18

Lisa Age Fifteen

High school brought more physical growth. I'd started my period two years before so I knew all about that and on the Internet I'd learned even more. I had shot up to a few inches less than six feet and my breasts had grown amply. I was embarrassed and excited at the same time.

At first I tried to hide them and my height by slumping over when I walked, stood, or sat around. Then I had tried standing tall and sticking out my chest. Neither strategy worked for me and sticking them out just got me lots of catcalls from the boys. I went back to basic baggy black, slumping over and tended to stay by myself, mostly in my own make believe world where I had friends and people who loved me.

I had seen the bully, Carl, beat up Randy and then pee on him. I had felt really badly for Randy who didn't seem to fit in either. I had wanted to go and help him but he shouted at me to leave him alone, and I knew if I were he I'd just want to be left alone.

Except for the sheer joy I felt when I drew, and being able to explore the universe through the Internet, I was terribly lonely. I read romance novels and dreamed of romantic relationships I knew I'd never have, though they reminded me of the loving caresses I used to get from my Uncle.

I lived in my imaginary lover's mind and inner thoughts; I believed that he perceived me with ambiguity and ambivalence like an enigma. In my mind I was angry with myself as well as with him and couldn't see how anyone could call my fantasies love. I tried to tell myself that it was love but failed miserably. The emotions I felt were almost overwhelming and contradictory. They were as strong as anything I had ever experienced. I was like fire and heat, like wood burning brightly until there would be nothing left of me. I thought that love was a puzzle I could not understand; I didn't know if I loved someone would they love me back?

I had "kind of" dated one boy and it was a disaster. He had seemed to accept me and didn't make fun of my ADHD and LD. He said he was dyslexic too. Pete was one of the guys who had asked for my help with using some computer software. I had met him again one night when we had a night drawing class. At break time we walked outdoors, away from the other students, out behind some trees where no one could see us. He took my hand and pointed out some constellation in the night sky.

I had pulled my hand from his. I didn't want him to get the wrong impression. I knew how boys were.

My mother had always told me, "Boys that age want just one thing. They want to get in your pants."

"Oh Mother," I had rolled my eyes. I'd heard the same thing so many times it was firmly rooted in my mind.

I'd heard some of the other girls talking about "making out." *I knew what it meant*, I thought. My mother wouldn't approve, I knew, as a small smile crept onto my face.

Maybe I did want to make out, like the other girls I heard talking about it. Maybe it was just because I knew my mother would disapprove. I took Pete's hand, kissed him, and put his hand on my breast. Making out with Pete felt nice. I liked his hands on my breasts and I had my first French kiss, as Pete had put his tongue in my mouth. We were both getting really excited; I could feel my nipples getting hard and the press of his stiff penis in his pants as he hugged me.

When the teacher called the class back in, I walked ahead of him.

I noticed him walking with his hands over his crotch to hide his erection. The French kiss had felt sensual and I remembered it lovingly.

A few days later, without meaning to, I'd overheard Pete talking to some of his friends. "Boy, Lisa may be weird, but she's hot. She's a real kisser and she let me feel up her tits. God they're so big and soft and she moaned."

He was bragging to his friends and I felt devastated and betrayed. I moved away quickly so that he wouldn't realize I had heard him.

I never let him 'feel me up'—well I had put his hand on my breast, but he wasn't supposed to tell, and such crude language.

I cried myself to sleep that night and later when my mother finally got me to tell her what I was upset about, my mother just said, "Well I told you so, now no one will want you." I refused to see "that boy" or any others again and tried to put the thought of having a boyfriend out of my mind. What had my mother told me? "No man will ever want you, you're defective." My mother said it so often it came to be my own belief about myself. So I consciously decided to protect myself from the hurt by rejecting almost any social life.

My energies and emotions I poured into my art, my computer and my fantasy life. I planned on majoring in computer graphic arts in college, certain I could get a job with those kinds of skills.

Chapter 19

Randy Age Sixteen

Since taking care of the bully, Carl, I had lost interest in taking kids out to watch my foster mother. I'd been living in the woods and bathing so infrequently for so long that even I realized how dirty and stinky I had become.

I continued to click my pen, play with fire and I started several small brush fires but was never caught. The fires were like something I could control. I was lonely, though I didn't want to admit it. With nothing else to do, I began walking the streets at night, my clicking pen was my only company.

On one night walk when I was taking a shortcut back to the woods, I passed a window with the light on and no curtain. A young woman was standing sideways and must have been looking into a mirror that was out of my sight. She was brushing her hair and she was naked.

I froze. Then I looked around to see if anyone was watching. When I was sure I was alone I stooped down and crept closer to the window. I'd only been able to see her from the waist up. She had both of her arms up to her head as she brushed and fussed with her hair. I loved the way her breasts with big pink colored nipples swayed back and forth. I could see her down to her knees now that I was closer and when she turned slightly sideways I could see the curly black pussie hair between her legs. Terrified she'd turn to the window and catch me watching didn't stop me. I couldn't stop myself. It was better than watching my foster mother, mostly because this woman didn't know I was watching.

This was something new. The woman in the window didn't know I was watching and the excitement of watching her and the possibility of getting caught had given me a huge hard-on.

I didn't know how long I stood there watching. When the woman walked out of the frame of the window, I bolted, afraid she was going to come look out the window. I ran most of the way back to my cave in the woods. As soon as I got there I started jacking off to the images of the naked woman. It took me less than a minute and it was one of the most powerful spurts I had ever had. I crawled into my sleeping bag and slept well that night.

Randy didn't know that his need for peeping would progress, eventually to wanting to do more than just peeping; he'd eventually want to touch his victims to make them his. He'd just have to work up the courage.

Chapter 20

Randy's Night Walks

I started taking more night walks, only now I was looking for someone to peep on. I'd been back to the same house but I never found her in the window again. In frustration I jerked off outside her window and left a stream of my spunk on some of her flowers.

One of my walks took me by a big house that was all by itself on a small hill. I was scared because of the open ground around the house that I would have to cross before I could get to the shade trees and bushes closer to the house. I waited until the moon went behind a cloud, listening for any sounds of dogs.

I'd learned that the hard way and had almost gotten bitten one night when I hopped over a fence to get closer to a house. Assured as I could be that there were no dogs, I climbed over the low fence and sprinted up to the bushes and crouched low below the only room with a light on. It was toward the backside of the house so I thought it might be a bedroom.

A quick peek in the window confirmed it. There were lace curtains but they were partially open and there was a red-haired girl sitting at a desk facing away form me. She was working on a laptop computer. As I watched she stretched, yawned and looked at her watch. She stood up and I ducked down. I recognized her. She was that weird girl from school who had tried to help me that time that bully, that stinking Carl and his buddies pissed on me. I couldn't remember her name.

I was clicking my pen rapidly.

When I looked in again she was taking her blouse off. She arched her back, reached behind her to undo her bra, and let her bra fall free. She turned sideways to throw her bra to the dirty clothes hamper, and I could see her full tits. My pen was forgotten. I was instantly hard as I watched her pull on a nightgown. She walked out of my vision and shortly thereafter the light went out.

Racing home to my hideaway I could see her tits as though they were real and right in front of me. When I got there I furiously jerked off to the images of her tits. I'd never seen anything so beautiful.

I was in love and was sure that she would love me in return. Part of the turn on was that she didn't know she was being stalked, as opposed to my stepmother who didn't seem to really care if I watched her having sex.

Chapter 21

Randy in Love

The next day at school I asked some kids I knew who the red-haired girl was. They told me her name was Lisa but not to bother with her as she was too stuck up.

What they didn't say to me, but I knew they were thinking was that I needed to at least take a shower before talking to any girl. I made it a point to be near her at her locker at the end of school.

"Hi," I said, "how's your computer project coming?"

"I don't know what you're talking about," Lisa said. She knew who Randy was and was still embarrassed for him.

"Yeah, well, see you around Red," I said, clicking my pen trying to be cool.

Lisa hated the name Red and any sympathy she had felt for Randy quickly vanished.

She looked daggers at me and turned and walked away.

I did a slow burn. How dare she treat me that way, I'd seen her naked after all. Didn't she know I loved her? Maybe some day I'd tell her and see what she thought of that!

Chapter 22

Randy Continues Night Walking

I continued my night walks looking for someone to peep on but I was obsessed with the idea of seeing Lisa again and took to visiting her house on a nightly basis. I got my wish a few times and got to see her get ready for bed and I couldn't wait to get home. One time, I jerked-off right there outside her window as I watched her. It was great cause I knew she loved me.

I had to get closer to her, yet she kept brushing me off at school. I'd overheard her telling someone she couldn't help him with his computer project as her parents were taking her to visit a college the coming weekend and they wouldn't be back until Sunday evening. This was great, now I'd be able to get something from her room, something of hers for me to hold at night.

Planning but not carefully, while clicking my pen, I went to her house on Saturday night and checked to see that the car was gone. I even knocked loudly on the door, ready to run if someone answered. The windowpane in the back door broke easily when I hit it with my sweater-covered elbow and I reached in and twisted the simple door lock open.

Inside the house I listened to the silence. A grandfather clock was ticking somewhere in the old house, otherwise it was completely quiet. The door I'd gone in was in the back kitchen and it took me a few wrong turns to find Lisa's room. I was using a flashlight, as I was afraid to turn on any lights. When I found her room I sat at her desk and fingered her laptop. Going to her dresser I rummaged through her drawers until I found her underwear. I felt her bras and panties. They were all cotton and then I found a pair of red silk panties. Putting them to my nose I was disappointed their weren't no scent of her.

Looking in her closet I saw her nightie. Taking it I sat on the bed holding the red silk panties in one hand and the nightie in the other. Lying back, I smelled the nightie and imagined she was there with me. Rubbing my cock with the red silk panties felt so good. In seconds I had cum and left all of my spunk on her bedspread. Wiping at it with her nightie, I quickly left, taking the red silk panties with me. I ran to my cave and jerked off over and over with the red silk panties until my dick was too sore to continue.

Chapter 23

Lisa Age Seventeen

The Bancroft's maid and butler had returned late Saturday night and found the broken glass on the floor in the back kitchen. They did a cursory look through the house and didn't see anything missing and so didn't report it to the police, as they knew Mr. Bancroft disliked any bad publicity. When Lisa and her parents returned home on Sunday evening the servants told them about the broken glass in the kitchen door.

"I'm tired mom. I'm going to bed," I said and went to my room. At first I didn't notice the things out of place in my room; I started to lie down on my bed and noticed that the bedspread was all wrinkled as though someone had been lying on it. Then I noticed a dried spot in the middle of the spread. I leaned closer and smelled it but couldn't tell what it was. The spot was about the size of a silver dollar and had little strands leading from it towards the side of the bed, as though someone had tried to wipe it up.

I noticed my nightgown on the floor next to the other side of my bed. I had left it hanging in my closet. Some of my dresser drawers were opened slightly. I went to them to see if anything was missing. My clothes in the drawers had definitely been rearranged but nothing seemed to be missing, until I got to my underwear drawer. I saw right away that my red silk panties were gone. The matching bra was there hidden on the other side of the drawer, so I searched again, but the panties were definitely gone.

That creep, I thought as I remembered that stinky boy Randy and wondered if he had broken in and taken them.

"What's wrong?" my mother asked as she came to wish me a good night.

"Oh, nothing mother," I replied. I tried to hide the red bra I was holding in my right hand. I turned my body sideways toward my mother hoping to hide the lacy bra.

"No. What is that?" my mother asked, reaching behind me. She pulled my arm out and gasped when she saw the skimpy bra. "Where did you get that?" she said accusingly.

"Oh God! Mother."

"Don't you use that tone of voice with me young woman," my mother snapped, holding the silky bra up to her own bust. "You're too young to have underwear like this. Where did you get it?" my mother repeated.

I sighed, and tried to hide my embarrassment in anger. Now I'd have to tell my mother but I wouldn't tell her everything. "Well if you must know . . ."

"Yes I must," my mother interrupted me. "Go on."

"Jamie and I went to the Victoria's Secret store over at the mall in Cleveland. I don't wear them. I mean I just got them because they're pretty and other girls were getting them to wear for their boyfriends."

"Boyfriends? You don't have a boyfriend you'd show these to? What do you mean, you 'got them?'"

"No I don't wear them for a boyfriend, mother."

Damn, I'd done it again, said 'them' that could imply two or more, I knew my mother would pick up on that and I would have to tell the rest.

"Well," my mother said holding and looking at the silk bra, "These usually come in matching sets, bra and panties."

"Yes, mother, I got the set."

"Well where are the panties?"

"They're gone, someone must have taken them," I said as I slumped on the side of the bed. "I think I know who took them."

I went on to tell my mother about the boy named Randy and his provocative comments. I showed my mother the spot on the bedspread and told her that I had found my nightgown on the floor beside the bed.

"Semen," my mother said as she sniffed the spot. "I know that smell. Thomas come here," she called to my stepfather.

They called the police and I was embarrassed to have to tell the whole story again and watch the uniformed policeman and a policewoman look at the spot on my bed and handle my bra. They took statements from me, the servants, and my mother and father.

"We'll have to take the bedspread and nightgown as evidence," the policeman said to Mr. Bancroft. They knew who he was and treated him with the differential manner due to someone of his standing in the community.

I just looked down at the floor and wanted them all to just leave me alone.

Chapter 24

Randy Age Seventeen

The next Monday morning I made sure that I was near Lisa's locker when she stopped by.

"So, I bet you'd look hot in red panties," I said, being so cool. She had to want me.

"You creep, get away from me," Lisa said and ran away.

"I'll see you later," I called after her, clicking my pen, planning my nightly trip to her bedroom window.

After school let out that day, I headed home. I hadn't been to my real home in several days and needed to get some more supplies. When I walked in the back door the police were waiting for me. If I'd come in the front way I'd have seen their car and run. They grabbed me before I could bolt and found the red silk panties in my jacket pocket.

Chapter 25

Randy and the "System"

The charges against me were Trespassing, Breaking and Entering, Burglary, and Sexual Assault in the Fourth Degree. They told me the sex charge included such things as stalking, exhibitionism, and any other non-touching sexual activity without the consent of the other person, like jerking of on Lisa's bed. Since I was still technically a juvenile and hadn't had any other charges, I was released to my foster mother's custody. Fortunately, she had been semi-sober and home when the police had come to talk to me about the break-in.

My case got lost in the logjam of the court system. I was assigned a Public Defender (PD). My foster mother couldn't afford to pay an attorney. The PD was a young kid, Samuel Johnson, fresh out of law school who had just passed the bar exam only a month prior.

Mr. Johnson met with me only one time and that was enough for him to know I was a loser. I was dirty and stank like something rotten. Mr. Johnson told me to bathe and wear a suit when we went to court.

The PD wanted to go to trial. He wanted the trial experience, even though he knew his client was guilty as hell. The police had gotten a DNA analysis and two months later they had a match with Randy and the semen on Lisa's bedspread and nightgown. And they had the red silk panties they had caught him with, which Lisa had embarrassingly identified as hers.

All this didn't matter though. The ADA (Assistant District Attorney) who was assigned to handle the case barely had time to read the police reports. It was a nothing bullshit case. He didn't have the time or inclination to try it. No one had been hurt, the panties were valued at less than $100, and nothing else was taken. So what if the kid had jerked off in the girl's bed? Lots of kids did things like that. That didn't make it okay, but it just wasn't worthwhile to waste time prosecuting. Mr. Bancroft wasn't that big a fish. He called the PD into his office and told him what was going to happen. The kid would plead guilty to disorderly conduct and be placed on probation until he was eighteen. They could have kept him in the system longer but the probation officers were already covering four times the number of cases that they could effectively keep track of. Although the new PD really wanted court time, he knew he wasn't going to get it with this case.

I was freshly bathed and in my suit, accompanied by my nearly sober foster mother and PD. I appeared briefly before a family court judge and I plead guilty to disorderly conduct. The judge asked me if I knew what I was pleading too. "Yes your honor," I replied. The judge sentenced me to one hundred hours of community service, a $200 fine, to get therapy for my sex problem, and probation until I reached the age of majority, eighteen, and then my record would be sealed. I could not come closer than fifty yards to Ms. Lisa Havenhurst under any circumstances. The whole thing lasted a quarter of an hour at most.

I had been scared. This wasn't as easy as firebombing Carl. I was worried that I might not be able to meet the conditions of my probation. The fantasies of Lisa were so strong. I successfully resisted the urges to go to her house that night. The image of the big policeman grabbing me was the only thing that stopped me. I had to settle for jacking off to images of Lisa and clicking my pen.

Chapter 26

Randy Seventeen

The next week my meeting with my Probation Officer was, if anything, briefer than my appearance in court. I met her in her office just off the courthouse street. Her dingy gray steel desk and most of the floor space around her desk was piled high with case files. There was barely room for the two chairs in front of her desk.

She didn't ask me to sit so I remained standing. She barely looked at my sentencing report and didn't even look at me.

She was going to tell Randy to come in once a month to report how he was doing and then noticed that he'd be eighteen in less than seven months.

Looking at his file, she said, "Hey kid, looks like you've got less than seven months until you're eighteen. Do what it says here," she said, handing me a list of my conditions of probation, "And stay out of trouble and you'll be off probation when you're eighteen. Don't let me see you again."

"Yes mam," I said and turned to go thinking *what a bitch she was.*

She looked up at him briefly. *Nice kid,* she thought hoping he'd do better than the others in the case files spread around her. She also wondered why he kept clicking his pen.

My foster mother had scraped up the money to pay my fine, but not without numerous lectures about how I was going to have to pay her back. I just listened as if to so much noise. I'd learned to tune her out long ago as I clicked my pen. I was somewhat more worried about my appointment with the shrink to talk about my "sex problem." I was to go to the court-appointed psychiatrist, Dr. Gerben, M.D., for my first session the next week.

Chapter 27

Randy and His First Shrink

"Welcome, Randy, come in. Take a seat over there." Dr. Gerben indicated a chair across from his desk. "Looks like you got yourself in some trouble here," he said, looking up from the police reports.

"Yeah," I replied nervously.

"You nervous kid? Don't worry, most people are the first time they see a shrink. I'm Dr. Gerben. Tell me about yourself."

"Nothing to tell, Doctor."

"How often do you masturbate? Two, three times a day? More?"

I shrugged my shoulders, "Yeah sometimes."

"So do you think about your mother when you jerk-off?" Dr. Gerben asked.

If he only knew, I thought, *I don't think about her. I've watched her and even done her.*

"No I just have ordinary fantasies, you know 'Playboy' stuff."

I relaxed. *This is going to be easy,* I thought. I proceeded to spin a line of bullshit about my childhood and how I loved my foster mother and was trying to do better in school but that the other kids picked on me.

Dr. Gerben asked me about why I was almost constantly clicking my pen. "Oh it's just a nervous habit," I replied, which seemed to satisfy Dr. Gerben. The forty-five-minute session was over in thirty minutes and I was given an appointment to come back the next week.

This continued on for three more appointments and at the close of the fourth appointment Dr. Gerben said, "You seem like an okay kid Randy. Pretty normal; except for clicking that pen all the time. I'll send the judge a letter saying you're discharged from treatment. Just keep your dick in your pants and no more stalking and breaking and entering," he said jokingly to Randy. "Hope I don't see you in the future."

"Yeah, me too," I said and I was out the door.

After Randy left Dr. Gerben was thinking to himself, *Given human nature being the way it is, my basic question to myself is, did one learn that not any of us are really capable of changing our lives. Knowing it is possible, but the patients I treat are often distrustful. It's easy for me and for them to see other people's patterns and mistakes. It's more difficult for them to recognize their own patterns of behavior, patterns of distorted thinking and self-deception that they repeat throughout their lives.*

They sometimes think these are fundamental patterns of truth about who they are and have been sense birth and will always be. Many think these traits cannot be changed whether it is optimism or pessimism, depression or happiness, gullibility or cynicism, laziness or tenacity. Some come in thinking that therapy might strengthen them or offset some problems, but in the main, people do what they do because they've always done things that way whether or not, the behavior is good or bad.

Indeed some choose to repeat the bad behavior because it is bad and it seems to be the only way they know. To predict what someone is going to do in the future, look at what they have done in the past. Of course it is possible to change, but first one must really want to change and put forth the effort in thinking and acting to do so. Dr. Gerben thought it wouldn't be long before Randy was back in the system.

Chapter 28

Randy's Consequences

I never got around to doing any community service but no one checked and a few weeks after my eighteenth birthday I got a letter in the mail from the probation office notifying me that I was released from probation since I'd turned eighteen and that my record would be sealed. There was also a gratuitous wish that I stay out of trouble. The letter wasn't even signed.

That night I went back to Lisa's with great anticipation. Probation had been so easy I didn't even care if I was caught again. But I was much more careful this time. She was more careful, too. Her curtains were closed and her blinds pulled down. I clicked my pen furiously. Lisa had graduated from high school and had a summer job at the multiplex theater at the mall. I would go there and smile at her when she took my ticket. She didn't acknowledge my clicking pen or me. I'd go to the back row of one of the R-rated movies and jerk-off thinking of Lisa's tits.

Since she was being so careful in closing her curtains, I quit trying to see in Lisa's window and went looking for others to stalk; I often got lucky and imagined that I was looking at my beloved Lisa. I never forgot Lisa and I kept track of her constantly. She was still my favorite fantasy for jerking off and that mostly took the place of clicking my pen.

Chapter 29

Lisa Age Eighteen

At the end of summer I left to go to the University of Cleveland. As a freshman I had to live in a dorm on campus and there I had a blond roommate named Sally Rafeal. I was relieved to find that I was on the 3rd floor so that no one could see in the windows from the street.

"So what's your last name?" I had asked the first day when we met in the dorm.

"No, that's it, Rafeal. Really. And no blond jokes."

"Okay," I said laughing, "but no red jokes either. Deal?"

We shook hands and became friends. I was gradually coming out of my "Black Period" as I later called it. I really liked the college atmosphere. It was so much more stimulating than high school and the students and professors were interesting. Since there were so many students, it didn't seem to matter that I didn't fit into any cliques. The cliques just weren't as important as they had seemed to be in high school.

I still had some troubling dreams about Uncle Vincent but in the morning couldn't remember what was troubling about them.

I was blossoming. I even started wearing dresses occasionally and different colors, though I still preferred my basic black jeans and T-shirt, which Sally said, looked stunning against my creamy skin. I added some silver jewelry. I'd gotten past the phase of wanting body-piercings. I still didn't feel comfortable dating and I didn't know if I ever would. I'd listen to Sally talking about her dates and really wanted to go on dates myself, but I refused to go out even on double dates because I just couldn't.

Eventually Sally quit pestering me and just accepted me as her quiet confidant. I poured my heart and brains into my studies of biology, graphics design, and my fantasy love relationships.

I had finally started in therapy and said I needed privacy, which I could only find in my therapy sessions. I prayed and longed to be loved. I needed something better than I had had so far. I believed, like so many other people of the world, that if I just had the hope and believed strongly enough and prayed long enough for God to send me love, He would. And so I prayed and tried to believe. I felt that I now understood enough to be able to recognize love if and when it came along. So many chances had gone by in the past that I was ready to accept the next offer that came my way. I gradually quit going to therapy; it didn't seem to be helping me.

Chapter 30

Randy Age Nineteen

When I had learned that Lisa had gone off to college I followed her. I knew she wanted me to. Getting a job as a night janitor cleaning the classrooms at the University had been easy. I had found Lisa's dorm and in the basement of the building I found an unused room behind the furnace. It was hard to get to. I had to crawl under some pipes to get to the door but that was perfect. No one would look for me there. I gradually moved in a mattress, hot plate, and a small TV. It even had a sink with hot and cold running water and I started to bathe more often. It used to be a mop room before they put in the new furnace. I had to be careful coming and going but there was hardly ever anyone in the furnace room and if there was someone, I'd just say I was looking for cleaning supplies.

I knew where Lisa's room was and I spent a great deal of time trying to figure out a way to see in or sneak in, but I couldn't think of anything. I'd tried the stairway, and I could get on her floor but she always kept the door closed and locked and checked through the peephole before she opened the door. In frustration I'd watched her get a delivery of pizza and had seen how careful she was. Following her on campus was impractical, not that I hadn't tried, because she was always with a bunch of other students and never went out at night, at least that I could tell.

Although I couldn't see Lisa, I had plenty of opportunities to stalk other co-eds and to imagine that they were Lisa. It seemed to me that they were almost asking to be looked at. In each dorm building I found at least one or two street-floor windows I could look in. Sometimes I'd see two girls at once. They'd sit on their beds talking, brushing their hair, and occasionally they'd be completely naked or wearing sexy nighties. They'd sit Indian style with their legs spread wide open and I could see their pussies. Sometimes I'd catch one using a dildo on herself and one time I caught two roommates in a sixty-nine, eating each other out. I was delighted. I always imagined the girls were Lisa and I was with her.

I started night walking again around some student housing on the campus and one time I saw a lady lying on her side on a day bed. It was a really hot night and she had left the door open and I could see her sleeping. Without thinking about it I walked up and opened the screen door and just stood over her watching her sleep. I could see one tit and nipple. It was an incredible rush, I was inside watching her sleep and she didn't even know it. I took my dick out and jacked off leaving my spunk on the side of her bed. I wanted to reach out and touch her but she rolled over and I was afraid she'd wake up so I left as quickly and quietly as I could. I couldn't believe what I'd just done and how exciting it was to be actually close enough to reach out and touch her while I jerked off.

I started getting careless and there were some complaints about a "stalker."

I couldn't stop myself. The more I couldn't get to Lisa the more I had to stalk others and pretend that they were Lisa. It got to the point where I didn't care if I got caught. I'd been caught before and nothing had really happened. If I just kept trying, I was certain I'd eventually get to my love. My supervisor warned me a couple of times about some of the female students complaining and that if I was doing anything wrong I'd better quit. I didn't listen.

Eight months into the school year there was a story in the school newspaper that the "stalker" had been caught by campus security "red handed" with his hard dick in his hand.

I had tried to claim I was just taking a leak but I'd been caught. This time, as an adult, I was put in the local jail. I was there for a week or more before I got a PD. The noise was unbelievable and I didn't have any privacy. A couple of the "Old Timers" had told me at length what I could expect in prison as a "sex offender." They said I'd be somebody's bitch within a day or two and would be forced to suck cock and get fucked in the ass. I was scared to death and listened eagerly to their advice on how to beat the charges.

When my PD came to see me for the first time, I had placed a little piece of soap under my tongue so that I would be able to froth at the mouth like the old guys suggested. The PD, who was an older guy this time, didn't seem to be falling for it. I knew I had to convince him I was crazy so that I could get an NGRI, Not Guilty by Reason of Insanity, verdict.

I didn't want to go to prison. My PD tried to convince me to knock it off. "With your lack of any prior record and the simple charge of exposing yourself, you probably wouldn't do more than six months max in prison and would more likely just get probation," he said.

I pretended to be listening, but knew I couldn't do even six months. The old guys had convinced me. I was terrified. Images of Carl and his friends beating and then peeing on me kept coming back. I started speaking gibberish in the direction of my PD and wet myself, and fell down so hard that I hit my head on the concrete and it knocked me out. I had done a good job. The judge sent me to the State Hospital to be evaluated by psychiatrists and psychologists to see if I was "fit" to stand trial, and if not, to keep me there until I was found to be "fit."

Chapter 31

Randy

I missed the brief notice of Randy's arrest that appeared in the local paper. Sally told me the "stalker" had been caught. I told her I'd known one of those in high school and was glad this one wouldn't be able to bother anyone else. After thinking about it, I decided that I really wasn't interested and didn't want to read the story in the local paper.

"I'd had enough trouble with my 'stalker' in high school," I told Sally. I never talked about it and Sally let it go.

Dr. William Float, Ph.D., was the first of the three Doctors to evaluate me. *With a name like that he'll be easy to fool,* I thought when I walked into the holding cell for the interview.

Dr. Float was in his late 50s, overweight, and had disheveled grey hair and coke-bottle size lenses in his glasses. His appearance added to my confidence.

"Hello Mr. Parson. I'm Dr. Float. Please be seated."

I just stood there as part of my "dumb" act.

"You can leave," Dr. Float told the guard who had brought Randy into the room.

"Okay, if you say so. But I'll be right outside the door if you need anything. Just push the bell button on the door or yell. But if you yell, it'll have to be pretty loudly. This interview room is pretty soundproof otherwise you wouldn't be able to hear each other because of all the noise out in the hall."

"Okay, officer. I'm sure I'll be fine," Dr. Float told the guard. He had done over a hundred of these "fitness to proceed" examinations over the years and had never been attacked or even threatened. Dr. Float was sitting behind a table studying his notes on Mr. Parson.

I just stood in silence staring off vacantly.

The guard who was new said, "Well, I'll check through the glass every quarter hour just to make sure." He turned and walked out and shut the steel door, which made a loud clang, and locked it from the outside.

Dr. Float looked up from the record and said again, "Please be seated Mr. Parson," indicating a chair that was bolted to the floor on the other side of the table. I just stood there.

"Okay. Suit yourself. For the record, can you tell me your name?"

I gave a slight nod but didn't say anything.

"Will you tell me your name?"

No answer.

"Are you Randolf Parson, Jr.?"

I just stood there.

"Well, this will be a short interview Mr. Parson. I'll just get the guard and tell the judge you refused to participate in the evaluation."

Thinking that I had to say something to prove I was crazy, I sat down and said, "Void where prohibited."

"What's void?"

"For a limited time only," I said and jerked my head around to the side. "Don't tell me what to do," I said as though talking to someone over my shoulder.

"Okay, Mr. Parson, you can drop the act. I'm not buying it. I'll see you later," and he started putting his papers back in his briefcase.

In desperation Randy said, "You got me Doc, but this place is driving me crazy," I said, thinking I had to keep the Doctor there.

"Yeah, I'm Randolf Parson, Jr., but you can call me Randy. Everybody does."

"That's more like it. Now for a few basic questions," and he went on to ask Randy his birth date, where he lived, basic demographic information. The Doctor already had this information in his file and he was probing to see if Mr. Parson would respond correctly to even innocent known information. The ones who were faking it often didn't.

"Where are you?"

"In this room."

"Look, don't try to get smart with me Mr. Parson, it won't work."

"You got me again. I'm in the State Mental Hospital on the holding ward. I don't know the name of this place."

"What's the date?"

"I don't know, Doc, you tell me."

Dr. Float laughed, realizing he'd have to look at his calendar to know the date. "You got me on that one, Mr. Parson. What day is it?"

"Friday. I know 'cause they got fish on the menu for tonight."

"Why are you here?"

"I don't really know, honest Doc. I never done nothing wrong."

"Who is your lawyer?"

"I don't know, some guy. I only seen him one time."

"What are you charged with?"

"I don't know."

"Do you know how long you might get if convicted?"

"What for? Don't know, Doc."

"Do you know the purpose of this evaluation?"

"No, Doc."

"Tell me the roles of the judge, the prosecution and your defense attorney."

"Those are easy," I said, thinking I could get back into my crazy act. "The judge is supposed to find me guilty, the prosecutor is to tell my story, and the defense attorney is supposed to make things up so I get out."

"What's your version of what happened?"

"Don't tell him," I said, talking over my shoulder. I wasn't sure how pretending to hear a voice was supposed to be done so I thought I'd just make some stuff up. *I mean how hard is it to act crazy?* I thought. "For a limited time only."

"You shut up," I said, looking over my shoulder.

Dr. Float still wasn't buying Mr. Parson's crazy act. He decided to try some standard questions that almost always caught the fakers.

"Do you always smell rotting fish when you brush your teeth?" The question was almost never answered in the affirmative when the person was really crazy.

I had enough cunning to realize that this might be a trick question so I said, "No. But I do smell burnt bodies when I roast marshmallows."

"Do you have to pat yourself on the head three times before you can cross the street?" Again I sensed a trick question. "No, I usually wait until the sign says don't walk. Do not, Do too," I said over my shoulder.

"Now I'm going to name ten items and ask you to name them back to me. Ready?" Dr. Float said, ignoring Randy's behavior.

"Sure, fire away Doc."

"Key, clock, stairs, bible, crayons, window, girl, flashlight, bottle, cat." He spoke them slowly, pausing for a second between each word.

Dr. Float waited thirty seconds and then asked Mr. Parson to repeat back as many things as he could remember.

"Gee, Doc, could you say them again?"

"No, just name as many as you can."

"Okay," and then after a log pause, "cat . . . dog . . . shit . . . car . . . key . . . ride . . . that's all I can remember, Doc."

"Okay, Mr. Parson, I'm going to show you some cards. Lots of people see different things on the cards." He took one of the ten Rorschach Ink Blot cards and showed it to Mr. Parson.

I recognized the card for what it was as I'd seen some like it used on a mystery show on TV.

"That one's two people trying to kill each other."

Dr. Float showed another one, "That's a woman's vagina, after she's been fucked. You didn't tell me you were gonna show me dirty pictures, Doc. Can I keep them?"

Ignoring Randy's question, Dr. Float showed him another one, "That's God praying for those sinners."

"What sinners?"

"The two who were eating each others pussies in the church last Sunday. They said it was an offering to God," I said.

"Do you hear voices, Mr. Parson?"

"Yeah, how'd you know? Do you hear them too?"

"Are they pleasant or unpleasant?"

I wasn't sure which answer was correct. Chance gave me a 50% probability of getting it right. "They're unpleasant."

I read the Doc's body language and knew I had answered correctly.

"Tell me about them."

"Sometimes they are loud and I have to fight to keep them away."

"How do you do that?"

I could answer that one easily. "I tell them to go away, or I listen to music or TV or sometimes I just hit my head on the wall." I'd seen some of the other inmates doing that.

"What do the voices say?"

"I can't tell you, they'd be mad and I can't really hear them that clearly anyway."

"Do they tell you to do bad things?"

"No . . . Yes." I didn't want to take a chance on giving the wrong answer.

About three-quarters of an hour later Dr. Float had finished with all of his questions and asked, "Mr. Parson, what were the things I asked you to remember about 30 minutes ago? There were ten things I named."

I couldn't name any.

Dr. Float said, "Mr. Parson, that's enough for today."

As he walked to his car, Dr. Float thought, *Mr. Parson wasn't completely sane. Either he was a pretty good actor or he definitely had some screws loose.* In any case, Dr. Float's opinion was that Mr. Parson wasn't fit to proceed with trial whether or not he was legally insane.

Randy varied his routine slightly with the two other Doctors who asked pretty much the same questions; they also found him unfit to proceed.

Chapter 32

Randy

The weeks at the State Hospital dragged into months. I believed that I had to continue to prove that I was "unfit" or they'd send me back to trial and I'd be sent to prison.

Randy didn't understand that the defense of NGRI, Not Guilty by Reason of Insanity, if successful, would send him back to the State Hospital for treatment and that once he was "cured" and/or found to be of no danger to himself or others, that he'd be released to the community and wouldn't do any prison time.

Anytime I'd see a shrink I'd start putting on my crazy talk and any other crazy antics I could think up. The TV was constantly on in the ward's "day room" and I picked up lots of ideas from watching the crazy things I saw on the TV.

I believed that the Doctors had put spies on the ward who were pretending to be patients, so I had to keep up my act, more or less, on a full time basis.

Other patients got to sleep in dorm rooms but because I acted so "crazy" I had a cell to myself, and no privacy.

The door was locked and had a twelve by twelve inch bullet proof glass in the door and nurses and graduate students were always "looking in" on the "crazy guy." I didn't disappoint them. When I saw someone looking in, if I wasn't already, I'd start jacking off. It became my only release and I did it constantly thinking of the times I'd seen Lisa's naked tits. I wished I still had her red silk panties. I developed a rash on my hands and used the hand lotion they gave me as lubricant for my jacking off.

I took the antipsychotic medication they gave me without protest as though this also proved I was crazy.

After a while it got so he wasn't acting so much as becoming crazy for real. Sometimes even he couldn't tell the difference.

Chapter 33

Randy

After the first several months, they began to let me out more often to be with the other patients in the day room. The months turned into years. I never had any visitors except for the once every six months "Fitness" evaluation by the mental-health professionals. I didn't see anyone except for the nurses, aids, Doctors, patients, and graduate students.

I had also been known to stand up to other inmates who tried to bully the smaller and weaker ones. They weren't my friends but I wouldn't let any of the other inmates pick on them.

Sometimes I'd participate in recreational activities and take day trips with other patients. One trip was to a dairy farm. We were allowed to wander in the pasture as it was reasoned there was no one for us to hurt and the fresh air and sunshine would be good for us.

In reality, the nurses just wanted to have the afternoon off. They had spread a blanket out on the grass in a cow pasture and talked about their boyfriends and griped about their supervisor. They didn't pay much attention to the patients.

I wandered off with another patient named Paul Stallworth, a paranoid schizophrenic who had been hospitalized several years ago on an NGRI after he had killed a city bus driver for no reason. Paul, a little over six feet tall and close to 300 lbs, was strange and yet was easy to be around and gave me plenty of real-life examples of how to act crazy.

Paul asked me if I liked "shrooms."

"What?" I asked, walking in a slight medication caused stupor. Paul was reaching down and turning over dried cow paddies.

"Look. The dried out-ones. Like these." He pointed to the small "shrooms," mushrooms he had uncovered. "Wrong kind will kill ya," he cackled, picking them up. "Try one." He offered one to me. I took it and chewed.

Randy didn't remember the rest of the day he was so tripped out, he thought he was with Lisa and started masturbating.

"Oh, not that again," one of the nurses said as she looked up from the blanket.

They decided it was time to hustle the patients back onto the hospital bus. They didn't know how much Randy was tripping as this was normal behavior for him, though it was a set back one nurse observed. Randy had seemed somewhat more sociable in his behavior. The nurses had giggled at the sight of Randy's penis and one whispered to the other, "I wish my boyfriend had one that big."

Chapter 34

Lisa

I continued my studies and by staying in school over the summer breaks I was able to finish a double major in four years in biology and graphics design.

I'd learned to use lists and constant reminders to keep myself on task and deal with my ADHD. The spell checker in my word-processing program made it possible for me to cope with my dyslexia. Still, I had to work a lot harder than the other students, and go over and over things if I was going to learn the material. My disabilities just made my work harder.

I was thinking of going for my master's degree but thought I'd like to take a break from school for a while. I'd already moved off campus and was living in my own apartment. Sally and I were still friends and occasionally I'd go out for coffee with a guy but we never seemed to hit it off. They either didn't call back or I found some excuse to avoid the ones who did.

I got a job with a local graphics design firm in Cleveland and it was an easy bus commute for me. I got to use my skills and was finding that I was learning a lot more on the job than I ever did in class. I'd take many projects home to work on my laptop at night and weekends. My boss was very pleased with both the quantity and quality of my work and that was all I worked for. It was the attention I needed. Encouraged by the praise I received and the pay raise, I expanded and started doing work on my own for pleasure and at the suggestions of some female friends and colleagues at work I entered some of my paintings in some local juried art shows.

I did most of my work digitally and then used the office printer to print it to paper for matting or canvas for stretching. After stretching the canvases I painted in acrylic on top of the printed image to add back in the feel and texture of a "real" canvas. The original underlying print only existed as pixels on my computer hard drive but the painted canvas or prints were one-of-a kind originals. Not wanting to do mass marketing, I never did limited-edition prints, just originals.

Over time I had won several honorable mentions for my work and even a first and a second place. I did both pure abstract and representational abstract. One of the local galleries in Cleveland asked me if they could represent and sell my work. I was thrilled. It wasn't much money; I didn't have the time to do that much painting, but it was very pleasing to know that others, strangers, liked my work well enough to buy it. I always sent a personal note, through the gallery owner, to the buyer. It was like they now owned a piece of me that I willingly shared.

An agency from New York even approached me asking if I'd be interested in having them represent me in the New York area. I was flattered about that but didn't think I had the time to do more art, in addition to my full-time job, which I loved. I did, however, use my skills to develop my own web page to display my digital art.

I seldom went home to visit my mother and stepfather. It seemed that they were always off on some trip somewhere in the world. Time seemed to fly by. Before I knew it, I had been at the firm for almost four years. I was at an office Christmas party when I got a call from my mother who was hysterical, sobbing and crying so much I could hardly understand her. I finally got my mother calmed down enough to learn that my stepfather had left my mom and gone off with his 27-year old secretary. I hurried home to be with my mother.

My mother and stepfather had tried some marriage counseling at my mother's insistence. As a couple they had been talking about their sex life and neither one was happy. He described her's as strange, like fucking a corps. She felt hurt by his statement and denied that her sex life was strange and then countered that he was the strange one. He agreed and shared his belief with her that with everyone sex was strange. No matter who you did it with, it was always strange. She didn't seem to understand what he was saying.

He tried to explain it further. He said that sex was the most important deepest thing in life for him and that each of the experiences he had were expressed differently, uniquely. Who you do it with, how you do it and what your fantasies are is what makes it the best. Sharing what you're thinking about what you're doing sexually makes it unique and that's why it's very intimate and magical.

My mother tried to understand and to share some of her own fantasies but it didn't work and only drove them farther apart. He, of course didn't want to disclose his own sexual activity that he had been having with his young secretary. He didn't want to admit that all his explanation of sex was his way of justifying to himself wanting to have sex with a younger woman.

"I'll get that bastard," my mother said through her tears, "He'll pay for this."

"It's okay, mom, we'll get through this together," I said as I hugged and rocked my mother.

"Now, I'm like you, damaged, used goods, no one will want me now," her mother sobbed.

I had almost stopped thinking of myself in those terms. I went with my mother to the attorney's office and helped her cope for several weeks. Finally my mother's constant complaining gave me the courage to tell my mother that I had to get back to my job.

The time with my mother had also given me ample time to think about how well my current relationships were going and finding I could be myself. I laughed for a long time but felt that it probably wasn't funny. When I thought about it I recalled how one guy had been laughing with me. I was laughing because he had been right and that was both the bad news and the good news. He had described me as being a certain type of woman and I realized that I was indeed trying to be someone I wasn't, like putting a square peg in a round hole. At times I was confused and awkward but at times I coped quite well with the world and wasn't overcome by the questions of the meaning of my life.

Chapter 35

Lisa

Three months later my mother called me in high spirits. The contrast to her prior distraught, depressed whiney mood couldn't have been greater. She was jubilant.

"I'm rich. Now I can do whatever I want. I may go on a long cruise. They are supposed to have some good looking cabin boys on those cruise ships," she said.

Mr. Bancroft, on advice of his attorney and not wanting a nasty drawn out divorce battle—and with a good deal of pressure from his current trophy wife to be had "bought" her out for a two-million dollar settlement and a home on the Big Island of Hawai'i.

I was happy for my mother. But the good times didn't last long. Within eight months, my mother was diagnosed with inoperable pancreatic cancer. She was given six months to live and she seemed to be determined to do just that, that is, not live any longer than six months. My mother loved her misery and wanted to leave as much of it as she could with me. We went through the Hospice procedure and the firm gave me a six-month leave of absence.

My work, that's who and what I am, I thought. It was my mantra and it had gotten to the point that I didn't think about it consciously and although I felt guilty about it, I couldn't wait for my mother to finish her dying so I could get back to work.

The time with my mother, without the constant timeline pressures of work, again gave me time to think about myself. I felt I could take care of my emotional and sexual needs by myself.

Admitting that I had needs was painful. I kept telling myself that I was the way I wanted to be. Since my social world was limited, I continually took great pleasure from all of my senses, taking time to smell and savor different aromas and tastes, trying to live in each moment.

Remembering the psychology course I had taken and all the things the professor had said about Freud, and sex as being a universal physical need, I told myself, *I can get along fine without it. I don't need it.*

Anyway, I told myself, I was happy the way I was, single and soon to be alone. Unfortunately, my mother's words were unshakable. *No one would have you anyway, and you're defective. I guess that that's who I am.*

I thought of the quote from John Milton's, "Paradise Lost, 'The mind is its own place, and in itself can make a Heaven of Hell, and a Hell of Heaven.'"

My mother died almost six months from the date when the doctors had told her she had six months to live.

After the funeral it took me—as I was the executrix of my mother's estate—several weeks to get the legal paperwork completed. When I could return to work, I found I didn't want to. And with my inheritance I didn't need to.

My mother's estate included a piece of property on the east coast of the Big Island of Hawai'i, just north of Hilo. It had a house that looked out over the Pacific Ocean. It was just off the highway south of Papaikou and was currently rented on a month-to-month basis. My mother and I had talked about going there for my mother "to die." But in the end it was easier for her to stay in her own home where she, at least, had a few friends who would visit and listen to her complaints.

Chapter 36

Randy

The staff at the State Hospital often left the newspapers out on the tables in the day room for any patients to read who might want to. Few did. I wouldn't have but I saw Lisa's picture above an article about a rich millionaires dying and leaving a beach house on Hawai'i to her daughter, Ms. Lisa Havenhurst. When the divorce had occurred it had been big society news. The article went on to say that Ms. Havenhurst would probably be moving to Hawai'i once her mother's estate was settled.

I had a new purpose; I had to escape. I had to have Lisa and knew that now she would be mine. The paper had as much as said so, talking about how unhappy she had been. *Of course,* I thought, *She must have been miserable since I've been locked away from her.* I began to plot my escape.

"Fliberty Jiberty, Jibbery, Jab. I think I've gone mad." That's what I said during my next therapy session. I talked to myself often and out loud, as I tried to understand the violent feelings I had.

Although not formally schooled past high school, I was cunning and a quick learner, especially when it came to using computers, using theatrical disguises, and reading people's body language.

I had also taken up with the "Nut House" thespian's group a year or more ago. The inmates had chosen their own name for the group. Anyone, not in lock down, was allowed to participate. The players, almost exclusively inmates, seemed to gather spontaneously right after the evening meal. They would wander in by ones or twos and get onto the "stage," the center of the ward's day room. Sometimes there would be long silences and then sometimes several inmates would be speaking at once. Some wore costumes. It was minimally controlled chaos and often-quite funny for the staff and inmates alike.

The inmates borrowed much of their "material" from various TV shows, especially the repetitive commercials.

"For a limited time only . . ." one inmate said with wide eyes not looking at anyone and pointing to something only he could see.

"Three easy payments of $19.95. If you call within the next 30 minutes," said another inmate.

"Void where prohibited . . ."

I loved the attention I got "performing" almost as much as "stalking." It was part of what made it bearable to be away from my Lisa. I was passionate about acting and made friends with the one local "civilian" who volunteered and "facilitated" the group three evenings a week, giving those who wanted them acting and stage craft lessons. I learned how to put on makeup and disguise my face and change my appearance so that I looked like a completely different person. Even the staff said they wouldn't recognize me if they didn't know me and even then they weren't sure. I'd learned how to alter my nose by inserting hollowed out corks and how to change the shape of my face using rolled cotton under my lips and in my cheeks. I could alter my height by wearing platform shoes or stooping over when I walked and stood. Of course I also learned about fake beards and mustaches, pancake makeup and fake wrinkles, and most importantly to become almost invisible by just blending into my surroundings.

I recognized that my acting was like an addiction. The longer I took the drug the more addicted I became; the longer I acted the more confused I became with reality and the character I played. I began to wonder who I really was. At times my true identity crumbled and I felt like nothing but a flat image on the movie screen of my life. I played the character of a man obsessed with a woman for so long that I became distraught with failure.

I felt gutted at the loss of Lisa. No one would believe me even if I told them and I didn't believe it myself. That's why I had to escape, to make my reality real. I was bitterly angry at Lisa, but still wanted her more than ever. Part of my rational mind knew I had no chance with her and wanted to smash things; I wanted to protect her; I wanted to hurt her; I was angry with myself for wanting her, for having my uncontrolled desires. I believed that I knew that she was seeing someone from her past and now there was no chance for me unless I could escape and rescue her.

Usually in our society the truth passes for what everyone else has accepted as a lie and agreed upon. It wasn't surprising then to find so much disagreement between what was real and what was fantasy.

No I said emphatically. I thought, *this is only my interpretation of reality. Put myself in her shoes and in her state of mind and I might begin to try to understand. Women fear, right? And the primitive urges of man are to kill and to rape. Any child who witnesses adults acting out these primitive emotions, as I had, could not help but be afraid. I wanted to be able to tell the child within me that there were real monsters out there but that being afraid only gave them more power. I thought of the mother and father I never had and how I wanted to protect Lisa.*

Chapter 37

Lisa Moves to Hawai'i

I was almost twenty-seven when I left Ohio to see if I could start a new life in Hawai'i. There was really nothing of importance left for me in Ohio and while I had really enjoyed my job, I just couldn't seem to get interested in returning to it. I asked for and received a very good reference letter from my boss, who was truly sorry to see me go and wished me good luck and told me that if I changed my mind and wanted to come back that there was a job waiting for me. He even gave me a lead to a job with a company that had just recently opened a new branch office in Hilo.

I hadn't realized at the time, but with the death of my mother I had been thrown into the abyss yet again of wondering what my life was about.

PART TWO

Chapter 38

Hart

I asked Dr. Longfellow if I could continue in therapy. I would receive my Ph.D. in Clinical Psychology in June. All I had left to do was to successfully defend my Dissertation.

"Come in, Hart," Dr. Longfellow said.

"Hi Doc," I replied as I walked in and flopped in the "patient" chair. I was smiling.

"What's the smile about?"

"Oh, I was just thinking how much happier I am since I've been seeing you. I just hope that someday I'll be as good a therapist as you."

The therapy process that was required as part of my training was over but I had asked Dr. Longfellow if I could continue. Dr. Longfellow agreed when I told her I was worried sick about defending my Dissertation and that I had met a woman and was thinking of asking her to marry me.

Dr. Longfellow had told me, "Hart, doing this therapy with me is part of your learning to be a therapist. When we're young we're afraid of the dark because we believe there are monsters under the bed; when we're grown up we're still afraid of the dark because we know there are real monsters in the dark out their waiting for us.

"The best teachers you'll ever have and from whom you can learn the most are your patients. Listen to them; they will tell you what their true problems are and even how to help them fix themselves. It's not as glamorous as being a surgeon but it is so much deeper. You get to know their inner-most secrets and feelings and have a more intimate relationship with them than anyone else in their lives. They can't be as honest with their family or spouse as they can and will be with you. Sorry for the lecture Hart. Now tell me about your lady friend."

"Yeah," I replied somewhat sheepishly with my eyes downcast, thinking about what she had just said. *That's who I want to be.*

Instead I told her, "You remember that lady I told you I had met?"

"Yes," Dr. Longfellow indicated nodding her head, waiting for Hart to go on.

"We had sex. I mean, we had done it before one time, after a party but this time it was great, Doc. I mean I couldn't believe it. I wasn't a virgin or anything like that. But this was different." I paused, "It was like my whole body was tingling with orgasm. She felt the same way." I breathed deeply remembering the wonderful feeling.

"I'm so happy you found someone, Hart."

"Yeah, me too. I want to ask her to marry me."

"Why?"

"I'm tired of living alone; I want to be married. I want to have someone to share my life with."

"And?" she said waiting for him to say something about love.

"She meets my requirements that I had told myself I was looking for in a mate. She enjoys sex, I mean really enjoys sex, she's not a neat freak, and she has enthusiasm for life."

"Sounds like you've thought about it."

"Yeah, I really think this is the one, Doc."

"Tell me about her."

"She's a year older than me and about an inch taller. She's beautiful, from a Eurasian background. Her mother is a Japanese American and her father is of Irish heritage. She's got that oriental slant to her eyes."

It was as though a spigot had been turned on as I rushed to describe my lover. "Her eyes are greenish amber, and she has jet black hair that hangs down to her rear. She's slender and has legs that go on forever, and a rack to die for," I said, holding my hands up as though I were cupping her breasts. "Oh, sorry Doc," I said and put my hands down in embarrassment.

"It's alright, Hart, no need to be embarrassed. I do sex therapy with couples and am used to talking frankly about sexual anatomy and the specifics of 'how to do it.' You'd be amazed at the number of guys who don't know what a clit is or where it is, and some women, too. The preparation to be a therapist isn't like that for surgeons, we don't scrub up our hands and arms: we have to clear our minds and emotions to be ready to help, often without even knowing what the problems are. We have to rely on our ability to make a real connection with the patient."

I looked forward to making that connection with my coming patients with their sex lives and any other problem they may bring to me.

Chapter 39

Hart

Since Hart was a student, Dr. Longfellow went on to share some more that she wouldn't normally have shared with a patient. "You know sex therapy is one of the most fun things to do professionally. You get to give homework assignments for couples to try between sessions and they have fun doing them and it's usually very successful. That's assuming that there isn't some other complicating psychological problem."

I was silent for a while feeling somewhat cold inside.

"What's her name? You don't have to tell me her last name, just the first will do, so that I don't have to refer to her as 'your lady friend.'"

"Alison. Alison O'Shear. She's finished law school and is studying to take the bar exam. Both her parents are attorneys. Her mother does trial litigation and her father specializes in patents in a big firm in Cleveland."

"How did you meet her?"

"We were at a grad student psych party, after the last semester's finals. We hadn't gone to the party together but

I had met her before at another party. It was getting pretty late and most people were pretty buzzed or stoned or both. There was a group of four of us, me and a guy and two girls that went into the only bathroom, turned the light out and were sitting on the bathroom floor, two on either side of the toilet, playing Primary Process.

"If someone wanted to use the bathroom, male or female didn't matter, they had to give us the password. Whatever they said was okay and we'd let them in and close the door and they had to pee in the dark.

"The guys didn't bother, they'd just back out and go outside and pee on the side of a tree or whatever. The girls would come in and some were very blasé, sat down, pulled their dress up or pants down, panties down, and started peeing. While they peed we'd all get quiet and say something outlandish like, 'she pees like a blond,' or 'her steam sounds a little weak. She must be anemic.' Some were too embarrassed and couldn't go.

"Then Alison came in and sat down in the dark on the toilet seat and when she'd finished, she took it one step further and asked if the service included wiping. The girl on Alison's left side got some toilet paper and reached over Alison's leg and wiped her. Shit, she was hot. I got up and followed her out of the bathroom when she left."

"How much do you know about her?"

"She was a little high that night. I asked her if she'd like to get some fresh air and we walked over to my place, which was just across the square from the party, and we just talked for a few hours. We didn't even kiss or touch, just talked and we seemed to sync. Like we could finish each other's thoughts.

"We talked about everything, sex, politics, religion, you name it. We could be quiet together too.

"She told me about her childhood and her parents."

"So how do you think she feels about marriage?"

"She married when she was younger but it hadn't lasted more than a year. She realized it was a mistake on her wedding night when her husband had had too much to drink and passed out on her before they could even get in bed. But she agreed to the marriage for the wrong reasons in the first place. It was expected in her social circle and her parents had kept pushing her to get married and give them some grandchildren. She told me she never even loved the guy."

"You say she likes sex. What do you mean?"

"Well she was, is, having sex with other guys and she told me she intended to continue even if we got married. She needs more sex than one man could give her."

"How did that affect you?"

"I guess I should have been horrified or mad or something like that, but I found it to be a real turn on that other guys wanted her; not just that they wanted her but that they'd had her. When she'd come to me, after just having sex with another guy and tell me about it, I'd get a real boner. We'd have great sex while she would tell me about how she had sucked another guy off and then had another one fuck her pussy and that I was getting sloppy seconds."

Hart was breathing heavily and he could feel himself getting hard just talking about it. He didn't notice that Dr. Longfellow seemed to be getting aroused too.

"Tell me the rest," she said in a husky voice Hart failed to notice.

"Sometimes she has me eat the other guy's semen out of her pussy. She'd have me hold some of it in my mouth and then French kiss her and we'd both swallow. She keeps her cunt shaved because she said it felt sexy and gave guys easy access to her vagina.

"She'd have multiple orgasms and sometimes her vagina would clamp down so hard on my dick it hurt, Doc.

"We agreed that if we get married she can have sex with as many men as she wants to as long as she is discrete and practices safe sex and knows the guy's sexual history. My only condition is that she has to share the details with me."

"Isn't that kind of sexual promiscuity kind of dangerous?" Dr. Longfellow said in a more normal voice, wondering about not just the physical STD dangers but also the emotional consequences.

"She usually goes after married men she knows haven't been fooling around or she goes for the silent virgin, inexperienced type."

Moving on to safer ground, Dr. Longfellow asked, "What do you mean about a neat freak?"

"I've seen her apartment, well more than seen it, I mean I often spend the night. Her place is a mess; stuff pilled everywhere. It isn't dirty, just real messy. I figured that someone who lived like that wouldn't be fussing at me for leaving things out or being messy. I had too much of that from my mom."

"What do you mean?"

"We had one room in our house, the 'living room,' though I could never figure out why they called it a living room. No one was allowed to go in there unless it was formal company, and other than that the furniture was always covered in transparent plastic and my mother was always after me to pick things up. My friends' homes all had living rooms like that, too. I knew I didn't want to marry someone who was going to fuss at me all the time to pick stuff up."

"You've thought a lot about this. Would you and Alison like to meet with me for some pre-marital counseling sessions?"

"That'd be great Doc. I'll ask Alison about it."

"We need to wrap up for today Hart. Same time next week? We still need to process your fears of doing your Dissertation defense."

"Okay see you then," Hart said.

Dr. Longfellow, had to get to all of Hart's past to help him, though she admitted to herself that some of it was long and tedious, and she wished she could speed him up in the process but she knew from her own training and experience that she had to let him set his own pace, no matter how tortuous it was for her; Hart would have to do the same for his patients in the future. She hoped she was teaching him well.

Chapter 40

Dr. Longfellow

Dr. Longfellow was glad she had a few minutes before her next session. It had gotten a little steamy there and Hart was an attractive guy. She needed to watch her counter transference and she couldn't wait to get home to jump her husband's bones. He'd wonder what had gotten her so wound up.

She wondered why Hart hadn't said anything about being in love when he talked about Alison. She made a note to ask Hart about that at the next session. It seemed to her that Hart was more in lust than love.

Usually graduate students who had some real-life experience, like Hart with four years in the US Air Force, became better therapists than those who came to graduate school straight from their undergraduate degree. She had some doubts about Hart but she wasn't sure why. She didn't think the relationship with Alison would last. Psychologists speak the language of feelings, through spoken or unspoken words, thoughts, body language, tone and pace of words and intuiting the meaning and feelings behind the words. Dr. Longfellow thought she was missing something with Hart and that Hart was missing something with Alison.

Chapter 41

Hart and Alison

Hart and Alison got married shortly after she had passed the bar and he had graduated with his Ph.D. in Clinical Psychology. They never got any pre-marital counseling; there was just too much going on with the wedding plans. The ceremony was small, just close family, her parents, and his mother, and a few friends. He didn't know where his dad was and really didn't care.

The sex continued to be great and varied. Alison had sex the afternoon of the wedding with Hart's best friend. Hart's best friend was shocked when Alison seduced him and would have been appalled if he had known that Hart had been complicit in this seduction. That night Hart was eager to hear about the details of the seduction and to enjoy sloppy seconds before they left to go on their honeymoon.

On the plane trip over to Kona on the Big Island, they were comfortable in their side-by-side first-class seats as the plane cruised at 35,000 feet chasing the setting sun. Alison got a blanket and snuggled into Hart's chest, her body covering him, as she jerked him off. Later, she had him finger her to orgasm.

"Is everything okay?" a young flight attendant had asked when Alison had moaned out, loud enough to be heard over the aircraft noise in the cabin.

Alison just smiled up from the blanket covering them and said, "Everything's fine. We're on our honeymoon."

"Oh, okay. I'll just leave you two alone," the flight attendant said with a knowing smile.

Chapter 42

The Honeymoon

The Big Island was a sybaritic paradise for their honeymoon where they indulged their sexual pleasures. Alison's only complaint was that she had only been able to find one married man she felt was safe enough to have sex with. She did fulfill one of her and Hart's fantasies by inviting Jamie, a woman she knew from college, to join her and her new husband for a threesome. Jamie was in Hawai'i for a post-divorce celebration.

I was beside myself when Lisa brought Jamie into our suite and instructed me to undress, and that she and Jamie were going to ravish me. I couldn't believe "every guy's" fantasy was about to come true for me.

Both women had shapely bodies and I just couldn't believe what was going to happen. Alison and Jamie started undressing each other, kissing as they proceeded. I was aroused as I watched the two nude women as I undressed and was eager when they invited me to a three-way kiss. Their tongues were twisting and swapping from mouth to mouth and bodies pressed together. I felt two hands on my already hard as steel dick and I was fingering two different pussies. I was pumped with excitement as I watched the two women entwined, their lips licking each other's nether lips.

Neither Alison nor Jamie had ever had sex with another woman before yet they seemed to be taking to the experience with great enthusiasm. For a while I just watched in escalating excitement and then joined in. Jaime was so excited she took a receptive, doggie-style position, and moaned in anticipation. Alison guided my throbbing dick into Jamie.

I was so excited I felt I might cum instantly. Alison licked my balls as I fucked Jamie and then Alison moved so that she could look up at me. I watched the rapture in Alison's eyes. It was too much for me, and I shot my load. I fell to the side of the king-size bed and watched the two women bring each other to multiple climaxes. I felt somewhat used and sad; it was just sex for Alison; there was no love involved.

Finally, temporarily sexually sated, and hungry, Alison called room service and ordered three T bones, "Very rare and I mean I want to see blood," she said, "With everything, salad, baked potatoes, and all the trimmings, and three bottles of a good red wine."

"What kind?"

"I don't care, you pick ones you like," she said and hung up.

Soon there was a knock on the door and a call of "Room Service."

I got up, "Just a minute I called," as I put on a robe. "You two cover up," I said. I went to the door, opened it and asked the young bellboy to bring in the cart and put it over by the table that came with the suite.

The young man walked in pushing the cart, and it wasn't until he was fully in the room that he saw the two women sitting naked on the bed. His jaw dropped open, staring wide-eyed, he was too shocked to look away. "Where do you want . . ."

"Just leave it," I said, pushing a tip into his hand and turning him to the door.

"You guys are heartless," I said to Alison and Jamie after I shut the door.

"Did you see the look on his face?" Alison asked. "That was a Master Card 'Priceless' moment."

"Did you see the instant tent in his pants?" Jamie asked.

"Maybe we should call him back."

"That's too much," I said.

"Your dick doesn't seem to think so," both women said at the same time, pointing to my hard dick sticking through the front of my robe.

We all laughed. We were having too good a time as we dug in and ate our steaks, potatoes, and salads, washing it all down with two bottles of wine.

Our hunger now sated, we were ready for more sex for dessert.

"Jerk-off for us," Jamie said. "I've never seen a guy do it except on porn flicks."

"Yeah. Do it Hart," Alison said as she sipped her wine.

"No," I said, "It's too embarrassing." I was feeling used again but I couldn't deny my arousal at the thought.

"Your dick doesn't seem to be embarrassed," Alison said again, pointing to my now very hard dick.

"Oh, okay," I said, dropping my robe, "Hand me some of that body oil."

"Oh," exclaimed Jamie, "He's done this before."

"Yeah," I said, "but not in front of two, just Alison."

"I got on the bed between them and Alison and Jamie took sips of their wine and leaned over me, their tits touching my arms, and kissed me, passing some wine from each mouth to mine, dribbling some on my chest. They leaned back and the two women and I rubbed my dick with oil.

"Watch his hand," said Alison, letting go of the shaft. "When it goes really fast he's going to cum."

We all three stared at my hand sliding up and down my shaft with the head peaking out between strokes.

"Talk dirty to me," I said in a husky voice.

"Your dick looks great. I loved it when you fucked me and then put it in your wife's mouth and then she put it back in me."

As they talked, I moved my hand faster.

"His balls feel great," said Jamie, as she cupped them and rolled them around.

"He's getting close!" Alison said. "Put your finger under the sack and rub at the base, just before his asshole."

"Oh, oh, god I'm cuming!" I moaned. Suddenly a rope of stringy white cum shot out of my dick and landed on Jamie's face. She had been leaning down to get a close look. Then two smaller spurts followed and fell on the side of my leg.

"Not bad for a guy who's already cum once tonight," Alison said.

"My god, that was fantastic. I've never seen anything like it. That's better than any porn I've ever seen."

I didn't know what to say; I somehow felt it was wrong but I couldn't deny I had enjoyed it.

Chapter 43

Alison

The sex continued off and on all night. They'd sleep for an hour or so and then someone would be having sex with someone.

The next morning the women were invigorated but I was exhausted. The women left me to rest while they went to see if they could "score some more" in paradise.

Jamie had to leave the next day and Alison and I explored the Big Island and both of us fell in love with the old town quaintness of Hilo.

On the flight back, I was relieved when Alison wasn't interested in any more sex under a blanket. She seemed to be in a pensive mood.

We don't often realize the hurt we cause others, but sometimes we do but we can't stop it. It has to come and there is nothing we can do but to accept the suffering and hope to learn from it. Sometimes we get a break and things turn out okay with no real harm done but that is not usually the way it ends up, but we have to go on living, she thought as the airplane sped through the night taking them back to new realities. *It doesn't matter what we reach for; what matters is that we keep reaching and trying to make whatever connections we can with other humans,* she rationalized.

For some reason I didn't understand, I was sad and thoughtful. *I was angry with myself for the way I had used Hart on our honeymoon. I remembered my childhood and how my parents had never been there to give me the attention I craved and needed.*

I had been seeing shrinks since kindergarten; they knew and I knew I was seeking attention that my parents couldn't or wouldn't give me. Then when I discovered sex I could get all the attention I needed. Yet even with all the sex, I knew that there was something missing. I had the sex to get closeness. And no matter how much sex I had, the more sex I had, the less closeness I felt. I hoped I could make it work with Hart. But I was having serious doubts about my admittedly selfish needs and myself. Hart was just too nice a guy. I hoped I wouldn't ruin it with him. All I could do was try. I really didn't want to hurt him.

Hart was pensive also. It's possible I thought to myself, *that a person can be callous and noble both at the same time; one can be self-sacrificing as well as self absorbed and display genuinely caring behavior while at the same time being a stone-cold steely-eyed sexual predator. In an instant life can change with no soundtrack to guide you or to let you know that the change was coming. There are no do overs or undo commands.*

When Alison thought of the truth about her parents she realized that they really did love her and that reminded her that love alone is not enough. *What each of us needs is a sense of identity and that can only be achieved by making mistakes and pushing against boundaries,* she thought.

Hart wished that they had gotten the premarital counseling from Dr. Longfellow.

When we returned to Cleveland, both Alison and I had new jobs waiting. I was starting as a new psychologist at the Cuyahoga County Mental Health Center and Alison was a junior assistant to the trial attorneys in her mother's litigation firm.

It wasn't long before I was defending cases on my own. The drama of the courtroom fed some need in me. Cross-examining and shredding expert witnesses was a great adrenaline rush, especially showing some academic shrink he was a dick-head and didn't know what he was talking about. Most of them were stupid and fell for the same old tricks. I remembered the first time I did it.

Tell me, Doctor, are you being paid for your testimony?

Yes was the usual reply.

How much?

How much, what?

Come on, Doctor don't be coy. How much are you being paid for your testimony?

$600 an hour.

So. You're being paid $600 an hour for your testimony.

Yes.

So basically you're saying you're a whore selling your testimony for $600 an hour.

Objection, shouted the opposing counsel. Too late.

Question withdrawn your honor.

But the jury had the message and the Doctor's credibility had been badly damaged if not destroyed.

Castrating men in public was fun and a real turn on, almost like fucking them against their will, I thought.

The torrid sex continued, although less and less frequently, as Alison was working eighty-hour weeks and often getting her sex at the office from coworkers. She had become tired of telling Hart about them. There just wasn't time. And she was becoming ashamed of herself. Secretly, Hart was happy that the sex was decreasing, as he just couldn't keep up. Alison always demanded that he bring her to three or four orgasms with his tongue, finger, dick, or a dildo. He'd still get rock hard when she told him about one of her blowjobs or fucks on her office desk.

Chapter 44

Hart

Less than a year after I had been working at the Cuyahoga Mental Health Center, I had made the decision to try private practice. It was what I had always wanted to do, to be like Dr. Longfellow and really help people. The pay was a lot better and the patients were a lot more interesting than the poor, uneducated people who went to the mental-health center. They weren't bad patients, but I wanted more. I'd had lunch with several colleagues who had made the switch from working in various institutions to private practice and they all encouraged me to do it.

Alison and I discussed it and she encouraged me too. She wanted me to develop some outside interest. She felt that I was becoming boring; I wasn't bringing any newness to the bed or the relationship. That seemed to be all her responsibility. She'd encouraged me to go out with other women but I was too shy, plus I was too afraid of STDs.

Thinking about it was half the problem between us. It had taken me some time to realize that Alison wanted someone who was much more open to experimental sex and it wasn't me. What was normal anyway I asked myself. For example she was motivated by sex and money and getting more of both. I on the other hand didn't really care much about money but wanted to help change lives and practice my profession.

I had enough savings to last while I started working part time at the mental-health center and opened a part-time private practice in a Doctor's office complex next to the University of Cleveland. The space I rented had two rooms, just a small waiting room and a slightly larger office. To keep overhead low I didn't have a secretary and did all of my own scheduling, billing, and all the paperwork. It wasn't long before I, like my wife, was putting in 80-hour weeks and we saw less and less of each other. We quit using birth control and tried to get pregnant. I had always wanted a child and we both thought a child might bring us back together.

Chapter 45

Hart

Within six months I was so busy in my practice that I had the courage to quit my part-time job with the mental-health center and go into full-time private practice. Most of my referrals were from medical Doctors and Attorneys and sometimes from child welfare. The medical Doctors were mostly either general practice or family practice MDs who didn't have the time to deal with the emotional complaints of most of their patients. The Doctors knew what many of their patients really needed was to have someone to share their issues with and who would help them learn to cope better with their problems. The MDs were only too happy to have another shrink to refer their patients to. Their psychiatrist colleagues were good for psychosis but for the average run of the mill anxiety, depression, and parenting/relationship problems, they found that their patients usually got better help from psychologists.

As I developed my reputation as a competent practitioner I was flooded with referrals and could be—and had learned the hard way that I had to be—choosier about who I saw. I did a lot of telephone screening before making the first appointment to keep out borderline personality disorders, active drug abusers, the frankly psychotic, and the back-door referrals from attorneys trying to snag me into being a "whore" for their client in a custody battle.

I rented a larger office, one that had a front and back door, so that patients wouldn't have to see each other passing in the waiting room as they came and went. Psychotherapy wasn't perceived as the stigma it used to be. Nonetheless there was still some stigma attached to seeing a shrink. *After all*, I thought, *healthy people don't see shrinks. And then lots of sick ones don't either and to be honest, most of the people I see are as healthy as I am. And how healthy is that?* I wondered. *Quit talking to yourself. At least I'm not doing it out loud. Yeah, not yet,* part of my mind said.

Alison had helped me screen the resumes of the people who responded to the ad for a psychologist's office assistant experience was not necessary. We couldn't put it in the ad, but Alison screened out all males and any woman who was over twenty-five. Alison wanted someone young and sexy who might be able to loosen me up and add some spice to our sex life. Attorneys were usually much more lax about the ethics of having sex with coworkers, subordinates, and/or clients.

She and I interviewed several competent young businesswomen. They were too competent and not sexual enough to meet Alison's criteria for my future office assistant and hopefully sex partner. Alison was beginning to feel more, abnormal for her, guilt about all of her sex partners and believed that if Hart had another partner, she'd feel less guilty. She could imagine him getting it on with his assistant on the couch in his office. Alison had narrowed the choice down to two young women, both twenty years old, blonds, with perky breasts and good figures. The choice between the two was made when one said how thrilled her boyfriend would be if she got a job working for a real psychologist. She was out. Alison wanted someone who would be available to me. Alison used one of her firm's private detectives to check the other girl out. The report came back that she didn't have a current boyfriend but had been dating an older man and may be a gold digger. *Perfect*, thought Alison.

I hired Peggy Sue Masters to start the next week. She was to work part time, four hours a day five days a week, as a combination receptionist who also did many of the other hundreds of details that went into making a private practice a success. She would also have time to continue her college work. She came in for her first day and was so excited she kissed me on the cheek and jumped up and down in excitement.

Alison came in the next week to check on the new assistant.

"That's my real name," Peggy Sue said. "My mother thought it was cute. Just call me Sue, all my friends do."

Alison thought she looked luscious and if Hart didn't jump her bones, she might. Still, Alison recognized that she had to suggest to Sue that wearing a see-though blouse wasn't appropriate for work, as she would be greeting Dr. Albertino's patients.

"Oh, I see what you mean," Sue said, looking down at her breasts, which were clearly visible through her blouse. They stood out nicely in a very brief pushup bra.

"Good luck Sue, see you later."

In addition to the big leather patient recliner and my own executive desk chair, I had a couch in my office and could and often did take naps there, especially when I had a "no show" patient. That evening after work, Alison came back and asked me how things were going with Sue.

"Fine," I said as Alison was pulling me to the couch.

"I hope you have good sex with her on this couch," she said as she climbed on top of me, unzipped my pants, pulled out my dick, and stuffed me inside her. She rode me to a quick climax. I enjoyed the sex but felt used.

Chapter 46

Hart and Alison

The months flew by and it seemed that Hart and Alison only saw each other on some weekends and holidays. She was often gone on "work" trips and there were fewer stories of her sexual affairs. We grew further and further apart.

I do my best thinking on the toilet, one of life's truly unappreciated great pleasures. That's what I needed to do with Hart, dump him. It just wasn't working. At first I thought he was truly a sexually free spirit like I was or wanted to believe I was. I had thought that the bathroom scene at the party where I'd gotten to know Hart was way out there. I really liked him and truly wanted what I thought was best for him and I had come to realize it wasn't me. I wasn't a bad person. That's why I tried to get him a sexy office assistant to ease the pain I knew was coming.

I had realized the end was coming long before Hart ever would. I had to make it seem callous on my part so that Hart could blame me. Truly, I wanted to set him free, even if I couldn't set myself free from my own needs. My sexual appetites were only a temporary substitute for what I needed. And I didn't know what I did need.

Although wildly promiscuous, even indiscriminate in my sexual behavior, I had tried to be careful. I even had the investigators from my mother's firm check the sexual lives of the men I planned on having affairs with. The men also had to get "tested" before I would have intercourse with them. Until then, they had to settle for hand jobs or oral sex with condoms. I never had unprotected sex without a clean bill of health.

Somewhere I must have slipped up. I had regular check-ups myself, especially since Hart and I had started trying to get pregnant, yet my last exam indicated I was HIV positive. I had it checked a second time with the same results. That was why I had quit having sex with Hart. It wasn't that I didn't care for him; I cared very much. I didn't want to hurt him and was too ashamed to tell him.

Although HIV wasn't the immediate death sentence it once was, I refused to expose Hart or any future baby. And I had protected sex with other men and women only after telling of my condition.

"But why?" Hart asked, not surprised yet deeply hurt nonetheless, when Alison asked for a divorce.

"It's just not working, Hart. You know it."

"We're both just working too much. We can cut back. We can work this out."

"Hart, when was the last time we had sex?"

"Not that long ago."

"It's been over three months and I've been fucking the brains out of the guys in my office and some of your colleagues," she lied.

"What?" said Hart, now shocked and angry. "You . . . We had an agreement. You were supposed to tell me."

"Yeah, well, it got boring. So sue me. No," she laughed, "I'm suing you, for divorce."

"But honey," Hart pleaded, "don't you want to try? We can get counseling."

"We'd have to go out of town. I've fucked most of the marriage counselors, male and female." She lied again.

"You what!"

"You heard me the first time. I've fucked your friends and colleagues. I even told some of them how you like to eat their cum out of me." She continued to lie to try to make Hart angry with her to ease his pain and her guilt.

"What!" Hart sputtered. "You didn't!"

"Yes, I did. It's over, Hart," Alison said as she turned to walk to the door. "I'll have my attorney contact your attorney. No children and we each take our own practices. It won't have to be bitter or even hostile."

Hart was crushed, devastated, not by her leaving so much, and not by her fucking his friends but by her not telling him all about the sexual encounters and telling others of his kinky sexual desires. How would he face his colleagues?

Life can turn on a dime, literally. And its changes can occur with split-second speed. You're moving on through your life making money and taking care of things. And then, suddenly, you find out your wife wants a divorce. What's more she doesn't want any counseling to see if we could work it out, Hart thought.

Chapter 47

Hart and Sue

Hart didn't realize it, yet he was vulnerable to any woman who would pay the least attention to him. He desperately needed reassurance and love. He started looking on the Internet and went out for coffee with several women who seemed interesting but it never worked out. He was too shy and hurt by the breakup with Alison. He never called them for a second date.

The legal process went quickly and within five months they were officially divorced.

Hart threw himself into his work. He told himself, *I'm happy going back to basics, helping others. I needed to focus my attention on my patients and their feelings, not on myself, and that helped me cope with my own feelings.*

Sue, who had the responsibility for opening the mail, saw the divorce papers before Hart did. She set about making herself more indispensable, and alluring. She took to wearing very sexy clothes and would let her breasts brush his arm any chance she got. She wore very short skirts and dropped things in his office, bending down with her ass up in the air, and knew that if he looked he would see she wasn't wearing any panties. She'd even shaved for him in anticipation.

It wasn't working; Hart didn't seem to notice my "offerings." I decided I'd have to take things into my own hands.

One day, soon thereafter, after the last patient of the day had left, I locked the outer door and walked into Hart's private office. He turned slowly in his chair. I sauntered over, knelt in front of him, and without a word I unzipped his pants, took out his cock, and proceeded to give him a blowjob. It didn't take long. Hart hadn't had sex in months. I carefully zipped him up using a Kleenex to clean him up. "Good night, Doctor," I smiled as I pranced out the door without another word.

Hart again felt used but also excited; he knew it was wrong both ethically and morally but he rationalized that she had started it. He just went along.

At the end of the next day, I went in and coyly took Hart to his couch. I undressed in front of him and placed his hands on my waiting breasts as I went about seductively undressing him. "Squeeze them, please, Doc. Suck on them. Play with my nipples. Oh, yes! That's it Doc," and I had my first climax even before fucking him.

It was the best sex Hart had had in a long time and he didn't have to have Sue tell him about having sex with other men to get off.

I know a good thing when I have one, Sue thought.

It took me only four months of more or less constant sex to get Hart to propose to me. I accepted and we were married a few months before I graduated. I continued to work for him and we bought a condo. I had him put it in my name and we got me a new car. We didn't go on a honeymoon. I said I'd rather have the money it would cost as a present to me.

Hart continued to work very hard having eight to ten 45-minute appointments a day with the last one at 6 PM. Sue didn't stay after the last patient any more.

"I've got some shopping errands to do, honey," she said when Hart complained that he wasn't seeing much of her anymore. The sex had gone from once a day to once a week to once every two weeks or so and then to once a month. Hart had to resort to fantasizing about Alison having sex with other men or Sue having sex with other men. In desperation Hart told Sue of his fantasies. Sue was shocked and flatly refused to participate in any such kinky sex.

I called Alison and arranged for lunch the next week. After the initial pleasantries, being served our drinks, and placing our orders, Sue got right to the point. "So is it true?"

"What do you mean?" Alison feigned innocence.

"You know, that Hart would eat you right after you had sex with another man."

"Oh, that. Yeah, it's true. You want to get it on this afternoon? I've got time before my next appointment."

"You've got to be kidding," Sue exclaimed indignantly.

"Oh don't act all prissy on me, Sue," Alison said, taking a sip of her wine. "I remember that blouse you wore on the first day to work. I figured you'd be humping Hart on his couch within a week. I knew you were after him. That's why I had him hire you."

"How dare you!" I sputtered, angry that Alison had seen through me so easily. I was blond but I wasn't dumb and I had figured I'd get a bundle off Hart if the marriage didn't work out. I got up and stomped out of the restaurant.

"Oh well," Alison toasted herself, "Can't say I didn't try." She did feel bad for Hart but didn't know what she could do to comfort him.

Chapter 48

Hart

That evening Sue told Hart he had to move out and that she was filing for a divorce. If he tried to fight her she'd file a sexual harassment suit against him for what he did to her before they were married.

I moved out, heartbroken again, and very depressed. I went back to see Dr. Longfellow and that, some medication, and my work with my patients kept me going.

Within six months I was divorced for the second time. Sue got the condo, half our savings, and her car. I didn't have to pay any alimony as she was working full time and making more than she had when she worked for me.

With the experience I had gained working for Hart, I had quickly found another job in a psychiatrist's office. The guy was older and I thought he might be vulnerable. I'd bide my time and then see if I could use my sexual charms on him. I knew men and how the world worked.

I worked through my feelings about the divorce with Dr. Longfellow and was doing okay but was still very embarrassed believing that all my colleagues knew the details of my private life. In *The American Psychologist* I saw an ad for a psychologist to work at the State Hospital in Kaneohe, Hawai'i. I applied for the position, and after a telephone interview was hired. The few possessions I had I packed up, transferred my patients to other psychologists, and left for Honolulu within a month.

PART THREE

Chapter 49

Lisa

There was no one to greet me when I arrived at the Hilo International Airport, which was how I wanted it, to start fresh and unknown. I arrived in the late afternoon, after transferring from my United flight from Cleveland to Honolulu and then on to Hawaiian Air to Hilo.

Lisa thought, *the airport car rental agency had been very friendly and helpful, giving me a map of the local area.* It was a short trip from the airport to downtown Hilo and I fell in love with the "old town" feel of the place. I drove around for a while just looking. Amazingly, I didn't hear a single horn honk. Somehow I felt more alive in the old town of Hilo, than I had for a long time.

I had made arrangements for the couple that had been renting my mother's house to be gone before I arrived and had the rental agency that was handling the place have it cleaned so that it would be ready for me when I got there.

Stopping at the real-estate agency I signed the necessary forms and got keys and directions to my new home. The power, phone, and cable had been left on in the realtors name and I would have to have them transferred to my name later. On the way to my new home I stopped at the Sack & Save and got some basic food and house supplies. Then I went back down to Bay Front and turned left towards Hamakua to go across the "singing" bridge and on to Papaikou and my new home. There was a palm-tree border in front of the house and a gravel drive leading around to a two-car garage on the side. The drive also made a circle in front of the front door.

There were stone crouching lions on either side of the big wooden double doors. It had an inviting yet formidable look. The key fit easily and I walked into the foyer that was a simple wall of koa wood from floor to ceiling with an opening to the right and left and a bench to sit on. Sitting down, I took off my shoes as I knew was the local custom. I stepped around to the left and was in a gorgeous main room. It had a soft black leather couch and easy chairs facing floor to ceiling sliding glass doors that opened out onto a twelve-foot wide by forty-foot long lanai. The Pacific Ocean view was breathtaking and unobstructed by any other houses.

My lot dropped off into the sea some five hundred feet slanting steeply below. The lot was only partially covered in wild grass and was mostly black lava. It extended three hundred feet on either side so I didn't have any close neighbors. Opening the lanai doors, I walked out onto the koa deck. A stiff ocean breeze and the smell of the sea greeted me. I leaned on the surrounding rail, my long red hair blowing in the breeze. I couldn't believe this was all mine. It was too beautiful.

Standing out in the open lanai at night in my new home in Hawai'i; I had wanted to see the sky, the vast distant enormous sky. The stars were like tiny pricks of light against the deeper black sky. It stretched to further heights, bigger than I could imagine. Billions of bright stars were far far away and they seemed to be unnaturally vivid as they showed outwards into the reaches of the universe. It stretched on forever. The feeling was like I was in a big clearing that was very dark and yet rich with latent shadows and possibilities. In the distance I could see life coming towards me and I wanted to go towards it too. Uncertain of the road or the trail as I was, I wondered would I ever reach where I was going. There seemed to be dark shapes around me with unknown intent. I was scared but moved forward through my tears.

Shivering in the cool sea breeze, I went back inside wiping my tears away and noticed the brick wood-burning fireplace on the far side of the great room. *Who would think you'd need a fireplace in Hawai'i?* I explored the rest of the house. It smelled of fresh cleaning. The kitchen was to the right of the entranceway and had a huge sub-zero refrigerator, and what looked like a professional oven range/cook top and microwave. There was plenty of room for cooking and even a small breakfast area.

On the other side of the great room was the master bedroom and bath with a built-in Jacuzzi big enough for two, a separate bidet, separate his and her sinks, and a separate shower also big enough for two. The king-size bed was plain by comparison to the rest of the house. There was a flat panel TV with surround sound in both the great room and master bedroom. *This place is fantastic,* I thought. My stepfather was rich I knew, but I had never realized that my mother had such great taste.

There was also a spare guest bedroom with separate bath and another half bath off the kitchen. I was overwhelmed. This would definitely be my home. The only things I could think to improve it were some of my own art and curtains and other decorations I would change in time. For now it was perfect.

After getting over the jet lag, I followed up on the job lead I had gotten from my old boss. I didn't really need the income since I had plenty to live on from my inheritance and yet I wanted to do something with my life.

The company, Designs Unlimited, was located in the Shipman Industrial Park, just south of Hilo half way to Keaau. They did custom designs and construction for luxury homes and business. As it turned out they had an urgent need for someone who could do both design and art work, both for interior decoration and for publications about their work. The person, who had been doing the job, had decided to quit to return to the mainland. He couldn't take the quiet life of Hilo and the third-world attitude of much of the government that seemed to be very anti-business.

I called Mr. Nelson, the president of the company, and he arranged to meet me for an interview the next day. I took a cab to the interview, and had my portfolio of my work and the letter of recommendation from my old boss. I was eager. Several of the other employees sat in on part of the interview and it was soon apparent that not only did I have the skills and experience they were looking for, but also that I would fit in well as a team player.

"We could wait to discuss it and call you back, but I don't think that will be necessary. The job is yours if you want it Ms. Havenhurst."

I was thrilled. I too thought we were a good match.

"The salary is competitive but the cost of living is high here," Mr. Nelson continued. "It does include full medical benefits, and a retirement plan. The hours can be long and they can also be flexible to meet your needs."

When I didn't say anything right away, he added, "and in six months, if things work out as I think they're going to, we will be able to offer you a 20% raise."

Barely able to talk, I stammer out a, "Yes, Yes. I accept. Thank you." The salary was almost twice what I had been making in the States or as I had quickly learned to say, on the mainland. Newcomers seemed to forget that Hawai'i is a part of the United States, although I had to admit it did have somewhat of a third-world country ambience.

"Good. When can you start?"

"Well, I do need to get a few things settled and to buy a car. If you can give me time off to do some of those things, I can start tomorrow."

"Done," he said and offered his hand. "I'll have the paper work ready for you to sign tomorrow. Welcome aboard."

"Mr. Nelson opened the door and called, "Joe, will you show Ms. Havenhurst her office and introduce her to the other staff. She'll be joining us starting tomorrow."

"Just call me Lisa please," I said to both Joe and Mr. Nelson.

"Okay," they said in unison.

"This way," Joe said as he took me around to introduce me. "We're having our usual Pau Hana get together this Friday and you can get to know us better then."

"Pau Hana?" I asked.

"Oh, that just means end of the work week."

"Okay," I said as Joe walked me to the door and drove me back to my home.

Somehow I seemed to find it easier to make friends here. I went to the Friday after-work Pau Hana parties and even went out on a date with Joe even though I didn't want to date anyone I worked with. He knew about my interest in doing my own art and had invited me to join him for a meeting of the Hilo Arts Group. They were a mixed group of painters, digital photographers, and artists that got together once a month to "talk story" and share ideas about art.

It was there that I had met Diana and Cheryl who were old time members and very willing to welcome me to the group. Both Diana and Cheryl were married, articulate, and knowledgeable on many subjects. They seemed to have some common problems with men and relationships, so I related to them on that level as well as on my interests in art.

I got my raise in six months and seemed to be fitting in and growing into my new life in Hilo. After the first year, I still loved the work I was doing and the people I was working with and even went out on a couple of dates with some guys. I had met them either through work or at the Arts group but they never lasted.

My friendship with Diana and Cheryl was lasting and developing, though they seemed to have more free time than I did. They had suggested to me that I quit working and just do my art, as it was selling well, but only on the mainland, and the demand exceeded my ability to paint new ones. I didn't want to quit working even though I didn't need the income. It was the social stimulation and intellectual challenges that the various projects involved that I needed. I was more often "on-site" interacting with designers and owners, than in my office at the company.

Chapter 50

Randy

I thought of dozens of plans to escape from the State Hospital. The nurses weren't watching me closely as it had been several months since my last "acting out" episode in the cow pasture. They took me off the "close watch" list and put me in a room with another long-term inmate, Paul Stallworth. Paul really was crazy yet he'd have lucid days and was an okay roommate if you left him alone on his "bad" days.

I started my escape plans by stopping my medication. Paul showed me how.

"You just put the pill in your mouth, close it, and move the pill with your tongue to your side teeth and then let it slip under your tongue," Paul told Randy.

"But doesn't the nurse check to make sure you swallow it?"

"Oh, sure. You got to swallow with your mouth closed so it looks like you swallowed the pill."

"I don't know if I can do that."

"Well you can practice with a small pebble."

"Like this?" I asked as I reached down and picked up a small pebble that looked, about the size of the pill I took every evening.

"Yeah. Now put it in your mouth and get it under your tongue and swallow. Then move it to outside of your back teeth."

I practiced a few times and found it was really quite easy to do. It was easy to pretend to take the pills. I'd just put them in my mouth while the nurse watched to make sure I was taking my medication. Sometimes the nurse would ask me to open my mouth and lift my tongue, but by then I'd let the pill slip to the side of my back molar. After I'd been off the meds for a few weeks my thinking seemed to be clearer.

Chapter 51

Randy

I spent my abundant free time using the library. The staff actually charted my library use as "therapy."

I used the computer in the library to Google escapes and hospital. A nurse or aid would check every now and then. They did for everybody to make sure none of the patients were using the Internet to watch porn. The checking was cursory at best; as long as they didn't see any pictures on the screen, they didn't look closely at what the inmates were doing.

I was amazed at the number of hits I had from my search over four hundred thousand. I started reading at random and decided I needed to narrow my search. I tried a number of different words but kept getting to many hits. Still I was getting some ideas. None of the staff carried any guns so I couldn't take a gun and shoot my way out. I could sneak a knife out of the kitchen, take one of the smaller aids as a hostage, and hold the knife to his neck and threaten to kill him unless they let me out. But then what? I'd make them give me a car and I'd force the aid to drive me off. I realized that that plan was no good. They'd just call the police and they'd follow me until we ran out of gas.

Googling Lisa's name and other information I had purposely remembered about her, I found her address on the Big Island of Hawai'i. It had taken some effort but I'd been determined and was elated when I found it. I was tempted to jerk-off right there in the library, but thought better of it. I had to plan and I didn't want to get "locked down."

I talked to my roommate about my various plans and frustrations at not being able to think of one that might work. It had been seven months since I had read the article about Lisa's move to the Big Island. I just had to escape. I knew Lisa needed me and I was determined to get to her.

"Why don't you just walk out?" Paul asked me.

"What? No way they'd let me do that."

"Oh, I don't mean on the day shift, you've got to wait until night."

"Still, I don't see them unlocking the door for me," I said.

"I didn't say they'd do that for you. Got to unlock the door for yourself."

"Yeah right, like I ask them for the keys and they say, 'Sure Randy, here you go.'"

"Well, I did it once."

"No you didn't," I said, thinking this must be part of the guy's delusional system.

"Did too. Was several years ago. Before you were here."

"They obviously caught you, you're back here now."

"They didn't catch me. I came back and they didn't even know I'd been gone."

"No way. You need your meds upped."

"You think I'm crazy huh?"

"Yeah."

Paul just gazed off into the distance as though he'd gone away in his mind.

After several minutes of silence, I asked Paul, "Okay, so how'd you do it?"

Paul was so long in waiting to answer that I thought he'd lost it for the day. "Was easy."

"Okay, I'm biting. How'd you do it?"

Paul looked shrewd and his eyes twinkled, "You remember those shrooms we ate that time in the cow pasture?"

I nodded.

"I had some shrooms and ground them up real fine and put them in their coffee."

"Who?"

"The two night-shift guys."

"Didn't they notice the taste?"

"Yeah, they complained it was bitter but there really isn't much taste to the shrooms."

"So then what?"

"When they were tripped out I just took the keys from one of them, unlocked the door, and walked out."

"How'd they catch you?"

"I told you they didn't. I found out I didn't have anywhere to go and came back in before the morning shift got in."

"They didn't know you'd been gone?" I asked in wonder.

"No they were still tripping when I got back. I put the keys back on the guy's belt and went to my room and went to sleep."

"Didn't they complain about being drugged?"

"I don't know. Nobody ever said anything to me. There wasn't any big shake down by the staff."

"I bet they were too embarrassed too tell anyone."

"Yeah maybe. I've still got some dried shrooms," Paul said, smiling.

Chapter 52

Randy

I made a small bundle of make up that I could hide inside a coat. That night I mixed the ground up shrooms in the aids' coffee and when they were tripped out I took the keys, and one of the aid's jacket that had a security badge on it and the words "Security" printed in big yellow letters across the back. I took the guys' wallets and credit cards. Between the two aids I got $120 in cash, which would be enough to buy a ticket from Honolulu to Hilo. I figured I could use the credit card with the badge for ID at least one time. After hugging Paul, I unlocked the doors and headed out to the dark parking lot. I had the keys to the aids cars'. There were only two cars in the lot and I picked the right one the first time. I unplugged it. The car was almost full of gas.

Since it was mid-February the cars were plugged in to keep the oil from freezing. It was one of the coldest winters in Ohio's history. *This doesn't make any significant difference for the weather in Honolulu,* I thought. I drove to the Cleveland airport and didn't have any trouble navigating as I had been there many times.

Parking in the unattended employees' parking lot, I walked to the tarmac like I belonged there. The few airline employees who were out on the tarmac loading and unloading luggage from the holds of the hug jets were all bundled up in long coats and fur hats. I hurried to a side door that entered the staff area and stopped the first guy I saw.

"Hey, I'm new here. Which way is the locker room? I need to get a winter coat before I go out there."

"What are you doing here?" the guy said, somewhat suspiciously. "It's not shift change," he said, looking at his watch.

"Yeah, I know. I was called in to fill in for a guy who got sick and had to leave."

"That must have been Bob."

"Yeah, I think that was the guy's name. The agency that called me said they had coats for guys who got called in on short notice. All I had to do was to check in the locker room."

"Okay. Glad you could make it, Bob was really sick." The guy believed I was there to fill in for "Bob," whoever that was, because he wanted to believe. "It's down the hall second door on the right."

"Thanks," I said in a friendly manner. "Sure is a cold one out there."

"Yeah I've got to run." The guy was still somewhat suspicious but said to himself, *fuck it, I ain't paid to be security.*

I got to the locker room and found a spare coat that fit and headed to the luggage area and luck was with me. I found a cage with a cat in it. All I had to do was change the tag to HNL for Honolulu. There were several luggage tags lying on a worktable nearby. I made the change, took the cat cage, and headed out to the tarmac.

"Hey buddy," I called to a guy who was loading luggage. "Where's the United flight to Honolulu? Someone forgot to load this cat," I said, holding up the cage.

"It's the second plane beyond this one. And you'd better hurry. I think they're almost through loading."

Luck was with me. The ramp to the plane's luggage hold was still in place and no one was about. That was a rare moment and I'd been prepared to lie about taking the cat in and then hope no one would notice that I didn't come back out. I went in and settled down with the cat and other animals in their cages. Moving over behind some luggage, I got a blanket and pillow and was far enough behind the luggage that if someone came to check on the pets, as they usually did on these long non-stop flights, no one would see me.

I had learned all this on the Internet. *A wonderful thing the Internet. I'll be with you soon Lisa.* I slept off and on for most of the trip. I'd found some bottled water but didn't have any food. I woke from my last nap when I felt the landing gear being lowered.

Chapter 53

Randy

Once the plane was stopped and the loading ramp in place, I waited for a few workers to come in to take out the luggage. I'd taken off the winter coat and hoped the word "Security" on the back of my jacket wouldn't alarm anyone. I didn't want to wait too long as I knew they'd come for the animals soon. Walking out, holding the cat cage in one hand and a small dog cage in the other, I passed one of the workers who just nodded to me.

I walked into the room where the luggage was loaded onto the conveyor belt; set the cages down on the floor and walked out the door to the baggage-claim area where passengers were waiting for their bags to come by on the circular carousel. I kept walking out the door and then followed the signs to Hawaiian Airlines, where I used the aid's badge and credit card for ID and paid cash to buy a round-trip ticket on the next flight to Hilo, which was on the windward side of the Big Island. I was proud of myself for remembering not to buy a one-way ticket, as that might alert security.

Chapter 54

Randy

When I got to Hilo it was all I could do to not go rushing to Lisa's house. I made an emergency stop in the restroom in the Hilo airport and entered one of the stalls, closed the door and jerked-off furiously thinking of images of Lisa. Since I had arrived around noon on a Tuesday morning I had the cab from the airport drive me straight to the local welfare office. *Wonderful stuff you can learn on the Internet,* I thought again as I walked into the welfare office.

As instructed, I took a number, one hundred ninety seven, and then sat in a dirty yellow plastic chair to wait for my number to be called. There were several dozen people waiting and I was lucky to get a seat.

"One hundred ninety seven?" was called out over the speaker a few hours later.

I got up and went to the open window and presented my number.

"ID please," said the petite Japanese lady on the other side of the counter.

"I lost it." *I knew I couldn't use the hospital aid's ID card.*

"Well you've got to have an ID to get any help. You'll have to go to the police to get an ID," she said and waited for me to leave.

"You don't understand. I lost everything. I don't have anything. No clothes, no money, no place to stay."

"What about your security job?"

"What? Oh that, I just found this jacket in the trash."

"Doesn't look like a jacket someone would throw away."

"Look Lady, please, I'm desperate; I got nothing. I need help, please."

"Okay," the lady said with a sigh. "Fill out this form and I can give you an emergency check for one month. But then you have to come back with an ID and you need to see Dr. Brandon to get certified as disabled." She handed me a well-used wooden clipboard with some forms for me to fill out. A stubby pencil was tied to the clipboard with a piece of string.

I took the forms back to my seat. I knew how the welfare system worked in Hawai'i, thanks again to the Internet. The crowd had thinned out considerably and it was almost four PM. I barely had time to fill out the forms. Most of it was easy; I wrote "none" for my address, occupation, and phone. The easiest part was using Paul's name, birth date, and social security number. I knew there weren't any warrants out on Paul Stallworth.

The clerk's window was just closing when I took the forms to hand in and I was able to get the emergency check. "There is a check-cashing store just a block down from the welfare office. It stays open until six PM," the clerk told me. "And the Methodist Church serves dinner at six thirty. It's just a short walk up Waianuenue Ave. You'll see the line out on the sidewalk."

I was able to cash my "emergency" check and made it to the church for supper. While eating the free dinner, I learned to "talk story" with some of the others, most of whom were homeless. One guy gave me the name of a boarding house.

When I went there after supper I was able to get a room in the back of a small house up the hill, or "Mauka," as I'd learned that was how the locals referred to going up the hill. Everything was Mauka, toward the mountain, or Makai, toward the sea, or as the locals would say, towards the name of a town. There wasn't any north or south, and windward or leeward were used for east and west.

Chapter 55

Randy

"You no dog, no cats, no food, no drink, no party, pay cash," said the older Filipino lady who ran the boarding house. I paid her and she told me, "You take number six, last on right, end of hall. No noise." She turned and left me standing on the porch, or lanai, as I'd learned it was referred to locally. She didn't seem to mind that I didn't have any luggage.

I couldn't wait any longer. I had to see Lisa that night. I'd Googled directions to Papaikou back in the hospital library. I walked down Wainuenue Ave. and started hitching north (or Hamakua way) on the belt loop road. It wasn't long before a Filipino farmer in an old Nissan pickup truck stopped and offered me a ride in the bed of the truck. There was someone else with the man in the cab.

"Where you go?" the man asked.

"Papaikou," I said, only I mispronounced it so that it sounded like Paypaycow.

"What? Never hear Paypaycow. You mean Papaikou?"

"Yeah that's it," I said, pronouncing it phonetically correctly this time as paw-pie-co.

The farmer pointed to the bed of the truck and I hoped in. It was only about twenty minutes before the truck pulled off the road and stopped.

The farmer leaned out the window and called back, "You here." I got out and watched the truck drive away. It wasn't hard to find Lisa's house, it was just a half-mile south of Papaikou, North of Hilo, and was just off a short road on the Makai side.

Chapter 56

Randy

I thought it was beautiful, a one-story, long low house with red-tiled roof, looking out over the Pacific Ocean. Night had fallen and I didn't think anyone would notice me as I walked silently towards Lisa's house. I walked down the drive and looked in a window but couldn't see anything. Then I went around the side and into the back yard of the house. The land sloped steeply towards the sea and I had to look up to the large lanai that projected out from the house. *I'm almost under her house. How am I going to be able to see in?* I wondered. I checked in the two-car garage but there were no windows and the door had a good solid lock.

Walking back out to the side of the house I almost fell down when I looked up again and saw Lisa standing there leaning on the wooden rail that ran around the lanai. She had on a sleeveless sundress that looked blue in the moonlight. She wasn't more than one hundred feet from me, looking out at the Pacific Ocean. My hand moved to my dick on its own. I could see partway up her dress. I imagined her curly red-haired pussy and remembered her hard pink nipples as I'd seen them from so long ago, as if it were yesterday.

She was beautiful and all mine. Her red hair blew in the ocean breeze. Her white skin was starkly beautiful in the moonlight. I called out her name softly as I stroked myself furiously. She couldn't hear me over the sound of the surf and the strong trade winds. The sea smell wafted over me and I imagined I could smell Lisa. It was over too quickly. My seed made a small white puddle in the moonlight on the shiny dark lava, just a short way from her lanai.

Lisa sighed and went in for the night. Spent, and both sad and happy, I walked back to the highway and quickly caught a ride back to Hilo. It was only nine thirty when I got back to my rooming house. I was met at the door by the woman of the house, "You no stay out late. I lock door," she said, glaring at me as if daring me to speak.

Chapter 57

Randy

In the day that followed, I learned the local bus system and found that it was free. I went to the police station with a made-up story that I was from Ohio and had been mugged and lost my ID and all my identification and needed a new driver's license. Using my friend Paul's name, birth date, and social security number was easy. I knew there weren't any outstanding warrants for Paul. I easily passed the written test and had gotten one of the guys at the rooming house to lend me his car to take the driving test. The local police were either to busy or lazy to even do a routine check of my name and SSN.

While I was at the police station filling out the paperwork to get a new license, I heard someone asking about a bicycle and I found out that I could get a bike from the police abandoned property department for $10. The bike was old and somewhat rusty and had decals of yellow ribbons to support the troops on both the front and rear fenders. I thought these must be left over from the Vietnam War. I peddled to Dr. Brandon's office in the Hilo Lagoon

Center and found Dr. Brandon's office on the third floor. I was disappointed when I found out I'd have to make an appointment and none were available for three weeks.

It must be my lucky day after all, I thought later that day when I got out of Ken's House of Pancakes with a job as a dishwasher starting tomorrow on the 3 to 11 PM shift.

On my first full day in Hilo I had gotten a bike, a driver's license, and a job. I needed the bike so that I wouldn't have to be hitching all the time. It was easy to hitch, but I didn't want to get known for stopping at Papaikou.

That night I was smiling with anticipation as I rode my beat up old bike across the "singing bridge," as the locals called it, and the few miles up the road to Lisa's house. It took longer than I thought it would, almost forty-five minutes before I got there. I knew Lisa would be waiting up for me. I wasn't disappointed. I again got to watch her on her lanai but got soaked in a sudden downpour. I didn't mind getting wet, but it drove Lisa inside and I couldn't find a way to peep into her bedroom window. It was too high up off the steeply sloping ground. There weren't any ladders I could use.

Chapter 58

Randy

Every night when I got off my shift at Ken's, I would peddle out to see my Lisa. I called it a date. I was frustrated, however. Out of twenty-five nightly trips to her house, I had only been able to watch her three nights. I'd called her phone a number of times but when she answered I'd hung up. "What's wrong, Lisa?" I asked out loud outside her house on the twenty-sixth night. My words were drowned out by the wind and sound of the crashing waves. "Why won't you come out and let me look at you?"

I was determined to find a way to be with Lisa even if I had to sneak into her house and hide in her closet. None of the windows were really good enough to see in. I figured she was probably at work during the day, so I would be able to break in and wait for her to come home. *She'll be surprised and happy to see me,* I thought, as I peddled out to her house.

When I got to her house, her car was gone, so I thought I would be able to break in easily. I tried the door but the credit-card trick I'd seen on TV didn't work. There were jalousie windows on both sides of her front door. I was in too much of a hurry and broke the second pane as I was drawing it out. When I reached to grab the broken piece I jabbed it deeply into my right hand.

I was bleeding profusely, yet I didn't care. I had to get into my Lisa's house. I got enough of the panes out and pushed the screen off so that I could reach around and unlock the door. I left a bloody palm print on the front door. At last I was inside and could smell Lisa's perfume. Turning left, I went down a brief hallway and found her bedroom. Lying down on her bed I fantasized about her walking in and seductively undressing for me. I began to play with myself. I didn't realize how badly I was bleeding. I barely noticed the blood dripping on my pants and the bed. It didn't take me long to cum. I had wanted to wait for her but was too excited.

Spent, I lay on Lisa's flowered bedspread and closed my eyes. I'd just wait for my lover. I knew she wanted me and we would fuck right there. I must have slept for an hour or more and woke up with a throbbing pain in my hand. The pain in my hand was so bad I knew I couldn't wait for Lisa. I had to take something to remember her so I went to her dresser and opened the drawers, searching until I found her underwear drawer. I took a pair of lacy panties and a matching bra and imagined her tits filling the cups. I stuffed my find in my pockets and got a small towel to wrap around my hand.

The pain was so great I had to leave; I had to get some help. Somehow I managed to hold the handlebar of my bike with my left hand and right forearm well enough to be able to ride back to Hilo. I saw the sign for a hospital and peddled up Wainuenue Ave. and on up the road to the Hilo Hospital. I walked into the ER and holding out my bloody hand, told the clerk at the counter, "I need help."

"Insurance card please."

I pulled out my license and said, "I ain't got no insurance. But I'm hurt," I said, shaking my hand wrapped up in the blood-soaked towel.

"Okay, it will be a few minutes though," the Filipino clerk told him. She'd seen it all and his injury wasn't that serious.

"You can sit over there," she said, pointing to the waiting area that was filled with other waiting patients.

I shuffled over to the only vacant chair and sat down. I grimaced in pain when my hand hit the armrest. "Ouch, ah shit!" I said. My pain was lost in the misery of the other waiting patients. I looked around. Some of the others in the waiting room were sleeping. A little girl with big brown eyes stared at me. She pulled at her mother's dress and pointed to the big man with the bloody towel wrapped around his hand. Her mother just told her not to point.

My eyes closed, I clenched my teeth in pain. "I don't know how long I can stand this," I muttered to myself as I rocked back and forth in my chair.

I couldn't tolerate pain very well. I opened my eyes and glanced at the big white clock on the wall above the clerk's window. *How long have I been waiting?* I wondered. My legs were shaky when I got up and went to the clerk's window.

"Hey, lady, I need something for the pain."

"The Doctor will be with you in a few minutes," she said and turned back to her computer monitor.

I just stood there for a few minutes. Finally, I went back to my chair and sat back down, began rocking again, and moaning. I looked at the clock again. Only five minutes had gone by. A nurse in scrubs came out and called a patient's name. She was taking a woman and her daughter toward the big double doors marked in very big red letters "STAFF ONLY."

"Hey!" I called out, "I need something for pain."

The steel doors closed. I looked at the clock again. It seemed like time was standing still; I knew how to get the attention of Nurses and Doctors. I'd had lots of practice at the State Hospital. I stood up and started screaming and shaking, cursing in a loud and incoherent way. I'd get their attention. They'd have to give me something for my pain.

He got their attention all right. Two big Samoan aids were suddenly on either side of him frog marching him down the hall. He was still screaming when they locked him in a secure holding cell on the psych ward. They came back in and held him while a nurse gave him an injection. It was like magic. *The drug must have been good,* he thought, as he instantly started drifting off. He'd gotten what he wanted.

Chapter 59

Randy

The next morning I woke up disoriented for a moment. Then it came back to me. My hand was wrapped in a clean bandage; it didn't hurt much. *They must have some good pain meds here. Where'd they put my clothes? I wondered. I've got to get out of here.*

I'd just gotten up to walk to the door when it opened and two uniformed policeman walked in, a big guy whose name tag said "Kama" and a thinner one whose tag said "Small."

"You're Mr. Paul Stallworth?" Kama asked, reading from a pad in his big hands.

"Yeah," I replied, sitting down on the bed. I felt naked in the small hospital dressing gown. "What's wrong? I just cut my hand. It was an accident. No big deal. I'm okay now. I got to get to work."

"You know a . . ." Kama looked at his pad, "Ms. Lisa Havenhurst?"

"No."

"Were you out at her house yesterday, Mr. Stallworth?"

"No. I told you. I just cut my hand."

"How'd you cut it?"

"What?"

"Your hand."

"Uh, I dropped a bottle."

"You can drop the act," Small said. "We're arresting you for breaking and entering, trespassing, and burglary." Then he read me my "Miranda Rights" from a card making sure to repeat it exactly so that some fancy defense schmuck couldn't get the case thrown out on a technicality.

Chapter 60

Randy

I had learned from my last arrest. I wasn't stupid after all, and there were lots of guys in the State Hospital in Ohio who had educated me on the NGRI process but I hadn't been ready to try it there. I needed to be sane enough to assist my public defender in my case. Then my attorney could plead my case for "Not Guilty by Reason of Insanity," NGRI.

I knew how to act now. I didn't need to be so crazy that I got sent to the hospital for evaluation of my "fitness to proceed" so that I could be tried for my charges. I just needed to be crazy enough to convince the three Doctors who would evaluate me that I was crazy at the time I committed the crimes and yet sane enough to be tried.

I could easily do that; I knew how to talk crazy and pretend that that was the way I was when I did the crimes. Then I only had to convince the jury that I was indeed "crazy," so that they could agree with the Doctors and send me to the State Hospital where I would stay and be "treated until cured" or clinically discharged as not being a danger to myself or society.

It took a little more than three weeks for the three Doctors to finish their evaluations and they all found him, aka Mr. Paul Stallworth, to be fit for trial. They also found, in correct legal terms, that he lacked understanding that what he had done at the time was wrong, and that he was also, at the time of the crime, lacking volitional capacity to conform his behavior to the requirements of the law—what the legal profession called insanity—for the charges of, Breaking and Entering, Burglary, and Sexual Assault in the Forth Degree.

The prosecution had all the evidence they needed. They had his blood type and his fingerprints in blood inside Ms. Havenhurst's house. They'd found her panties and bra in the pockets of Randy's jeans. When they got the results of the DNA tests on the semen from Ms. Havenhurst's bedspread, they'd added the fourth charge of Sexual Assault.

My PD had very little trouble convincing a jury that his client was "crazy." I knew how to play the part and indeed, for part of it, I wasn't playing. I was crazy. I believed that Lisa loved me and wanted to marry me. "You don't understand," I cried out from the witness stand, "she loves me. I had to do it! She made me."

It didn't take the jurors long to find Mr. Stallworth "Not Guilty by Reason of Insanity." He was sent to the Hawai'i State Hospital, the "Red Roof Inn," on Oahu, to be treated until cured.

At the trial Lisa had thought the man looked vaguely familiar but she didn't make the connection from the sight of the current crazy man in court and the kid who had stalked her when she was a teenager. She did wonder if she was doing something to attract such weirdoes.

Chapter 61

Hart

My first ex-wife and I had visited Hawai'i for our honeymoon and I had decided after my second divorce to move from the mainland to Hawai'i; to try to start my life over. I had liked the small-town atmosphere of Hilo and there was a University there.

As a stepping-stone for the eventual move to the Big Island, I started as a clinical psychologist working on a ward at the State Mental Hospital in Kaneohe on Oahu, or as it was known locally, the Red Roof Inn. I had left my thriving private practice in Ohio and knew that eventually I wanted to open a private practice and wanted to have a solid basis before I started, so I took the hospital job.

The first time I looked out on the Bay from the hospital grounds I was struck by the beauty. The hospital was located on the foothills on the windward or east side of the Koolau Mountains and looked out over Kaneohe Bay. I had thought, *Wow, if I ever need to be in a nut house, this is where I want to be committed.*

However, the reality was that there were very few "people like me" that were patients. The majority of the 600+ patients were old, burned out schizophrenics and some forensic patients; and some were even sex offenders.

It was the first time I had worked in an inpatient setting since my internship years before. At first I tried to get some group therapy started for the patients on my ward. I was the only psychologist on the ward and the position had been vacant for several months, so there wasn't much in the way of verbal therapy going on, just medication, activities, and crafts. The Red Roof Inn, however, wasn't like the mental ward on which I'd interned back on the mainland. Those patients had been able to talk and interact with each other and me if they chose to. Talking to the schizophrenics at the Red Roof Inn was like talking to someone who wasn't there and I usually didn't get any reply in return. Getting a group of five or more patients to just sit together, and not get up and wander away, was a huge accomplishment; getting them to talk or process their feelings or thoughts was impossible.

This is driving me nuts, I thought as I tried to do something positive on the ward. I talked to other psychologist in the hospital who seemed surprised that I was upset that the patients couldn't interact more, like "What did I expect?"

There was, however, a group of patients who could and did talk. These were the sex offenders. Some were child molesters and some were rapists and some were stalkers and/or exhibitionists. They were housed in the forensic section of the hospital and were required by the courts to participate in sex-offender treatment. When I first heard about the sex-offender inmates, and their required group therapy, my reaction was the same as most people; "Yuck! How can anyone stand to work with those perverts?"

As the days and weeks wore on I became more and more frustrated with the lack of interaction that I was used to in therapy. Finally, reluctantly, when an opening occurred for a new therapist for the weekly sex-offender group, I accepted the position. *At least these people can talk*, I thought.

I talked to other psychologists who had run the group. I read what I could find on the subject of sex-offender treatment and gradually became more comfortable working with the men. I began to see them as human beings who had very distorted thinking about life and sex and how they had gotten to the place where they could rationalize and justify their behavior to themselves. *I had a fleeting thought about my own kinky sex life, but at least it was legal,* I told myself.

I knew there was no justification for their offending behaviors. I believed that I was helping them change their thinking and behavior. I knew that these men would, eventually, be released and hoped that they would make enough change in their lives so that they wouldn't hurt anyone else by reoffending after they were released.

Chapter 62

Hart

I had been moved to the admitting ward, which was much more interesting. This was where patients were first admitted to the hospital for evaluation, classification, and diagnosis. Most of the admissions were of inmates who had been admitted and discharged many times over. Some were acute drug reactions, some were suicide attempts, many were burned-out schizophrenics who had a specific psychotic breakdown, some were acutely psychotic in a manic state, and some were the forensic NGRIs.

It was during a night shift, and I was in receiving, when a "John Doe" was admitted. No one knew his name. He'd been found in Chinatown in Honolulu wandering around, disoriented, muttering over and over, "Got to finish, got to finish." That wouldn't have mattered to anyone but he was scaring the tourists so the beat cop had stopped him.

"ID pal," the cop said.

"Got to finish."

"Spread em," the cop said as he pushed the man to the wall behind him and frisked him. "Send the wagon," he said into his shoulder mike. "We got a nut."

The "John Doe" appeared crazy. He didn't have any ID and was incoherent. He was a slight man, about five and a half feet tall, and dressed only in a nylon T-shirt, red shorts, and expensive running shoes. He didn't offer any resistance to the police.

John, as the staff had taken to calling the unknown patient, gradually became more coherent as the days went by. He'd been severely dehydrated when admitted and his cognitive processes had been severely impaired. The medical staff thought he might have had a small stroke.

When I saw John for the second time a week after his admission he was talking in whole sentences. They still didn't know who he was. There weren't any missing person reports that matched his description.

"But I'm a dentist, Doc. I've got my own private practice. Just call . . ." he was stumped.

"What's your name?"

"I don't know," he said with a puzzled expression on his face.

"Where's your office?"

"It's in . . ." he couldn't say.

"What is it you had to finish?"

"What?"

"When you were admitted, you kept repeating over and over 'got to finish.'"

"I don't know."

The over-worked social work staff were making efforts to identify him and not having any success.

Chapter 63

Hart

It went on like that for John Doe for the next two weeks. The admission ward had an arts and crafts room where patients, who were judged as not dangerous, were allowed, under supervision, to use crayons, acrylics, watercolors, poster paper, and other "craft stuff" but no scissors. It was soon apparent that the unknown Chinese patient, John, had a real talent for abstract art. He spent hours every day painting. He painted in bold reds, yellows and blues, fantastic shapes. He seemed to get lost in his paintings. The staff members really admired his work. One of the nurses asked if he would sign the painting he had given to her. He took it, put his initials on the bottom right front, turned it over, and wrote his name, Kwon Cho.

The nurse didn't recognize the name but told the social worker, Ms. Clark, who was trying to find out his identity.

"I'll check the phone book to see if there are any Chos and if any of them are artists or missing."

There were lots of Chos in the white pages. Then the social worker had an idea. She knew that the patient claimed to be a dentist and sure enough, there he was in the Yellow Pages, Cho, Kwon DDS. She called his office listing.

"Dr. Cho's answering service, can you hold?" and she was put on hold before she could reply. A few minutes later when the operator came back on, she said, "I'm Ms. Clark a social worker at the State Hospital. Is Dr. Cho missing?"

"Missing? Let me check," she was put on hold again. When the operator returned, she said, "I'm sure Ms. Clark. Our records indicate that Dr. Cho is on vacation until next week."

"May I have his home number?"

"I can't give out that information."

"Yeah, I figured you'd say that but it was worth a try. Can you call his home number and ask him to call me back?"

"Yes, I can do that."

"Okay. Please tell him it's urgent." She gave the operator her phone number at the hospital.

Chapter 64

Dr. Cho

It wasn't until the next day that someone from Dr. Cho's home returned her call.

"Hello, Ms. Clark social-work services."

"Hello. You call for Dr. Cho?"

"Yes. I'm a social worker at the State Hospital."

"Doctor no here."

"Where is he? I need to talk to him."

"He run."

"What?"

"He run."

"Where did he run?"

"Somewhere, mainland, long run. No here."

"Wait, please don't hang up. Is there anyone there I can talk to who would know how to get in touch with him?"

"No one here. All holoholo. All gone. Back next week. You call then."

Ms. Clark heard the click of the phone being hung up. *At least I know there is a Dr. Cho who is a dentist.* It was late on Friday afternoon, too late to call the local dental association to see if they could be of any assistance. *The family will be back next week,* she thought, as she got ready to go home herself. She left a note about John's possible identity in the patient's chart. That was all she could do for now.

Hart had ended his week at the hospital processing another new patient, an NGRI, Paul Stallworth, from the admission ward to a longer term care forensic ward and had started him in sex-offender group therapy. Hart wasn't aware of the patient's history of similar hospitalization on the mainland or his real name.

Chapter 65

Dr. Cho

The next Monday Dr. Cho's wife called Ms. Clark.

"Hello, social work, this is Ms. Clark. How may I help you?"

"Yes, this is Mrs. Cho. You called about my husband Dr. Cho?"

"Yes, we have a patient here who claims to be a dentist. We just recently found out his name is Kwon Cho."

Mrs. Cho interrupted her, "Dr. Cho is out of town and not accepting any new patients now."

"Where exactly is Dr. Cho?"

"I don't think that's any of your business. I'll have him call you when he gets back."

"Mrs. Cho I'm not trying to refer any patients to Dr. Cho. We have a man on our admissions ward at the State Hospital who claims he is a dentist but doesn't have any ID and we just found out his name is Kwon Cho."

"He can't be there," Mrs. Cho interrupted again. "That's crazy, he's running a marathon in Arizona. He was supposed to have left just after he finished a local marathon."

"Just let me describe the man we have." Ms. Clark described Dr. Cho and when she mentioned his painting she heard a gasp of recognition from the other end of the phone.

"That's impossible. He can't be there. Is he all right? I'll be there in an hour."

"He's fine. Do you know where the hospital is?"

"Yes, he used to see patients there 20 years ago. Didn't anyone recognize him?"

"I'm afraid not. Staff turnover is pretty high here and he's been on a closed ward."

"He's fine? This is really crazy."

Ms. Clark heard her call in the background, "Hey kids, this is funny. Your dad's at the Red Roof Inn. No," she replied to the children asking if he was seeing patients there again, "As a patient. They finally caught him. Ha, what a laugh. Hang on."

"Ms. Clark, you still there?"

"Yes."

"He is fine? Right? I mean he can still work can't he?"

"He's fine."

"Good. I'll be there to get him in an hour, no better make that two hours with all the traffic," and she hung up.

Ms. Clark shared the good news with the staff and they hurriedly called an emergency staff meeting to process Dr. Cho's discharge. There was no reason not to discharge him. He had regained all of his cognitive functioning, if not all of his memory, and he had family coming to get him. His disorientation that had lead to his hospitalization must have been a combination of dehydration, stress, and probable mild transient ischemia attacks, or "Brain farts," as the staff called the mild strokes.

Chapter 66

Aloha

"So you really are a dentist, Dr. Cho," I said at our last meeting prior to Dr. Cho's discharge.

"Hey, call me Kwon."

"Okay," I laughed, "Call me Hart."

"It's good to be going back to the 'real world,' though I did enjoy the time painting."

"Take care of yourself and look me up when you go to the Big Island for your next marathon. And thanks for the tips about practice there."

Even before the social worker had found out the truth, Dr. Cho had convinced me that he really was a dentist and we had talked of many professional issues. Dr. Cho helped me mentally make the transfer to the Big Island. We also talked about Dr. Cho's painting and how he did most of it digitally, and I found my own interest in painting re-awaking. I thought I'd start doing some digital painting and photography once I got settled in Hilo.

"It's a different pace over there. If you get bored you can always set up shop in Kaimuki. How about it Doc, there's space right next to my practice."

"No. The times I've visited the Big Island I could tell that I liked the slower pace of Hilo. It's like I was meant to be there."

We hugged each other and said Aloha. A few hours later, Dr. Cho drove off with his wife.

I liked the word Aloha and knew that it meant both hello and goodbye. Wanting to learn more about the local Hawaiian culture I had taken a course on the culture at the local community college. It was there that I learned more about the language and meaning and spirit of Aloha. One of the assistant student teachers had taken the time to fully explain the concept to me. It was much more than hello, it was a statement of sharing of the breath of life. I loved the way the concept had been explained to me and tried to live my life with Aloha; to share the breath of my life with others. I used the word often and I hoped the depth of my feeling came through when I greeted my patients and friends with "Aloha," even though I was a transplanted haole, which meant foreigner, but had come to mean Caucasian.

Chapter 67

Hart

Although things were better at the hospital, now that I was on the admitting ward, I still knew that I wanted to get back into private practice as I missed the therapy process of dealing with less disturbed people, people I felt I really had a chance of helping. I had made the move gradually.

Although my life history didn't seem to support it, I was cautious by nature. After more than a year at the State Hospital and several trips to the Big Island, I made the decision to start my practice in Hilo. I'd visited Hilo briefly before on my honeymoon with Alison and had fallen in love with the small-town atmosphere I found there. Financially, it made great sense to start my practice there, as the Big Island was the only place in the State where one could find affordable housing. $250,000.00 would only buy you a one-room shack on the island of Oahu whereas in Hilo you could get a nice house for that amount. I'd been assured by several of the local psychologists in Hilo that I had talked to that I'd be "instantly" as busy as I wanted to be.

I let the hospital know of my pending plans. The staff didn't want me to go, as they also knew a good doctor when they saw one, but they were supportive and agreed to let me work four days a week while I made the transition to private practice in Hilo, commuting every week back and forth for several months. The only patient in the hospital I was concerned about was the newly admitted sex offender whom I knew as Paul. I was concerned that Paul wasn't taking his treatment seriously and seemed to be obsessed with the image of one woman. It was almost as though his very life depended on the woman, and there was nothing I could do to reach him. Indeed, Paul's descriptions sounded more like delusional stalking and I was afraid for the woman's safety and would have warned her but Paul wouldn't reveal her name.

PART FOUR

Chapter 68

Hart and Lisa

After I moved to Hilo and had my practice going, I decided to do more with my creative ideas and returned to painting digitally on my computer, and using digital photography to make abstract collages. Although I was scared of any future relationships with women, I wanted to meet someone at least for friendship and to go to concerts and movies with. I couldn't date any of my patients and I didn't meet anyone through my work. I thought I'd try the local Arts Group I had heard about from Dr. Cho and see if I could meet a kindred spirit there.

"Nudes" was the topic for the next Hilo Arts Group. That was sure to attract a larger than usual number of members to attend the meeting. There was something about the nude human body that spoke to everyone no matter how many clothes they had on. Members were to bring matted prints or canvases to show and be open to constructive feedback. Although, artists being what they are, the feedback sometimes wasn't supportive and was even harsh. The harshest criticism usually came from those who didn't often present any of their own work for comments. They could only feel better about themselves by putting down other's work. *"How sad and lonely they must be,"* I thought.

The members milled about eating potluck appetizers and commenting to each other on the offered works. The crowd wasn't large, about thirty or so, mostly older and more women than men.

"The breasts on this one look good. Almost like you want to reach out and touch them," someone said.

"Yeah, but the fingers seem wrong."

"I like the way he posed this one. See the bare buttocks and curved back that just blend nicely into the long neck and the head disappears into darkness. A really powerful image."

I listened to the conversations and comments of several members I didn't know. It was my first time attending the group and I hadn't brought any of my own work, though I didn't usually do nudes as I felt it would offend too many people.

I was surprised to see two of my current patients at the meeting, Cheryl and Diana. They seemed to know each other and were talking with a third woman I could only partially see. I didn't see anyone else I knew in the group and felt that it would be rude or at least awkward not to say hello to them.

"Good evening ladies," I said as I joined their small group.

"Hi," Diana and Cheryl said at the same time.

I noticed the third woman with them.

"Lisa, this is Dr. Albertino. Dr. Albertino, Lisa Havenhurst," Cheryl made the introductions.

"Hello Dr. Albertino," Lisa said, extending her hand.

"Hart," I said. "Just call me Hart." I took her hand and felt an immediate connection. Her eyes held mine and I realized I was holding her hand too long and quickly let it go.

Lisa turned her head to look at some of the prints. She had felt the connection too.

"Are these yours?" I asked, pointing. "These are really beautiful. They're night painted. Right?"

"Yeah," Lisa saw the blank look on Cheryl's face. "I'll tell you how I do them later. I want to see some of the others before the meeting starts," Lisa said as she turned to go.

Sometimes special gifts come completely by surprise, I thought as I watched her walk away.

The formal meeting was being called to order and we all sat down to listen to the evening presentation. I got separated from the three ladies and found a lone seat near the front. When the meeting broke up, 30 minutes later, I looked for Lisa and couldn't find her.

"Diana," I called, waving to her across the room.

"Where's Lisa?" I asked when I got to her.

"Oh. She had to leave. She has an early work day tomorrow."

"Oh. Where does she work?"

"I'm not sure of the name, Design, something."

"What does she do?"

"Oh, she does a lot of stuff for them, interior design, decoration, and a lot of art work for commissions and for their brochures."

"Oh," I said, wondering if I could find the company. I didn't feel comfortable asking Diana for anymore information about Lisa.

"Got to go. See you later Doc," Diana said, knowing that Hart wasn't the only one who could read body language. Hart was definitely interested in Lisa. Diana was happy for him but it made her own situation seem all the worse.

"Okay," I replied.

The next day I searched through the Yellow Pages looking for design companies and found that I had to look under Graphic Designers. There were less than a dozen firms listed and many of them were on the Kona side. I was not about to give up, and eventually found the firm where Lisa worked.

I worried about the call to Lisa a long time before I picked up the phone to call her. I hadn't dated since my last disastrous divorce. I was as nervous as I remembered being as a high school kid asking for a date to the senior prom. I had liked Lisa's work and there was that instant spark between us at the Arts Group. The language of emotion was clamoring at my heart. What was it the researchers said, something about the primitive brain being able to make instant judgments, to size up another person in 30 seconds or less. My gut told me to call and to let caution take care of itself. *Yes*, I thought, *and that is how I got into trouble with Alison.* Sue had been another story altogether. There had been no spark with Sue. She had hunted and trapped me like a wounded member of the heard.

I finally made the call.

"Hello. Designs Unlimited. How may I help you?"

"Ms. Havenhurst, please."

"May I say who's calling?"

"Dr. Albertino."

"Just a moment. I'll see if she's in."

"Dr. Albertino," Lisa said. "What a pleasant surprise. I was just thinking about you. Was your nose itching?"

"Aloha, Ms. Havenhurst." I hoped she didn't hear the nervousness in my voice. "Please call me Hart," I replied, trying to keep my tone light.

"Okay, Hart and you must call me Lisa."

"Well, I am calling you, Lisa."

"Yes?"

"Well, umm, would you like to go out for coffee or dinner sometime?"

"I'd love to, Hart."

Lisa had indeed been thinking about Dr. Albertino the same as he had apparently been thinking about her. She too had felt the instant connection at the Arts Group meeting and had been hoping he would call.

"If it's not too last minute, how about this evening say at seven. I can pick you up or we could meet someplace?"

"Seven's fine. Let's meet somewhere." Lisa hoped she didn't sound desperate agreeing to his last-minute invitation. She preferred to meet and drive herself to the meeting so that she could leave easily if she wanted to.

"Okay. How about the Kaikodo?" It was one of the few fancy restaurants in Hilo.

"Okay. I'll see you there."

"Okay. Aloha," I said hanging up.

They were both breathless on their respective ends of the phone lines. Had she been too eager with him? Had he been to forward with her, they wondered separately.

Hart and Lisa arrived at the doors to the Kaikodo at the same time. There was a light misty rain coming down which was usual for Hilo at this time of year. They stood just under the protective overhang above the doors.

"Aloha, Lisa." I thought she looked stunning in her deep purple dress.

"Hello, Hart." Lisa thought he looked very handsome in his classy Aloha shirt and dark grey slacks. It had taken her a while to get used to the idea that dressing up for men in Hilo didn't mean a coat and tie. Only lawyers and judges and unknowing tourists wore coats and ties.

We embraced briefly and I held the door open for Lisa. The Kaikodo was elegant and quiet. It was one of the few restaurants in Hilo that had white linen tablecloths and napkins. The maitre d' tried to seat us at a table in one of the big windows facing Keawe Street. I asked if we could have a table in the back away from the distractions of the street. It was a table for four. The maitre d' pulled back a chair for Lisa and I took the chair next to her.

The waitperson introduced himself and took our drink orders a Manhattan straight up for me and a Vodka Gibson for Lisa.

"It's so good to see you again," I said nervously, hoping that I wouldn't come across as too eager.

"You too," Lisa replied, equally as nervous.

I looked around at the half-empty restaurant. I noticed some abstract paintings on a near wall.

"I like those," I said pointing.

"Me too. They're mine," she said with a twinkle in her eye.

"Yours?"

"Yes. I'm glad you like them. Most people don't get abstract paintings."

"Yeah. I do some abstracts too, and people often ask me 'what's it supposed to be?'"

"Me, too," Lisa said.

"They don't get it," we both said at the same time.

"The good ones evoke feelings or thoughts and each day you can see something different."

"It depends on your mood," I said. "I see love in those two."

"Strange," Lisa said, "I usually see loss but tonight I can see love, too."

There was an embarrassed silence for a few seconds.

Appearing silently at their table, the waiter said, "Would you like to start with an appetizer?"

"How about we split the coconut ginger fried calamari?" I asked.

"Sounds good to me."

"Would you like another drink?" the waitperson asked.

I looked at Lisa who shook her head no.

"No. But bring us two glasses of your house dry white wine. Is that okay with you Lisa?"

"Fine."

We talked some more about painting and soon the Calamari arrived. It was delicious with a spicy honey wasabi sauce.

"Ono," I said, chewing slowly and savoring the taste of the sauce and the dry wine and Lisa's wonderful company.

"Who could think that fried octopus would taste so good?" Lisa commented as she too savored the delicious flavors and the frisson she got from watching Hart.

When the waiter came back to take their orders, both of us were surprised the time had passed so quickly. We hadn't even looked at the menus. The waiter started to recite the special of the day but I politely interrupted.

"I think I know what we want," I said, looking at Lisa. "How about we get an order of filet mignon and one of blackened seared Ahi and we can split them. How does that sound?"

"Perfect," said Lisa, "And rare for the steak?"

I nodded and also ordered a bottle of Pinot Noir.

The meal was fabulous and we ate slowly, savoring each bite and each other. The conversation ranged from God, to the meaning of life, philosophy, and local politics.

We both were amazed to find how easy it was to talk and how comfortable we felt, like we had known each other for years. I respected the depth of her thoughts and she appreciated that I seemed to really listen to what she had to say. We were both surprised to find that it was 10:30 when we finished our coffee at the end of the meal.

I left a generous tip on the credit-card slip and pulled Lisa's chair out for her to get up. We stopped just outside the restaurant door.

"I've had a wonderful time, Lisa."

"Me, too, Hart."

We hugged and kissed briefly, very lightly, on the lips and each of us felt the spark of electricity between us.

"I'll call you tomorrow."

"Please do," Lisa said.

We parted slowly.

We started seeing each other for lunch or dinner two or three times a week for several weeks and we spoke for an hour or two on the phone daily. I told her all about my two previous failed marriages and the death of my brother. I was almost four years older than Lisa.

Lisa told me of her lonely childhood. She was thrilled when she found out that I did abstract paintings. I also had some real personal understanding of her problems. I had ADHD and was dyslexic, too. So I knew how difficult life could be coping with these disorders. I had several of my paintings in my waiting room and she enjoyed seeing them when I took her to see my office.

On many of the days after seeing Hart I was pensive and introspective. As usual, without thinking about it, I enjoyed the physical sensations of the feel of my bare feet on the soft carpet in my bedroom and the feel of the muscles in my legs as I moved. I looked at myself in the mirror above the sink in my bathroom. I still irrationally despised my appearance. *After all, as mother said, I'm defective.*

I remembered my plaintive whining from childhood from when I began to know I was "different." *Why can't I be normal? Why do I have to be like this? It's not fair!* But no matter how often I asked, I never got any answers that helped me. I tried to focus on the one area where I felt competent, my work and art, yet still on dark lonely nights, or whenever I wasn't busy with something, I'd return to *Why do I have to be like this?* I still didn't have any answers. Being with Hart seemed to make me more aware of my loneliness when I wasn't with him.

I was always excited to see Lisa and to talk to her on the phone. I felt more than just a physical attraction towards her. I had even been dreaming about her. There seemed to be some deeper connection between us. We shared common symptoms of ADHD and dyslexia and a joy of painting.

My dreams were very erotic yet never complete; they always left me wanting more. Sometimes I felt guilty about having the dreams. I knew the initial excitement of any relationship usually didn't last.

Chapter 69

Lisa

Someone was trying to kill me. *God, how cliché is that*, I thought, *everyone must think like that at sometime. I'm just being paranoid.* The few patrons in the bar had all turned to look at me when I had walked through the door. I looked around to get a feel for the place. I took a stool seat by the door so that I could see out while I waited for the rain to quit.

When the barman asked, to be polite, I ordered a cup of coffee.

I had thought I had first seen the man who was following me when I had ducked into the dark tavern to get out of the sudden downpour. The man reminded me vaguely of my Uncle Vincent. The tavern was dark and dank like the weather. I could feel sweat dripping down my chest between my breasts.

"Black," Lisa replied to the barman's question about cream and sugar. The other customers quickly lost interest in me. I paid when the barman brought the coffee so that I could leave quickly. It had been weeks since I'd been out for a nighttime walk. I thought I'd be safe but I was lost in thought and when the rain started down I had found myself in a strange neighborhood. I waited patiently, sipping my coffee, watching the rain sheet down the bar's window. The dark brew was hot. The heat from the mug felt good as I cupped my cold hands around it. It was strong, the way I liked it, and somewhat bitter, matching my mood.

Someone outside walked slowly past the window and looked in. I locked eyes with him briefly and then looked away. I hadn't recognized him and knew it was dangerous to make eye contact. The stranger came in and took a stool at the far end of the bar. All eyes except mine had turned to the man as he entered. I kept my eyes down. The background conversations were low and quiet. There was no music in the tavern, which seemed to make it give off a desolate feeling.

"Coffee," I heard the man say, as the barman approached him.

As soon as the rain let up, I left the tavern. Over my shoulder I saw the dark shape of the man get up and follow. I panicked. He must be the one who had been calling. The calls had been annoying. No words after I answered the phone, just silence. Not even any heavy breathing. I'd only had a few of them and simply hung up when no one replied. I hadn't thought much about them until now. Was he the caller? Was it another stalker? How had he found me? How did he know I'd be there? I searched for my cell phone to call for help but couldn't find it. Where had I put it? Too late, irrational, my panic pushed me down the street away from the safety of the people in the tavern.

I ran through the rain-slicked streets. The surrounding buildings were barley visible in the few streetlights. The sky was black. I was breathing rapidly and my heart was beating in my chest like a sprinter at the end of a 100-yard dash. I looked for someone, anyone to call for help; running on blindly until I felt I had to stop. I couldn't breathe and wanted to scream. *What was it you were supposed to cry, not rape, no one responded to that*, I thought to myself.

I remembered the story in the newspaper about the woman who was raped and killed by a man. The whole time the woman had been screaming "Help, someone, rape, he's raping me." But no one in the surrounding apartment buildings had responded or even called the police. Some even looked out their windows but didn't do anything. No one wanted to get involved. They all thought someone else would have called the police.

My blouse was torn open but I didn't know how that had happened. I'd lost a shoe somewhere along the way and my gait was lopsided but I didn't have the time to stop and take off the other shoe.

I ran some more until I didn't think my legs could go on. I looked and saw the figure moving through the swirling mist that rose from the street. He didn't seem to be hurrying, just coming steadily on.

Turning to my right, I ran down an alley but didn't realize until I got to the end and actually ran into the brick wall that it was a dead end. I'd fallen when I hit the wall.

I got up on shaky legs. *God, he's going to get me this time,* I thought as I turned to face him he got larger and larger and I could see what looked like a knife in his hand.

Trying to find a weapon I looked for anything, but only saw a few garbage cans. They were too big for me to lift and the tops were useless but I picked one up anyway and found a door in a wall on the left side and beat on it in desperation with my free hand. "Help, open up. Help me, PLEASE PLEASE HELP ME!" I shouted, beating on the metal door. No one replied.

As he got within a few feet of me he raised the knife to his shoulder. I couldn't make out his face but saw that he was wearing a dark hat and a long trench coat that hung open revealing his erect penis. He didn't seem to be in a hurry. His mouth opened but I couldn't see any teeth, just a dark maw.

"Now you're mine," he said in a whisper. "You know you want me."

He moved closer and I heard a ringing sound. Maybe it was a police car, but that didn't sound like a police siren. The ringing got louder. *Maybe he has a cell phone.*

I gasped and clutched the bed sheets as I came fully awake and realized it was my cell phone that was ringing. The same nightmare, *"God when is it going to stop?"* The person in the dream was someone I knew. Someone who had hurt me in the past but I couldn't remember who. Although I knew he had hurt me somehow, I kept returning to him in the dream. By the time I had reached my phone it had quit ringing and there was no message. *Who would be calling me? It must be a wrong number,* I thought.

I couldn't go back to sleep for hours; just lay there gazing at the shadows on the ceiling and walls, hearing the wind-blown rain and small tree branches occasionally brushing against the side of the house.

I could feel goose bumps on my skin and took pleasure in feeling them. The sensations reassured me that I was alive.

Chapter 70

Lisa

I thought that Hart seemed to have the same compassion and understanding as my Uncle. Of course, Uncle Vincent understood me because, although I didn't know it at the time, he had ADHD and was dyslexic, too. I thought it strange, yet interesting, that both Uncle Vincent and Hart had the same problems. I wanted to please Hart as I had tried to please Uncle Vincent, who was the only one who really paid much attention to me as a child.

Uncle Vincent had said, "In time you'll come to accept it and it won't be so hard." I kept wondering, *when will that time come?*

I was frustrated with my relationship with Hart. I wanted it to go further but I was scared. I was really very comfortable with Hart and looked forward to each date, each phone call. I wanted to cuddle and kiss and touch and be touched yet each time we started to touch I would get scared and withdraw.

Chapter 71

Hart and Mrs. Cheryl Downhill

I shoved the stick shift into second gear, enjoying the surge of power as I drove to work. I could never understand how anyone would choose to drive an automatic if they had the opportunity to drive a straight shift. I loved the way it gave me a sense of "feel" for the road. It gave me a sense of control over at least part of my life. I knew it was illusory yet it felt so good at the moment of shifting gears, of being in control. *Too bad that it wasn't that way with most of my patients or other parts of my life.*

It was morning and I was on my way to the office. Classical music from my CD player filled the interior as I sipped hot, black coffee from my personalized, insulated cup. I moved my head from side to side and tapped my fingers above the steering wheel as though conducting the music, *probably Bach*, I thought, again consciously aware of wanting control, to be the conductor.

My office was in a professional building with many medical Doctors. Their ready welcomes and many referrals had helped my private practice prosper. Most of my patients were emotionally insecure, sexually frustrated, and bothered by real-life concerns, such as working, paying the bills, parenting, caring for aging relatives, and all the other hundreds of things that filled their lives, depressed them, made them anxious, and left them little time to care for themselves.

My first patient of the day was Cheryl Downhill, a high-society older woman with a serious cocaine problem. I had first met her at the Hilo Arts Group before she became my patient.

At the first session, I had said, "Aloha, Mrs. Downhill. You may call me Dr. Albertino, Hart, or whatever you want. I want you to be as comfortable as possible. Some people prefer first names and some prefer Doctor. Is it okay if I call you Cheryl?"

"Sure Doctor," Cheryl replied, already feeling more relaxed.

I didn't sit behind a desk. My desk was against the wall; my diplomas and "certificates," paper credentials I called them, were hung on the wall over my desk. My leather chair faced the couch and there was a big recliner that was the "patient's" chair. It was more like sitting in a modified living room than a formal Doctor's office with the Doctor sitting behind his desk and the patient in front; the desk serving as a barrier keeping the Doctor safe from the patient. I didn't want that to be the patient's impression. I wanted my patients to feel that I was there with them not separate or above them. I often thought of Dr. Longfellow and how she had taught me to do therapy. I didn't need to be protected by a desk barrier. My open arrangement seemed to work for me. I hadn't sussed out during my phone screening that Cheryl's problem was severe cocaine addiction or I probably would not have accepted her as a patient.

Therapy was about breaking down barriers so I could help my patients. I would sometimes explain to patients, "the most important variables in successful therapy were the relationship between the patient and the therapist and the motivation the patient brought to their therapy." Part of breaking down barriers and building the therapeutic relationship was, for me, also to disclose parts of my own personal past.

For most of the first session I listened to Cheryl's history, occasionally asking questions and taking notes on my laptop computer. After listening for a while I asked, "May I make a suggestion?"

I knew that changes in a person's life could occur slowly or quickly in one swift moment of action. I suspected that for Cheryl it would be slow unless something from outside her life occurred to shake her up.

"Sure, Doc," Cheryl replied. She was terrified of hearing the things she didn't want to hear. She knew them already, and was traumatized by the depth and pain of her dark thoughts. That's why she couldn't cope and used coke. She felt utterly helpless and hid her fears and hopelessness from her friends and acquaintances, presenting a hollow shell of competence to all around her.

I went on to suggest several practical things Cheryl could try to help her cope more effectively. I was trying to reach her on an emotional level but was always left on the surface. I remembered what Dr. Longfellow had told me, "If you don't feel the hurt from your patients and/or your own mistakes, you can't learn from them. Therapy is more like art, only your life is the canvas and you're the painter, I'm just the coach or teacher."

After several sessions, I began to wonder if Cheryl, like many other patients, didn't want to let go of her issues. "It's what you know, and as painful as your life is, you seem to have gotten comfortable with it. It's more painful to deal with the trauma of your past. You've learned to manage your addiction and use it as a way of coping."

"No," she had stated firmly, "I wouldn't do that, I don't choose to be addicted, I didn't ask to be born this way. You're stupid."

I was happy to hear her direct expression of her anger towards me. "It's a sign of progress that you can express your anger directly to me. Thank you." I'd finally reached her on at least some emotional level, now if I could just build from there.

"You're welcome," she'd laughed lightly breaking the tension.

Chapter 72

Cheryl

Cheryl was late for her next week's session. I took my usual few minutes prior to seeing her to review my notes from the last therapy session, so I'd have some idea where we had left off. Because of my own ADHD, I was very easily distracted and couldn't remember things unless I wrote them down.

"Aloha, Cheryl," I said as I opened the office door and beckoned her to enter.

"Good morning, Doctor," Cheryl replied automatically as she walked in, smoothing her short skirt over her thighs, and sitting in the patient chair.

"So what's happened since our last session?" Her body language was shouting that she was high on coke and anxious about something. Her pupils were wide open.

Like most people who used drugs, she had a thousand reasons for doing it: she was happy, sad, anxious, it was a holiday, everybody does it, I'm not hurting anybody, nobody knows, what difference does it make, it's someone's birthday, it's Monday, it's the end of the week, it's the weekend, it's cold, the list went on and on. But mainly it was a long-term failed attempt at self-medication, to at least temporarily avoid dealing with the other problems in her life, her failed marriage, no children, and why she wasn't living "happily ever after." Of course the coke had long since started causing more problems.

"Hey, Doc. Same ol', same ol'," Cheryl replied. She leaned forward and then back in her chair. She avoided eye contact. "Haven't used since our last session," she lied.

"Any more nose bleeds?"

"No, No," she sniffed mucous from her nose, shaking her head. She'd had one in the last week.

"So how's your sleep?"

"Like a baby," she lied again. Most of the therapy sessions were lies and more lies. She knew she wanted help but she kept rejecting it. I knew she really wanted help but I couldn't break through her exterior armor to the core of her feelings. I felt frustrated.

"Look Cheryl, if you want me to help you, you've got to be honest with me. I won't be mad at you." I strongly suspected she was still lying to me, as she almost always did.

"Okay, Doc. To be honest with you I used a couple of times," she lied again. She'd been snorting daily since the last session. She would vow she was going to quit and then found herself looking down at lines on her hand-held mirror. The anticipated relief was so great.

I knew she was deliberately minimizing her use. It was part of the pattern and part of our therapy dance. "What about some of the other things I suggested?"

No reply.

Did she try any of the things I suggested to break up the pattern? I wondered, *Is she doing anything to break the cycle of thought, urge, feelings of panic, and the anticipatory anxiety which always led to her use.*

I even had her rehearse these strategies. She did them with some nervous laughter in my office. Outside the office was a different story. When the urge hit, she didn't use any of the strategies. She didn't even practice them when she didn't have the urges, as I had suggested.

"So Cheryl, did you rehearse any of the coping strategies?"

Cheryl started to lie automatically, but then stopped. What was the use? "No, Doc. I didn't."

"Thank you for your honesty Cheryl."

"The only time I don't use is when I can't get any. And then I'm going out of my skin. I can't stand it."

"What did you do before you started using?" We had been over this many times and I kept asking in hopes of finding some motivation, some emotional vein that Cheryl could tap into to help herself.

"You know I eat, and look at me," she gestured at her skinny body. "I eat and still lose weight. It's a great weight-loss program Doc," she said with a laugh. "The rush is so great Doc. It's better than an orgasm. Not that I have any of those anymore. My husband hasn't touched me in years."

I noticed that she hadn't answered my question. We had talked of exercise, laughter at a good joke, of humor being the best medicine, and a good cry, and even pleasuring herself to an orgasm. Laughter and crying worked but only sometimes and Cheryl just wasn't willing to touch herself "down there." She'd grown up in the old school and nice girls didn't do such things.

I was typing notes on my laptop computer. I sighed in frustration. I couldn't use my "big gun" of paradoxical intention, telling her to snort more coke. It wouldn't work in this case and would have been grossly inappropriate. I wished I had something I could use to get to her. Yet, in the end, I knew Cheryl had to find the motivation within herself.

"You're still not going to narcotics anonymous, NA?"

"No, every time I went, it's like I told you before, it's like all those junkies get high on just talking about their use. And most of them are stoned on something anyway. What help is that?"

"Many people find it very helpful," I said for the umpteenth time. "What about your sponsor?"

"Oh, she's great. She knows where to get the best stuff," Cheryl replied sarcastically.

So it went for the rest of the session, I prodded and Cheryl resisted. Throughout the session Cheryl fidgeted, tapping her fingers, and sniffing as though she could be sniffing some of the white powder. She was thinking about finishing the session and having a "line."

I noticed the time on the little clock behind Cheryl's head. "It's time to wrap up for today," I sighed in frustration. "Same time next week?"

"Sure, Doc, whatever." Cheryl was in a hurry to leave.

Chapter 73

Hart

I had Cheryl leave by the back door. I didn't want her to see my next appointment who was her friend. I was thankful for the 45/50-minute hour that left me time between patients to return the numerous phone calls that piled up on my answering machine and to go to the bathroom.

The time with my patients was their time and I tried to not let anything interrupt it. During treatment sessions I turned the volume off so that I wouldn't be bothered by phone calls. This worked, but often resulted in many backed up calls I had to return. *Nothing urgent*, I thought, as I listened to the answering machine.

Many of the calls were of the phone tag sort, where the person left a message saying that they were returning my call and I had left them a message saying I was returning their call. Sometimes it got to the point where I couldn't remember who had called who first. I chuckled to myself thinking about the old Abbott and Costello "Who's on First" routine.

Chapter 74

Cheryl

Cheryl left her appointment thinking about Dr. Albertino's suggestions. *Who does he think he is, the old fart?* She appreciated that he gave her some good suggestions on how to cope. Of course, she didn't follow them. She wanted to but didn't want to.

What she liked most about him was that he seemed to really listen to her and was willing to share part of his own life. *It makes him more human,* she thought, and went to a place where she could take a snort. As she'd told him, "Doc, it's my favorite coping strategy." One time she had offered him some pot someone had given her but he had declined, and didn't make her feel bad for offering. She'd tried pot, but nothing worked like coke.

She'd been to a half dozen different therapists and liked Hart the best even though she wasn't getting any better. She really believed Dr. Albertino could help her quit if she'd just let him. She kept hoping that something would come along that would make her quit.

Chapter 75

Mrs. Diana Akuna

Diana Akuna, my next patient, happened to also be in the Hilo Arts Group. She still wasn't making much progress with her intimacy issues and her sexual frigidity.

I opened the waiting-room door, "Aloha, Diana. Come in."

Diana was wearing a very revealing dress that didn't flatter her Rubenesque body. As she moved to the therapy chair, the sun from the window made the dress almost transparent, as she had hoped it would. Three buttons were open on her already low-cut blouse and her breasts were pushed up like melons being offered as a prize. She sat in the chair with her legs flopping open and the dress bunched high on top of her thighs.

I didn't want to look, but I couldn't help noticing her white panties and the dark patch of her pubic hair. As though she hadn't noticed how she was sitting, Diana pushed her dress down and sighed. She hoped Hart had gotten an eye full.

For some reason the sight of Diana caused me to think back to my therapy with Dr. Longfellow who had told me "You'll know the moment you become a true therapist and if you notice you may not notice the change it makes in you." I didn't think this was such a moment.

Diana usually did something overtly sexual to attract my attention but never as blatantly as today. When I was in session with Diana, I usually wished I had a nurse who could sit in with me to verify that I hadn't done anything sexual with my patient. Her blatant sexual acting out was beginning to be a huge concern and something I would have to deal with in the session. I couldn't let her go on acting out like that.

"Diana, please button your blouse. You know that's not appropriate."

"Oh, this?" Diana sweetly said, looking at her pushed up breasts. She buttoned two of the buttons and left the top one open.

"That better, Doc?"

Maybe this was that moment.

Chapter 76

Diana

I thought back to the first few sessions when Diana had started therapy. Unlike most patients she had been straightforward about why she was coming to see me. Her maiden name was Diana Jane Knobwoody. I could just think of the teasing a name like Knobwoody would bring to a young girl in high school.

"Doctor, I need help with my sex," she had said without any preamble or pleasantries. "I mean, how much sex I have, well, not how much I have it. I have plenty, but the lack of feeling I have."

Many patients came in saying they had one problem and didn't get to the real problems until a few sessions later, as though they had to test the waters first to see if they could trust the Doctor. Diana's immediate openness was either a sign of her desperation or her characteristic way of interacting, or a combination of both. Again I thought of Dr. Longfellow's views. *Therapy begins with, waiting and listening and hope that the patients will heal themselves.*

Diana had always dressed and acted seductively from the first session. I had probed her history as I usually did during the first few sessions. Diana told me her history in excruciating detail, what for many women would have been emotionally embarrassing, in a flat monotone, as though she was talking about someone else.

"It started when I was seven or eight, or at least that is the earliest I remember. We all slept in the same bed, my older brothers and me. They were 14 and 15 I think, Bubba Ray and Billy Bob. They'd wake up with hard-ons.

"Of course, back then I didn't know what a hard-on was. I remember asking why I didn't have one. I pulled my nightie up, well it wasn't really a nightie, just a big old T-shirt, and looked between my legs. 'That's okay,' they said, 'you've got something special that makes all the guys happy.'

"I was young, and you know, I wanted to please them. Mam and Pap were always working and usually gone before we got up. We didn't have any neighbors so the only attention I could get was from my brothers. They started rubbing me between my legs and told me I could feel their dicks if I wanted. One got on each side of me and they put my hands on their dicks. I knew, you know the way kids can sense things, that they wanted me to hold them or as they later instructed me 'to play with their dicks and rub them up and down.' It did feel kinda good having them rub my cunt and clit, though back then I didn't know what they were either.

"Every morning would be the same with them playing with me and me stroking them. They started sticking their fingers in me and said, 'all the girls love this.' Then they did the same with their tongues and they had me put their dicks in my mouth. They usually came pretty quickly. I didn't know what that was back then either; only this white stuff would come out of their dicks. They seemed to like it when they'd come in my mouth and really liked it when I swallowed it. It didn't taste bad, just a little salty. They told me, 'All the guys like that,' and that, 'you'll be really popular if you do that.'"

I was shocked, though I tried not to show it. I knew these things happened much more often than was reported, especially in the back-woods areas of the Appalachia Mountains in West Virginia where Diana grew up.

I knew it happened in almost every rural area and in many areas of the cities. Her parents were dirt poor and Diana was lucky to get one "new" hand-me-down dress once a year from the church people. The family went to church every week and holding their one Bible was an honor that was passed around each Sunday. The choir would sing wondrous hymns of the joys of the Lord and the preacher would shout and rant for an hour or two about hell and damnation and the wages of sin and fornication.

Monday morning Diana would wake up (both parents had left for work long before daylight) and get fucked by her brothers. When Diana said something about the preacher saying fornication was a sin, her brothers would say, "We're not fornicating, this is just fucking."

"But mostly they liked getting quick blow jobs before we had to get ready to catch the bus to school. I guess that's why I didn't get pregnant because almost all the time I was eating their sperm."

I was silently crying inside for Diana as I typed the details in my laptop computer. Diana continued on in her emotionless voice.

"I didn't have many friends in grade school. They all made fun of my old clothes and me. I only had one dress and my shoes always had holes where my brothers had worn them out. I really wanted to have friends; I was so lonely.

"Then by the time I got to high school, I must have been 13 or 14, and I had developed breasts and had hair on my pussy. My brothers liked it better when I had a hairless 'beaver.' They wanted me to shave it," she paused, "but I didn't want to do that."

The matter-of-fact clinical way she described her physical anatomy, made it both less disturbing and at the same time more horrifying. I suspected she had had to develop this emotional distance, as though she were talking about someone else, to protect herself from the otherwise horrific emotional hurt.

"From the first day in high school things changed. I didn't have a bra. Well the church ladies gave me one shortly after they noticed me at church without one. So anyway, I guess the boys could see my tits through the old T-shirt I was wearing that day at school. After the bell rang ending the day, a couple of them asked me to go and sit under the bleachers in the shade to wait for the bus. They said it'd be about a 30-minute wait. They were older so they knew these things. My brothers had already graduated and were working in the local sawmill, so I was on my own.

"I went with the boys behind the bleachers. I didn't see any other kids around but I wasn't scared. I was happy someone was talking to me. We'd barely gotten out of sight of the school when the biggest boy hugged me and started kissing me, sticking his tongue in my mouth; I felt other hands on my bare tits under my T-shirt. That's what they called them, tits. They pulled my shirt up and over my head so they could look at my tits and get hold of them without my shirt being in the way. They squeezed my nipples and laughed when I'd cry out but they didn't pinch as hard after that."

Tears were rolling down her cheeks. I handed her a Kleenex.

"I remembered how my brothers told me I'd be real popular if I gave good 'head.' I felt someone's hands on my shoulders pushing me down. I went willingly and wasn't surprised to find the guy already had his cock out and was stroking it. 'Go ahead,' he said in a husky voice, 'Take it in your mouth.' I did and he began 'fucking' my mouth. I didn't even have to use my hands. He came pretty quickly and then I had another cock in my mouth. It went on like that for quite a while and word must have spread, as there were a lot of them, maybe 10 or 12, I don't remember.

"Eventually, when no one was left, one of the older boys offered me a ride home. I'd missed the bus. The boy was polite and thanked me for the blowjob. Of course he wanted to feel me up as he said goodbye and then he had my head in his lap and his cock in my mouth for another quick blowjob."

Chapter 77

Diana

I was flabbergasted. I'd heard a lot in the past but the clinical lack of emotion in her voice was the most disturbing.

"It went on like that throughout high school. I got a real good reputation as the school slut. It was almost always blowjobs though, as if I wasn't good enough to fuck or that they weren't cheating on their girlfriends, as blowjobs weren't considered sex."

She was silent and looking down. I thought she might be going to show some more emotion. "It's okay to cry, Diana. What happened to you is terrible. You were assaulted."

"Oh, it's not that," Diana said looking up. "I was just wondering why they call it a blowjob when it's really sucking. Well sometimes they do say, 'suck me baby.' That seemed more honest to me."

Since her brothers were now working and considered "men" her parents didn't think it was appropriate for Diana to be sleeping with them so they made her a bed in a closet off the front parlor, near the front door. Since her brothers now went to work at the same time as her parents, the morning sex had stopped too.

"Strangely, I felt really popular. I didn't mind that the girls didn't like me. I had lots of boyfriends. Sometimes the boys gave me a note asking me to come out that night and meet them in their car down the road from my house. It was easy to sneak out. Everyone slept hard after working all day in the mill. I'd even thought to oil the hinges on the front door so it wouldn't squeak.

"I'd sneak out about midnight and walk down the road to a car. Usually there would be two or three guys waiting with their dicks in their hands. Sometimes we wouldn't even say 'Hi.' I'd just get in the back seat or on my knees in the grass and start 'giving head' to one, while the others drank beer and waited their turns.

"There was only one time I refused sex with a guy. Some guys wanted to force a 'good church' kid to have sex so he would fit in. They kept daring him and calling him a sissy if he didn't do it. It was clear he didn't want to do it, so I just told them I wouldn't do the kid. When the other boys tried to bully me into doing him, I just gave them a real mean look and said 'You really want me to talk to your girlfriends?' So they backed off and left the kid alone."

I wanted to say, "Diana, that's enough." But I knew she had to get it all out. It seemed to almost be over.

"That sort of thing went on all through high school. It wasn't until my senior year, when I took a class in Personal Psychology, that I really knew what I was doing was terribly wrong. I'd known it was wrong but not really, that it was really wrong. You know what I mean, Doc?"

"Yes, Diana. You can sense something is wrong and not know it intellectually, or maybe you couldn't admit it to yourself as you didn't know how to deal with it at the time."

"Yeah, that's it Doc. Only I still don't know how to deal with it. That's what I want you to help me with. I took a community college course in psychology when I came to the Big Island and they talked about people like me, sexual addicts they said, and that psychologist could help with treatment."

"How did you feel about it all?"

"You know I really enjoyed the attention at the time. I mean I was popular and had all the boys lined up to see me. I liked it so much I began to feel ashamed. To deal with my shame I decided to take it out on this star quarterback. He acted like he was hot stuff and didn't want to do it with me, like he was doing me a favor. I was mad and made fun of his small dick until he lost his erection. Then I spread the rumor that he couldn't get it up and was probably gay."

"How'd you feel about it?"

"Well, I felt really guilty about it, so I punished myself by taking on the whole team, at least the ones who wanted to fuck the 'whore.' I was sore for a week after that.

"What's really strange Doc, is I never came, not once with all the sex I had. I didn't even know what an orgasm was until I came here and one of the women (she hadn't wanted to say who it was) told me about how you can make yourself cum with a dildo. So I got myself some books on sex and a vibrator and found out. WOW! I'd never known what I'd been missing."

"So you've learned how to pleasure yourself?"

"Yeah, but then, and now, I'm jacking off all the time, though I like to call it 'Jilling,' it's more feminine." She had unconsciously or consciously started to rub herself right in front of me.

"That's not appropriate Diana." She stopped as though she had been doing nothing more than biting her nails.

"I did have one girlfriend in high school, Sally Jean, though she went by Jean. She wasn't very pretty, pencil thin, and no curves at all. But she was the only girl who was nice to me and I was nice to her. We got to be really good friends. I think I was her only friend and she was my only girlfriend. We'd share secrets and she couldn't believe how many BJs I gave out. After graduation her parents, who owned the mill where most of the town worked, gave her, and a friend of her choice, a trip to Hawai'i and she invited me to go along.

"When we got here it was wonderful, like starting all over. No one knew me and there were all the wonderful restaurants and clubs in Kona. We had a blast. Jean got laid for the first time in her life, and I don't mean the flower kind."

"And," I said when she had stopped talking.

"Jean had her first ever orgasm and then before we knew it, it was time to leave. I thought about it and decided I wasn't going to leave Paradise. There was nothing for me on the mainland but poverty and hard work. I was 18 and decided to stay."

"How did you survive?"

"Oh it wasn't hard. Ha ha, I guess that's a pun. I met lots of guys in the clubs and I was back to my old tricks. Ha, another pun. I was a 'working girl' but not a pro. I quickly got a reputation. I'd walk into one of the bars I'd frequent and they saw me coming. If there was a new guy or even one of the regular ones, I'd sidle up and we'd talk for a while and then we'd go back to the guy's place and I'd give him head. I'd learned to use condoms by then. I'd fuck the guy with my mouth while he'd play with my tits. I didn't feel anything. Most of them would give me $50 to $100 and I'd be off until the next night. I didn't hate them; you know it was just a way to get attention, and make some money. Sometimes I'd do two or three in a night. So I wasn't hurting for money.

"I met one guy who made fake IDs and got one that said I was 21, so I didn't have to worry about being 'carded' in those bars that bothered to check. I also got some pressure from a guy to 'work' for him but I told him I wasn't a prostitute. Guess I was deluding myself. Luckily the guy must have been new to the pimping business himself, as he didn't know how to beat me into submission.

"Eventually I got a small room in a boarding house way off the beach."

"So how long has this been going on?"

"It's been going on since I was seven or eight, I told you Doc. Weren't you listening? I haven't quit. That's why I need your help. I've tried, but I can't quit. It's like a compulsion, I keep going back, and the money's not bad."

I was impressed with her openness and her very good diction. "Where did you learn to speak so well?" I asked.

"Oh, I pick things up pretty quickly and I was hanging out with the rich crowds at the hotels in Kona. I took a few college courses at the community college.

"The problem is, I can orgasm all I want by myself but I can't make it with a guy. I guess I can't really be intimate."

She has hit the mark right on the head, I thought.

Chapter 78

Diana

I welcomed Diana in for our third session. "Where would you like to start today?"

Diana had met an older stockbroker, Warren Stewart, at one of the clubs. He was also involved in real estate. Warren was shy and must have been a virgin or at the very most hadn't had very much sexual experience. The sex with Diana was the best he'd ever had, the only BJs he'd ever had, and she'd even let him fuck her. He was in love. He didn't know enough to even wonder if she orgasmed, so she didn't have to bother faking it.

Warren proposed marriage a few months after they had met. She accepted. He was nice enough and had lots of money and bought her nice jewelry and took her clubbing when she wanted. He didn't see the knowing looks or hear the whispered comments and snickers behind his back when his friends learned that he had asked her to marry him. They couldn't bring themselves to tell him she was sucking them all off even when she was engaged to him. They figured it would all end quickly anyway and no one wanted to be the one to tell poor Warren he was going to be cuckolded.

The wedding was a big society event. One of the most eligible bachelors was getting married, Champaign flowed, the flowers were numerous and beautiful as was the bride in her white dress. Some of her college friends served as bridesmaids. Warren's sister served as her head bridesmaid and his best friend, Teddy, served as best man. The best man had some trouble hiding the tent in his pants when he thought of how many times Diana had sucked him off, as recently as the day before the wedding.

Since no one else was available, Warren's dad served to give away the bride. After their vows were exchanged and rings of tokens of love and fidelity were given, the happy couple kissed deeply. Many of the men knew how Diana's lips had felt wrapped around their cocks.

During the reception Diana excused herself to go to the restroom where she met the best man, and kneeling in her white dress gave him a quick goodbye-for-now blowjob.

To fit in with the other society ladies, and to have something to do, other than sucking cock, Diana started to do digital photography and at Cheryl's invitation joined the Hilo Arts Group.

Chapter 79

Diana

Diana was saying, "It's not that I'm a bad person, Doc. I love Warren. I take care of him but I just can't be intimate with him. I mean I have sex with him but it's not the same thing. I can't seem to have an emotional relationship with anyone. I feel really bad for cheating on him but I can't seem to stop. I tell myself I won't do it again and the next thing I know I'm on my knees with some guy's cock in my mouth." With all the sex she was having she was aware of how ironic her comments sounded.

"Guess that's stupid, huh, Doc?"

"No Diana, it's a common response to sexual trauma. Some victims freeze up and won't let anyone touch them. Others, as seems to be the case for you, act out sexually over and over again trying to achieve the one thing they can't have, the intimacy that was stolen or repressed when they were assaulted or abused. In your case the assaults weren't physically brutal but took place repeatedly over a long period of time and with no intimacy, no love or caring for your feelings."

"I think I gained weight so guys wouldn't find me attractive but even the weight doesn't keep them from getting hard when I wrap my lips around their cocks. Ah fuck it, I'm sick of it all. I want to stop."

"It's like an addiction Diana. There are even groups similar to AA but for sex addition. The sex becomes a way of avoiding dealing with other problems in your life."

"Yeah, well enough BS for one day."

I was looking at my computer and before I knew it, Diana was on her knees, blouse open, a tit out in one hand and the other hand reaching for my crotch.

"STOP it Lisa, I mean Diana," I shouted. I was aroused despite myself. I'd been thinking of Lisa while Diana was describing her sexual behavior. I got up, turned my back on Diana and went to the door. By the time I reached the doorknob Diana had covered up and was standing up.

"Spoil sport," she said, still flirting with me, back to her old coping style. "What would it hurt?"

I wanted to end the session on a positive note. I wanted to say, "It seems like you're making a little progress. Keep up the efforts." All I could muster was, "Goodbye Diana." I'd have to stop seeing her if she did anything like that again.

My mind was again focused on my next date with Lisa. I couldn't believe I'd said Lisa's name when Diana was exposing herself to me.

Chapter 80

Hart and Lisa

With anticipation, I waited for my next date with Lisa. I made sure my beard was neatly trimmed and wiped the shine off my forehead, trying to convince myself that it had nothing to do with my anticipation of seeing Lisa. *Was I becoming as delusional as my patients?* I wondered briefly, and then dismissed the thought.

As I was driving to pick Lisa up, I thought back about my move to Hawai'i. I had sought a change of life with new scenery and adventure, another similarity I shared with Lisa. At my age, I was still looking for love, still caught in the web of fantasy of most of my patients, wanting my beautiful maiden and to "live happily ever after." Just like the fairy tales I'd warned my patients about.

At lunch Lisa sat primly with her skirt pulled over her knees. Her breathing was slow and controlled. Watching her breasts rise and fall I felt was an analogy for our relationship. We were on the same track in almost all areas except for physical intimacy. We both wanted it but Lisa always pushed away if I got too close.

"How are you doing Lisa?" I said in what I hoped was a neutral tone.

"I still feel down when it comes to touching. I don't know why. I'm so sorry Hart. It's not you. I just need more time. I enjoy just being with you."

"I'm happy to hear that you are having some good times," I replied with some frustration.

"It's not you. Even the goldfish I buy for pets end up dying on me. It's like an analogy for my life, someone buys you, and takes you home and you die. I've started so many relationships, especially since moving to the Big Island, and they have all died out. Because, well you know."

I wanted to break her out of her pattern; I definitely didn't want to be dropped out. I'd gone through the usual questions of why with her, and how long she had been this way. She couldn't remember a time when she wasn't afraid of touching except with Uncle Vincent.

I thought Uncle Vincent would be a key relationship to explore in more depth, but whenever I probed in this area, she seemed to be very adroit at changing directions.

We had become very comfortable in talking about anything and everything except her fear of touching. "You seem very lonely, Lisa. Have you always been lonely?"

"Yes," she replied shyly. "Except for when I was with Uncle Vincent."

"How did you handle the loneliness?"

Silence. A shrug from Lisa.

I tried again. "Did you ever date when you were younger?" I didn't want to be her shrink but I wanted to get past whatever was in the way of getting closer to her.

A shrug again. Lisa didn't want to tell me about her one attempt at dating. It was too embarrassing, but she trusted Hart. He wasn't like any other man she had known. She told him about the boy she had dated in high school and how since then she'd freeze up if someone tried to touch her. And now even when she wanted Hart to touch her she had the same reflexive response.

I tried to probe. "How did you handle the loneliness?"

"I don't know."

"Do you have fantasies about love?"

"Yes."

"Will you tell me about them? I've told you mine."

Lisa thought of the soap operas she watched and the romance novels she read, the handsome men, rescuing suffering maidens. "Sometimes I dream about being held."

"What happens when you're being held?"

"I feel safe."

"And what happens next in your fantasies?"

She knew I was asking about sex. But she didn't want to tell me. It was too secret, too private. "You mean sex?" she asked.

"Tell me what you think?"

"Why do we have to talk about sex?"

"Why do you think? We talk about everything else, why not sex?"

"I don't know, why?" Lisa shrugged. "You've had sex so it's no big deal to you," she said irritated.

"I don't want to make the same mistakes I made in the past, Lisa. When you think of sex, what comes to your mind?"

She didn't reply, she just looked at her hands in her lap and sat silently.

We were at the impasse again.

Chapter 81

Hart and Lisa

Getting ready for our lunch date a week later, I took a longer shower that morning than I had taken in a long time. I let the hot water spray beat on my neck, shoulders, and back and then down my face, between my breasts and legs. I took a long time soaping myself, rubbing my mons. After the shower I felt tingly and invigorated. I loved the feel of the goose bumps the fluffy towel made as I dried myself.

I finished dressing, going "commando," or without panties, as I had started doing soon after Hart and I met. I told myself I didn't know why. The fresh air felt more natural and sensual.

I met her for lunch at Pestos. I gazed lovingly at Lisa. In the intimate space of my mind, Lisa was my fantasy lover. I was hoping to make the fantasy real; was solicitous and frustrated. I knew that she was destined someday to find her "knight in shinning armor" to sweep her away to live "happily ever after." I wanted to believe it like everyone else. Unfortunately, I knew from personal and professional experience that people were most often sadly disappointed when the reality of life didn't match the fantasy. I hoped that I could be her Knight and that it would turn out much better than the reality of my last two attempts at marriage.

Jealousy was just under the surface of my feelings for Lisa, jealous of whatever was keeping her away from me. Making her happy was what I wanted to do. *That's irrational,* I thought to myself. *I want her to be able to touch and be touched.*

Helping Lisa should be my only concern. Perhaps using hypnosis would help her get through her past. I know that she trusts me and I'd never do anything to break that trust, I thought as I looked at her. *How can I broach the subject with her?* We talked about simple ordinary things for the rest of the meal.

"I need to get back to the office. Would you like to come there for lunch tomorrow?"

"Okay, Hart," she replied and we both got up. I walked her to her car. I was again extremely aware of her physical beauty and was tempted to give her a hug, just so I could feel her pressed against me. The way I had on the night that we had gone dancing at "Uncle Mike's," a popular dance place that had line dancing, hot hyped-up jazz and slow dances, when I would hold her close and know that she could feel my hard penis pressed against her mons.

Chapter 82

Hart and Lisa

I couldn't seem to stop myself from fantasizing about taking her to my car and then to my home, and my bed. I'd fantasized so often that it was almost as if I had explored every inch of her body with her willing participation. I was her phantom lover and she didn't know it.

He, however, didn't know that he was her phantom lover.

After our polite goodbyes, I departed for the safety of my home. I was finding it more and more difficult to hide from Hart. I remembered the visits with Uncle Vincent. For some reason Vincent was more on my mind since I had been seeing Hart. I had some vague memories about Uncle Vincent that were somehow pleasant and yet unpleasant, and I couldn't figure out why. After my dates with Hart I was more acutely aware of my senses, my breathing, the movement of my muscles, and the beat of my heart. I felt more alive.

Chapter 83

Lisa

It had been three days since my last date with Hart. So this afternoon I was thrilled with anticipation and excitement for that evening's date with him.

I enjoyed my invigorating shower. I now stood, naked, in front of the bathroom mirror. As usual I didn't like what I saw.

I put some blush on my cheeks, adding just enough eye shadow to add interest but not so much as to appear sluttish. Batting my eyes to inspect the change in the mirror, I was pleased with the accent it added to my face.

I continued to make myself more alluring as I carefully rolled on some glossy rose lipstick and added understated silver earrings. I thought of Hart as distinguished looking and handsome and wanted him to think of me as beautiful and elegant.

Still naked, as a final inspection and to empower myself, I thought, *There, now what's not to like about this face if you're a man looking for love?*

The symbolism escaped her notice that she was doing all this in the nude, inviting inspection of not just her face but also her body.

I noticed my nipples and impulsively thought of adding some rose lip-gloss to them, but didn't. I enjoyed the thrill of anticipation. Of course, deep within, I still saw myself as damaged goods.

My face was ready to go; I suddenly wanted to hide from my body. Quickly I slipped on my thin black dress. It had pleating from the waist all the way down to the tea-length hemline. I put on a golden ankle bracelet. My feet were nestled in high-heeled shoes. I continued trying to deny to myself that I had any sexual feelings.

Only a few minutes later, I heard Hart's car drive up. I bounded out my door, happy to see him. Hart was out and opening the car door as I approached him and gave him a hug from the back.

"Hey, cut that out," Hart teased. "I won't be able to drive."

"Why, silly?"

I turned and she saw why.

"Oh, sorry," I said, blushing but secretly pleased with Hart's reaction to me.

We were going to Hart's office to eat sandwiches there. I had wanted to look again at his abstracts on the walls of his waiting room and to see in more depth where he spent most of his working time.

Chapter 84

Hart and Lisa

I opened the door of my office.

"Aloha. Please come in," I was offering her a roll to play as a patient. Lisa smiled, "Why thank you, Doctor," and gracefully walked into the room and took her seat in the leather recliner.

I folded my hands, a frown of concern on my face. Seated in my chair catty corner from her, I leaned forward and asked, "What's going on, Lisa?" I noticed and appreciated the makeup that made her beautiful face more radiant and sensual. A quick glance when I thought she wasn't looking and I noticed her nipples through the fabric of her dress.

I could only play at this game, of me being a patient, for a few minutes.

"How about your dreams? Am I in them?" Hart hoped.

"Yes you are, darling, but that monster keeps coming back, three times this week. Fortunately you're usually there to scare him off. I don't know what's wrong with me," I said with a sad look. I got out of the "therapy chair" and sat on the couch. I didn't want to play the roll of a patient any more.

Stroking my beard, I doubted she was consciously aware of her use of the slang word for orgasm when she described the monster as "coming" three times. She hadn't said she had dreamed of the monster three times but that the monster "came" three times in her dreams. She didn't seem to be aware of her repressed sexuality.

"Could you see his face this time?" It didn't hurt to ask again.

I knew about how Lisa's stepfather had been emotionally distant from her. As a child the few walks her biologic father had taken with her were her best memories of her real father. I suspected that the vague figure of her dreams was her dead father.

"No," I said. "It was just a blur of darkness."

I tried to shift directions. "Lisa, I've got a great idea."

"Yeah? What do you have in mind?" I looked warily at him.

"We could try to use hypnosis to help you uncover these dreams and it might help you to be able to be touched."

"I don't know. Maybe. But not now, let's go eat."

"Will you think about it?"

"Yes."

"We could do it here in my office or in your home if you'd be more comfortable there."

I could see his anxious concern and I did trust him. "Okay," I said reluctantly but hopefully, "We can try it sometime."

"You can stop the hypnosis at any time you want."

"I said, okay!" I was a little miffed at him for pushing and at myself for holding back.

Chapter 85

Hart and Lisa

We talked about it some more over dinner that night.

"What have you heard about hypnosis?" I asked.

"I watched a stage hypnotists on TV once back on the mainland. He made people do all kinds of crazy things. I laughed, but I'm sure it wasn't funny to the people when they realized what he had done."

Lisa, like most people, had only been exposed to this entertainment type of hypnosis and had the mistaken belief that the hypnotists <u>made</u> people do things. She was somewhat frightened and apprehensive about it.

I remembered my own first encounter with hypnosis when I had gone through training and my own apprehension and then amazement as I allowed the therapist to guide me into the hypnotic state.

"Clinical hypnosis is not really like stage hypnosis," I told Lisa. "Those people on stage aren't really doing anything they don't want to do. The hypnotist just gives them the suggestions to free them from their social inhibitions so that they can act out the roles he suggests to them. And before he selects them he asks a number of questions to determine if they would be good subjects.

"Okay. We'll talk some more about it. It doesn't require any effort on your part. I know you'll do great. You've got a great imagination."

We finished the dinner talking about painting, photography, and the Hilo Arts Group where we had first met.

Chapter 86

The Photo Shoot

I had agreed to go on an outing with a small group of members of the Hilo Arts Group. We had agreed on shooting at the Volcano National Park. Although everyone going, except for Lisa, had been there many times before, there were always many interesting scenes to shoot.

I worried briefly about a "dual-role" conflict with Diana and Cheryl being my patients and going on a shoot with them. But the ethics' rules made exceptions for rural communities and it wasn't as though I was going with them. I was going with Lisa, and Diana and Cheryl were just members of the group. Several others had also been invited to go on the shoot.

We had agreed to meet at the information center just inside the Volcano National Park. I had offered to pick up Lisa since it would be her first time.

It's okay, I told myself. *It's just the kind of thing to do on a date, something we're both interested in.* I hoped I could get even closer to her.

When I parked in front of Lisa's house, Lisa was already out the door, camera bag, and tripod in hand. I went around the car to open the door for Lisa and helped her load her gear. I put it next to mine, alongside the small cooler that contained some sodas, bottled water, and a couple of sandwiches I'd picked up at the Sack and Save. There was a physical tension between us that we both tried to ignore. Lisa was stunning in a white short-sleeved blouse and kaki shorts. She wore sensible shoes ready for hiking in the park. I had trouble keeping my eyes off of her.

"I've got an extra rain parka and coat for you. It can get pretty cold in the wind up at the Park."

"Thank you, Hart."

"No problem, it's a pleasure," I replied somewhat stiffly as I closed her door. It wasn't long until we had reached the highway leading to Volcano. I had a classical CD playing softly. We had both kept our windows most of the way up so that the wind wouldn't drown out the music or conversation.

"It's a beautiful day," Lisa said, breaking the silence.

"Yeah. Can you believe those beautiful clouds? We have the most beautiful clouds here and they're free."

"Do you ever shoot them?"

"All the time. I've got hundreds of photos of clouds. They're like that almost every day."

We gained altitude as I drove on, going up to Volcano. There was the usual light to moderate traffic but I was in no hurry. I'd made the trip many times and knew it would take about an hour. I enjoyed the music and having Lisa sitting next to me. I pointed out some sights along the way.

My hand had brushed Lisa's bare thigh once when I was shifting gears and we were both electrified by the touch. Neither of us mentioned it, as though not talking about it would mean it hadn't happened. The tension had returned.

Chapter 87

The Orchid Farm

When we got to the Orchid Farm, about halfway up the road to Volcano, I pulled into the mostly empty parking lot. "You're going to love this Lisa," I said to her as I shut the engine off and set the parking brake. I unbuckled quickly and went to her side to open her door but Lisa hadn't waited for me and was already out of the car by the time I got to the other side. We walked side by side to the glass front door and I opened it for her.

"Thank you kind sir," Lisa said with a small mocking smile.

"You're welcome, gentle lady," I replied in a courtly manner.

When we were inside, Lisa gasped and held her hand to her throat. "Oh! Look at all the flowers. There must be hundreds of them," she said, looking at the beautiful sea of orchids. She walked ahead of Hart enthralled by the beauty and variety of the orchids, deep reds, blues, purples, yellows, pinks, and all the colors she could imagine. I walked behind her enjoying the sight of her curvaceous hips, rear, and long legs. I was enjoying her joy of seeing the orchids.

"Look Hart," Lisa said. And then, a minute later, saying it again as she pointed out yet another beautiful orchid. Some were smaller than the size of a dime and others were larger than a grapefruit. She couldn't believe the number and variety.

"Will they let you photograph them?" she asked.

"Sure. Why not?"

"Oh. I can't believe this. And it's free. I've got to get my camera." She turned and headed toward the door. I followed quickly behind her and when she was almost to the car I pushed the electronic key to unlock the doors. Lisa reached in and got her camera and tripod and I got mine. Cameras ready, we walked back to the orchids. There were very few customers in the huge building. We went about the place snapping shots of the beautiful flowers. I would sometimes shoot Lisa.

I couldn't help thinking the thoughts I had every time I looked at some of the purple and red orchids, how they reminded me of a woman's genitalia. I wondered if Lisa noticed it too.

He needn't have wondered. Lisa was well aware that many of the orchids looked like inviting vaginas. She could feel herself getting wet. She hoped that she wouldn't embarrass herself with any wet spots in the crotch of her shorts. "That's enough," she said. "They're too beautiful." She needed a moment to collect herself. "I've got to go to the lady's room." She left me to hold her camera. Inside she breathed deeply to calm her unanticipated arousal.

When she came out to where I was waiting, her face was a little flushed. I asked, "Are you okay?"

"Yeah," she replied in a husky voice. She cleared her throat. *If he only knew*, she thought. "Here," she reached for her camera. "Let's go. I can only take so much beauty at one time. Like being in a museum. After about an hour or so I can't take any more and have to leave."

"Yeah," I said as I handed her camera to her and followed her out to the car.

The sexual tension was heavy in the car as we buckled up. Both of us were aware of how Lisa's breasts were accentuated by the seat belt shoulder strap pressing between them.

After she got into the car she didn't do anything for a moment. Then she put her hand on my thigh. I started the car and drove down the road and to a secluded patch of woods. Her hand stayed on my thigh and moved higher. When we stopped she felt no need to explain; I felt the same way. The cloudy sky was bright and clear as I kissed her, and we opened our mouths and held each other as our tongues explored. Our breathing was heavier and the sound of the motor running and the branches blowing in the breeze were the only sounds. I turned off the car, letting the heater die, as the windows began to fog. She moved onto my lap still with our mouths connected, tongues touching. For a few moments we were able to forget about the world outside.

Then as if in panic I started the car and pushed away from her. "I'm sorry I stammered."

"I'm not." she said, as I turned up the music, and kept my eyes on the road as we continued the journey to Volcano.

"It's not fair, I mean far," I stammered.

"I love the greens in those trees," Lisa replied as she looked out her side window.

Chapter 88

The Shoot Continues

"Well, we're here," I said, a short time later as I turned into the Park entrance. There was only one car ahead of us. I pulled up to the entrance booth, showed my yearly pass, and got another map of the park. "Here," I said, handing it to Lisa, "This will show you where we are."

"I know where we are dummy," Lisa said with humor. The tension was broken again.

I found a parking spot and we got out of the car to look for the others at the information center. We spotted Diana.

"Where's Cheryl?" I asked.

"I talked to her this morning," Diana said. "She said she hadn't slept well and wasn't going to make it. No one else seems to be here either. So I guess it's just us."

"Okay," I said. "Where do you want to start?"

"What took you guys so long?" Diana asked, looking at her watch. "You're thirty minutes late. I'd just about given up on you."

"We stopped to look at the Orchid Farm . . ."

"Oh," Diana said.

"How about we drive to that spot where you can see the misty smoke from the crater. There's a good car park there and we can then walk the 'Crater Rim Trail,'" I said.

We got back in our cars. Several minutes later we were unloading our camera gear and getting ready to start out on the trail.

Lisa was shivering in the cool stiff breeze that pushed her blouse and shorts against her body. I glanced at her and had to tear my eyes from the sight.

"Here," I said, handing her the extra coat and getting one for myself. She took the coat and quickly put it on and zipped it up.

There were a few tourists looking at the mist rising from the crater, snapping pictures with their point and shoot cameras. Within half a mile down the trail however, we had the scenery all to ourselves.

For the next two hours we walked to various spots and whenever someone felt like it they would stop and start shooting. We were soon spread out along the trail. I even let Lisa out of my sight as I shot an interesting shadow on the wall of the crater. We eventually stopped and regrouped in a small clearing. The sun was out, the wind had slackened, and we were all warm from the walk. We had stopped to shoot so often that we probably hadn't gone more than a mile or so. Still, we were all ready for a break.

We seated ourselves in various spots in the clearing, Diana on an old concrete fence post that had fallen over. I sat near Lisa on an outcropping of Pahoehoe, the relatively smooth type of lava. Lisa sat on a fallen log. We were all silent for a while. We retrieved our water bottles from our backpacks and drank quietly.

It's incredible how delicious just plain water can be, Lisa thought as she swallowed.

I watched her throat as she leaned her head back to swallow. Diana watched Hart watching Lisa. *Something's going on there.*

"So what do you think Lisa?" Diana asked.

"It's incredibly beautiful. It takes my breath away," Lisa replied.

"Yeah," I said, "I'd forgotten how mystic and inspiring it is up here. Let's go to the Lava Tube."

I stood up. The lava was too hard to sit on for very long. I extended my hand to Lisa and helped her up.

The walk back to our cars didn't take as long since we didn't stop to shoot. Back at our cars we stowed our gear. "See you at the Lava Tube," I said to Diana.

In the Lava Tube's parking lot there were several Robert's of Hawai'i tour buses, engines idling, diesel smoke polluting the air, one loading a large group of Japanese tourist, and one letting off an equally large load; one bus was sitting empty, engine idling.

"We should have come here first, to beat all the tourist," Diana complained.

"Well, we're here now. Let's see what we can get," Hart said.

We got our gear and headed to the steps leading down to the tube. We were the only ones with tripods.

Although the lush green growth gave us some good shots, there were just too many tourists ahead of and behind us. We were back at our cars within 45 minutes. Two other buses were busy loading and unloading tourists.

"I think that's it for me," Diana said.

"Yeah, me too," Lisa replied.

"Next time, let's meet here about 7 AM," Diana suggested.

"Sounds like a great idea," I agreed.

"Hey, guys," Lisa said, "Thanks for letting me hang out with you. I'm only an amateur. I'm sure you noticed."

"No such thing as amateur," Diana disclaimed, "Just different stages of growth. And you're the one who's actually sold some work."

"Okay, until next time," I called out as Lisa and I got into my car.

"There is a little spot not far from here. Shall we stop and eat our sandwiches?" I asked Lisa.

"Too many tourists."

"No. This spot is too small and out of the way. I doubt anyone will be there. Let's check it out."

"Okay, you're driving," Lisa replied, as she buckled her seat belt.

Chapter 89

Randy

Randy, aka Paul Stallworth, had headed straight for Hilo when he was released from the Red Roof Inn due to over crowding. He wanted to see his beloved Lisa again. He couldn't wait because he knew she missed him.

After arriving in Hilo in mid-afternoon I easily found another rooming house. Of course, I was supposed to register as a sex offender, yet I never bothered, as I knew the "system" was so overloaded that no one would ever know. I got another bike from the Hilo police station, another one with yellow ribbon decals on both fenders, *what a coincidence* and by nightfall was peddling my way to Lisa's.

Damn. That's not fair. How am I supposed to see her with that fence all around her house? And she has dogs too, I thought. *She must be afraid of somebody. Don't worry, Lisa honey, I'm back, I'll take care of you. I won't let anyone hurt you,* I thought. *She's mine. No one else can have her.*

I couldn't get closer to her so I jacked-off and again left her a white "calling card" outside her fence.

I realized that I'd have to replenish all of my makeup stock with corks, fake beards, mustache, pancake makeup, and wigs and other things to use to disguise myself so I'd be able to follow Lisa and not be recognized.

I started watching her again the next day after I'd replenished my makeup supplies. I didn't have to work immediately. I had some money in my savings account from my last job at Ken's, enough to buy an old non-descript Nissan pickup truck—there were thousands just like it on the Big Island.

Over the next few weeks I gradually learned who Lisa's friends were and her daily routine. She belonged to the Hilo Arts Group and seemed to have some close friends. And there was that same damned psychologist, the one I'd seen on the admissions ward at the Red Roof Inn. I saw the shrink's name on the outside of his office door, "Dr. Albertino." *Got to think of a way to get rid of him.*

I continued to be very frustrated at my lack of ability to get to my Lisa.

Once I get rid of her friends, she'll have to come to me.

Chapter 90

Hart and Lisa

The spot Hart drove to was only 15 minutes up the road and was on a very long turn off from the main road. There was a small picnic table under an iron wood tree. No one was there.

"See," I said getting out, "We've got the place to ourselves." I pulled the cooler and my backpack from the back seat and we walked over to the table. I took some paper towels from my pack and cleaned some debris off the benches and tabletop. When I had finished wiping the benches, Lisa sat and watched me clean the tabletop.

"Here," I said, extending a sandwich to her. "Tuna fish. Hope that's okay. I should have asked you what you like."

"Tuna's fine," Lisa replied, taking the sandwich and unwrapping the cellophane.

We ate in silence for a while, sitting side-by-side, leaning our backs against the edge of the table.

"I'd forgotten how good a tuna sandwich could be," Lisa said.

"Maybe it's just the sun and breeze and the outdoors," I replied.

Lisa continued to eat. She took small bites and chewed with her eyes closed. I watched her jaw muscles work as she chewed. I didn't want to get caught staring at anything else.

She opened her eyes and smiled at me. "Yummy," she purred. "What's the Hawaiian word?"

"Ono. You've got some mayo on you lips," I said as I reached my finger to her lips to wipe it off. It was too personal a gesture. Lisa impulsively nibbled at my finger, then sucked it into her mouth. "Ono," she said.

She was thinking about how well our current relationship was going and finding she could be her self. Hart found himself stirring in his pants.

An old Nissan pickup pulled into the small spot. There was a lone man in the driver's seat. He had on big round glasses and turned away after briefly glancing at Hart and Lisa. Neither suspected anything.

"Guess we'd better go," I said.

"Spoil sport," Lisa teased. "We're just having a snack." *Now I've done it*, Lisa thought, *He's embarrassed*. I didn't say anything else as he picked up our rubbish and put it in a trashcan.

"Let's go," I said, taking my backpack and the cooler and her hand. I opened her door, put the cooler and backpack in the rear, and held the door for her.

We drove back to Hilo as dark clouds formed overhead. Every now and then one of us would comment on the day's shoot. I was careful to not touch her leg when I shifted gears.

Chapter 91

Hart and Lisa

Parked outside of Lisa's house, I blurted out impulsively, "Lisa, you look ravishing tonight."

"Why thank you, Hart."

Lisa leaned over and kissed me on the lips. I kissed her back. We both parted our lips.

I reached out and hugged her; she responded instinctively, extending her body to me. I wished he'd cup my breasts. I was so ready for this.

We were both breathing heavily when I finally managed to regain some control and pushed back.

In a breathless whisper I said again, "I'm, I shouldn't have. I didn't mean to."

"Yes you did Hart, and I wanted you to."

Lisa reached up and kissed me again. She wanted and needed my physical touch. She felt a deep sense of relief as our lips and bodies pressed together. Then she giggled.

I pushed away again, confused this time. Lisa didn't say anything. She was breathing slowly and holding my hand. The giggle became a laugh.

The laughter helped me get control. I managed to ask, "Now what the hell are you laughing about?"

"I'm . . ." Lisa said, still giggling. "It's your mustache. It tickled my nose."

"Oh," I said. I was happy to see Lisa laugh. I wanted to kiss her.

I could feel my arousal stirring again. Lisa knew what she was feeling and only wanted Hart to hold her and kiss her again. The laughter of a few moments ago was gone.

There was a moment of awkwardness as we separated and I got out of the car. This time Lisa waited for me to open her door. I took her hand to help her out and then got her camera bag, camera, and tripod. She grabbed my hand again as we walked up to her front door.

I reached for my beard and nervously fidgeted with it. I wanted to kiss her again. "Hey, I better get going, it's getting late," I said.

Yet my hands reached out for her shoulders. I leaned forward. She closed her eyes, lifting her chin, and her lips seemed to quiver in anticipation.

We ended up in a passionate embrace and deep kiss. This time my mustache didn't tickle.

Breathing heavily, I backed off. "Okay, goodnight and sleep tight. I'll see you this coming Wednesday for lunch as usual, right?"

"I'll be there Hart," I replied, sounding disappointed. I yearned to have him hold me and take me inside and to bed like the phantom lovers of my dreams.

I smiled awkwardly, then turned around and started down the walk toward my car. I was smiling and humming a tune in my mind, something from "Ain't Misbehaving."

I wasn't close enough to hear her softly say, "Goodnight, Hart."

Both slept very poorly that night, remembering the kiss.

Chapter 92

Dr. Cho

The next day I was in my office when I took a call from Dr. Cho.

We exchanged pleasantries for a short time.

"I'll get to the point. You remember when I was a guest at the Red Roofed Inn?"

"How can I ever forget," I said, smiling to myself.

"Ever since then," Dr. Cho continued, "I've been more interested in it. A few weeks ago in the Honolulu paper there was an article on the front page about the place. The court is making them release patients due to overcrowding. I've been meaning to call you about it but I kept forgetting."

"Well, it was always overcrowded when I was there," I said. "I've been meaning to call you too."

"There is one inmate you might be interested in, and I doubt it made the news over there in the boonies."

"Hey, you're just jealous because you're stuck with Honolulu traffic," I said, laughing. "But you're right, I didn't see anything about it in our local paper but then I don't read it too closely."

"Let me finish and you might not be laughing so much. They let out a bunch of inmates and a couple of them were sex offenders. I think you saw one of them when you were on the admissions ward. Same time I was there. A sex offender from Hilo, who was an NGRI was one of them. I didn't recognize the name but thought you'd want to know."

"So what's the name?"

"The article in the paper said it was Paul Stallworth."

"Yeah that name sounds familiar," I said. "I think I remember him. He was obsessed with some woman but would never say her name."

"I thought you'd want to know. Since he's from Hilo, he's probably headed your way."

"Shit. Not good news. I only saw him for a short time and I never decided if he was really crazy or just acting but if he wasn't acting he was real scary with his obsession with one woman. He would never share her name though.

"Hey thanks for calling, I've got to go. My next appointment just walked into the waiting room."

"Okay, Hart. I'll see you when I'm over there for the Volcano Marathon."

"Aloha," I said and we both hung up. I was worried and frowned at the news about the sex offender but I didn't have time to think about it now. My next patient was waiting.

PART FIVE

Chapter 93

The FBI

FBI Special Agent Strickland (Special Agent in Charge, SAC) saw nothing but trouble in the call he got about the "Anthrax Case," as it was being called. The fake anthrax letter had been postmarked from Hilo. It meant a hell of a lot more "High Priority" work for his already overworked staff. They were undermanned yet the usual leads had to be checked out. He'd sent an agent to Hilo as soon as he'd been briefed. He would also send one of his agents to the State Hospital in Kaneohe. Since the substance wasn't anthrax, he was thinking it might be a nut case who might have spent some time in the State Hospital but it still had to be checked out.

"Nagata," Strickland called out his open office door.

"Yeah, boss." Agent Kim Nagata was pretty, well proportioned, and most importantly, a 'local.'

"Go over to the hospital in Kaneohe and check their records."

"Sure thing, boss. What am I looking for?"

"I don't really know. Not any current patients but any cases that were sent here from Hilo, or who have relatives on the Big Island."

"Okay, boss."

Strickland watched her ass as she walked out of his office. He'd already tried to put a move on her when she had first been assigned to the Honolulu office fresh out of the Academy. "We'll meet at the Delaney bar when you get back," he called to her as she left. "Take the Pali highway. It's quicker this time of day."

Agent Nagata didn't say anything; she just turned and gave him a slight nod with not even a hint of a smile. *Shit he thinks he knows how to get around this island better than I do; I was born and raised here,* she thought.

Damn, Strickland thought. *Well at least she's local and more likely to get cooperation than that idiot Richardson.*

Kim Nagata had grown up on the leeward coast of Oahu and had learned to be tough and not take any shit from anyone. Her father and two brothers were police officers in the Hawai'i Police Department. She knew a few of the nurses at the Red Roof Inn. She'd gone to college with some of them.

Kim made the cross island trip in 45 minutes. *Not bad,* she thought as she parked and got out of her car and headed straight to the Admissions/Records Office.

"Hey Kim, what brings you out here on such a fine day? Did you catch the surf this morning?" Karen said as she greeted her old friend from the other side of the office counter. "I saw your auntie the other day at the park; she was all banged up. She okay?"

"Yeah, her old man beat on her, but I can't make her leave him. Hey, what about your cousin Harry?"

"What?" Karen said with a smile.

"What? What? You know what. He still around?"

"Oh, he's around."

"Quit teasing. Is he with anyone?"

"No. But you need to be careful with him. I no want you hurt again," she said, slipping into pidgin.

"No worries mate, I'm grown up now and an FBI agent. Speaking of which I'd better get to business. I had a late night shift last night. We got a hot one to track down. You got any Big Island inmates . . ."

"Is water wet?" Karen interrupted her. They both laughed.

"Yeah, stupid of me to ask. This one would have to have been released at least a month ago."

"Hold on, let me boot up the patient ID screen."

"While you're there, can you go back and check for the last 12 months?"

"Hell, I can go back five years if you want but any further and we'd have to sort through the old paper records.

"Here we go. Looks like we have ten inmates from the Big Island who were discharged in the last twelve months. Eight males and two females."

"Can you give me a printout of their names and addresses? And pictures if you have them?"

"Sure Kim, but they may not be very accurate. Lots of these people are homeless. You might need to check the patient's charts to see if there are any more addresses or contact information. I'll have to go to the patient records files to print up pictures and I'll double check for current addresses. It may take an hour or so."

"That's okay, we need to get right on this and the names and addresses will give us a start. Can you fax the pictures to the SAC's office?" Since they were all forensic cases and their admissions were public knowledge, Karen didn't have to worry about any consent from the patients.

"Let me just print this out then." Karen selected the names she wanted and hit the print key. "What's so hot about this one Kim?" she asked as she handed over the one page list.

"You've been in this long enough to know I can't say," she smiled at her friend to take the edge off of her reply and then added, "It's just a false lead on a fake letter, no real danger."

"Okay," Karen said not taking any offense. "You surfing this Saturday?"

"Maybe. I've got to run, see you later. Please don't forget the pictures."

"Okay, tell your mom and dad hi."

Chapter 94

Agent Richardson

Kim had to get to the office and fax this list to Special Agent Richardson. He should be in Hilo by now.

Agent Richardson took the fax from the secretary in the Hilo Police Station.

"So where are the pictures, honey?" he asked in a condescending, lecherous manner.

He had a way of irritating people without even trying. It was a talent he wasn't aware he possessed. He wondered why she was glaring at him.

"There weren't any pictures."

How am I supposed to ID anyone without any pictures? Richardson wondered.

There were only two men on the list that had Hilo addresses but a total of six that had addresses on the east side of the Big Island. They all had to be checked out but these six would be first. He had to ask the Chief for help and wasn't getting any until he told the Chief about the "Anthrax Case." The Chief assigned two men, Ted Oshiro and Clay Barton, and they each took two cases. Richardson took the ones in the Hilo area, as they would be easier for him to find. *Oshiro and Barton? What kind of names are those, sounds like some kinda Japanese/Italian meat,* Richardson thought.

Checking out the "Hilo" addresses wasn't that easy. The first address Richardson never did find. The street, Kinoole, just ended and there was no number 96000. The other address was at a Filipino rooming house. He spoke to the old lady who ran the place. They were standing on her front lanai. In his coat and tie, he stood out like headlights on a dark country road at night. None of the locals wore suit coats or ties.

"You want room. No noise, no dog, no cat. You pay cash."

"No. No. I'm checking on a man who used to live here."

"You want room?"

"NO," Richardson said raising his voice as though volume would make the crazy woman understand. *Why do I always get the crazy ones,* he wondered.

"I no crazy," she shouted as though she had read his mind.

"I never said you were crazy," Richardson said. His voice was still very loud.

"You go. You trouble maker." She turned to leave.

"No. Wait, please." He searched for the local word, "Kokua?" he asked, hoping that was right.

She turned, squinting at him.

"Did . . ." he looked at the list in his hand, "a Mr. Stallworth live here?"

"Stallworth?"

"Stallworth," Richardson repeated.

"English?"

"No, American."

This is crazy, I must be caught in an Abbott and Costello time warp. I may as well ask her 'who's on first?'

"Was a man named Stallworth living here?"

"What Stallworth?"

"It's the man's name."

"Stallworth?"

"Yes. Stallworth."

"No Stallworth."

"So no Stallworth lived here?"

"No Stallworth," she turned to go.

"Wait, Kokua. A Paul Stallworth?"

"Paul, he no good. He leave, no come back."

At last he was making progress. "So Paul Stallworth lived here?"

"No Stallworth." She turned to leave again.

"No. Please wait. Paul Stallworth stayed here?"

"No Stallworth."

"Paul?"

"He no good. You make trouble. You leave." She turned and went inside and firmly closed her door.

Richardson shook his head in frustration. "Damn locals," he muttered. He wasn't at all sure she hadn't been playing with him. *Now I'll have to get one of the local boys*

296

to come with me. Should have had a picture anyway. What kinda shit was this sending a guy out to ID someone and not even have a picture to show.

Richardson returned to the Hilo Police station to see if any pictures had been faxed in and to check on the progress of the other two officers. They had had some better luck than Richardson had. Two of the former inmates had moved back to the mainland and had forwarding addresses that could be checked. Of the remaining two, one was located at another boarding home address and had agreed to come in for questioning but their gut reaction was that this wasn't the guy they were looking for. He didn't seem to be able to read or write so they didn't think he could have addressed the anthrax envelope. The fourth man's address had checked out but his sister reported that he had gone fishing with her husband and they wouldn't be back for a few days.

That left Paul Stallworth, the one on Kinoole Street, and the two on the leeward side, still to be interviewed. Oshiro and Barton got a good laugh when Richardson told his story of trying to interview the old Filipino lady.

"That's the lady they call 'Crazy Being.' Nobody can get anything out of her."

"Well you guys can go try again when we have a picture to show. And you can get someone on the Kona side to check those two. Anything else come in?"

"Yeah. We got summaries of their treatment records. This guy, Stallworth, was treated by one of our local shrinks, Dr. Albertino."

Richardson glanced at his watch. It was only 4:30 in the afternoon. Maybe they could interview him this afternoon. He put in a call to Dr. Albertino's office but only got his machine. Richardson left his name and the local office number and asked Dr. Albertino to call as soon as possible on an urgent matter.

Chapter 95

Hart and the FBI

Twenty minutes later while Richardson, Oshiro, and Barton were still talking over the treatment summaries of the other inmates, Dr. Albertino returned Richardson's call.

The Police Chief's secretary had come in annoyed. It was only because she had stayed late to type up a report for the Chief that the call was even answered. All the staff had left, and these dickheads were too lazy to answer a phone after their shift as that might require some actual work. She was in a pissy mood anyway. Oshiro hadn't called her since she'd "put out" for him more than a month ago.

"It's for you," she said sarcastically, nodding at Richardson. *Asshole*, she thought, *Men are all alike*.

Richardson picked up the phone on his desk and punched the lighted button for line one.

"Agent Richardson?"

"Yes . . ."

"I just finished my last appointment. Your message said it was urgent," Hart interrupted him.

"Dr. Albertino thanks for returning my call so quickly. We're working on a case that might involve a patient you treated at the State Hospital, or as we call it the Red Roof Inn."

"That was some time ago."

"Is it okay if I come over to your office? It'd be a great help, Doctor."

"Okay," Hart said, looking at his watch. "If you can make it right away. I've got a meeting to get to in an hour."

"I'll get the local guys to show me where your office is. I should . . ." he looked at Oshiro and Barton who held up five fingers, "be there in five minutes."

"Okay, just come into the waiting room. I've got a camera and will know when you get here."

Five minutes later Agent Richardson was saying, "Thanks for seeing me today, Dr. Albertino. It's really important."

"It's okay. Call me Hart unless you want to be formal."

"We'd better keep it formal, Dr. Albertino."

"Okay," Hart said and waited for Agent Richardson to continue.

"Do you remember treating a patient named Paul Stallworth when you were at the State Hospital?"

"Yeah, as a matter of fact I do. Normally I guess I wouldn't remember, but it was his name. And a friend of mine on Oahu called several weeks ago to let me know that Stallworth might be heading to Hilo."

"Here's a copy of your treatment record," Richardson said as he handed over a one-page summary.

Hart took a few minutes to read the report and then looked up expectantly.

"What can you add to this?"

"What do you want to know?"

"Would you consider him dangerous?"

"Why do you want to know?"

"I can't tell you that."

"Well, it doesn't matter as I couldn't tell you."

"If you're worried about patient confidentiality, Dr. Albertino, I can get a court order if necessary."

"It's not that," Hart told the agent. "It's been too long since I last saw him. So I wouldn't have the necessary forensic data to comment on his current dangerousness."

"Can't you tell me anything, Dr. Albertino?" Richardson said in frustration.

"I can tell you, that at the time I did see him at the State Hospital, I did consider him dangerous because of his continued delusional obsession over one woman but he never did reveal her name, though in the past he had been stalking a woman who I'm currently dating, Ms. Lisa Havenhurst, so it may have been her. He was hospitalized on an NGRI for that stalking. If he goes back to stalking her again, I'd have to say he is dangerous, and certainly in need of some long-term treatment. Unfortunately, I haven't seen or heard anything about him. In the past when he had been stalking Ms. Havenhurst, I didn't know her at that time. So to sum it up Agent Richardson, I'd have to say he is dangerous, especially to Ms. Havenhurst."

"Well thank you for talking with me, Dr. Albertino. If you see him or hear anything about him please let me know ASAP."

"Okay," Hart said. "Do you think he's dangerous Agent Richardson?"

"Based on what we know so far, I think so, but with these nut cases you never know."

I was pensive after Agent Richardson left. I didn't know if I should tell Lisa about Stallworth. Although I did believe that Paul was a danger to her, I really didn't want to alarm her; I would see that she was safe, and as far as I knew Paul had never committed any violent behavior, just stalking, breaking and entering, and sexual assault in the fourth degree. Now that she had her guard dogs and the chain-link fence around her house, it was unlikely that Stallworth would be able to break into her house again. On balance, I decided not to tell Lisa, as I believed it would only unnecessarily frighten her and I felt she already had enough to deal with. Besides, I was there to look after her now.

Had he known Paul's full history his opinion would have been quite different.

Chapter 96

Hart and Lisa

Even though I believed that there was nothing to be concerned about, after meeting with Agent Richardson, I was more worried about Lisa. I used that as an excuse to go to her home. We came together naturally and just held each other for a long time. I didn't tell her about Paul Stallworth.

The background of fear and concern about Stallworth and his prior stalking of Lisa seemed like a primal force pushing me towards Lisa. The holding became mutual caressing and kissing. Without words we leaned back on Lisa's couch and started to undress each other. Lisa slowly unbuttoned my shirt and felt the strength in my arms and chest.

I unbuttoned Lisa's blouse and marveled at her breasts. We kissed gently. This time my mustache wasn't tickling, and then I reached behind Lisa. She leaned forward to give me better access, and I unclasped her bra, freeing her luscious breasts. We both gasped; Lisa from the cool air on her nipples and me from the sight of her. I devoured her with my eyes and gently caressed her breasts. I was leaning to kiss and suck on the nipple of her breast, when I heard her sigh and she pushed me away. She was shaking and crying.

"What's the matter, Lisa?" I asked with concern.

"It's not you," Lisa replied through her tears. "It feels so good to have you hold me and caress me. I want it. It's just that I have this terrible memory that it's wrong and dirty, that I'm no good," she cried.

"No you're not, you're beautiful and wonderful."

"I'm spoiled goods," she cried again remembering the words from her mother.

I tried my best to comfort her yet the mood had changed. We awkwardly buttoned up in silence.

"I guess I'd better go," I said as I got up. I hoped she would ask me to stay.

"Okay," Lisa said. She wanted him to stay and yet she couldn't ask him.

Chapter 97

Hypnosis

Lisa had invited Hart to her home for dinner the next night. When Hart came into her foyer, they greeted and hugged awkwardly. They sat on the edge of the couch, trying not to talk about the last time they'd been sitting there.

"We need to talk."

"I know," Hart replied.

"It's no use, Hart. I don't want to hurt you any more."

"Lisa, I think using hypnosis will fix this," I said.

"No. Nothing can fix me. Nothing."

"At least let's give it a try. Please."

"I'm afraid, Hart," she said meekly.

"There's nothing to be afraid of. Just trust me. Just a little. We'll stop at anytime you want to."

Reluctantly, Lisa agreed to try. "What do you want me to do?"

"You just lie back on the couch. And close your eyes. Concentrate on the sound of my voice," I said as I pulled over a straight-backed chair and sat down next to the couch.

I didn't waste time and Lisa was responsive. I quickly took her into a hypnotic state.

Lisa was now in a very deep trance and I had taken her back in time to her childhood. Her eyes were closed and her body was resting comfortably on her own couch. I had explained to her that she would be able to talk to me and remain in a trance state.

I asked, "Please describe where you are."

"I'm in my bedroom. It's nighttime and I'm in bed."

"Are you alone?"

"No, Uncle Vincent is with me."

"How old are you?"

"Eight." The voice was that of a young child.

"What is Uncle Vincent doing?"

"He's reading me a story. Now he's tickling me. It feels good." Lisa giggled like a little girl.

Lisa's face was soft and relaxed. "What's going on now?"

"He's caressing my legs and arms. It feels good."

"Then what?"

"He's getting some hand lotion and putting it in his hands. He is rubbing my legs some more. He wants to take off my panties so I'll feel better."

Lisa's face was an expression of sexual arousal. She didn't know it. I was alarmed. "What's going on now?"

"He's rubbing my privates. It feels good and warm." She wiggled her legs as though she could feel Uncle Vincent rubbing the mound of her sex.

I was really alarmed now and disgusted. I now knew what had happened. The Uncle Vincent who Lisa loved so much, and felt so close to, had sexually molested her. Of course, it felt good to a young child who craved attention. That only made the betrayal worse for her, as she was old enough, to know at some level, that it was wrong.

So that's where she got the idea that sex is wrong, I thought. I wanted to stop. It was disgusting and I felt like a voyeur. Yet I knew I had to help her by letting her remember it all.

"What next?" I was cautious not to lead her or place any false memories in her mind by suggesting any specifics to her.

"He is putting his finger in me. That hurts." Her face scrunched up in pain.

"What next?" I repeated yet again.

"He is putting my hand on his thingy and rubbing it up and down."

I didn't think I could take any more revulsion and disgust, yet I went on, "What next?"

"Some white sticky stuff came out. He says I made him very happy. That makes me feel good." Her face was a relaxed Mona Lisa smile.

"And next?" I felt like I really didn't want to hear it.

"He is tucking me under the covers. He is telling me he loves me. He left and I am going to sleep."

"Whew," I said under my breath. I hoped the worst was over. "What do you remember next?"

"I am taking a bath. I tell mom about Uncle Vincent. She is really upset and yelling a lot. I am scared. I knew I had done something wrong." She lapsed into silence.

"Then what?"

"I am crying. Mom says, 'You're damaged goods now. Now no man will want you.'"

Chapter 98

Tears of Joy

I hoped that Lisa would be all right since she had remembered the abuse under hypnosis after repressing it for years. Sometimes the memories caused more trauma before any healing could begin.

"What next?"

"It's the next day. I am putting my colors away. I don't want to color anymore."

"What next?" I repeated.

Lisa didn't reply. She remained relaxed and breathed deeply and easily. I was ashamed of myself for watching her breasts rise and fall, as though I were violating her just like Uncle Vincent. I remembered that she had told me that Uncle Vincent had died some years ago.

When Lisa still didn't reply after a few minutes I said, "Okay, Lisa. I think that is enough for now. I'm going to count backwards from three to one and then I'll snap my fingers and you'll come all the way back to the present, open your eyes, relaxed and refreshed. You will only remember what you experienced if you want to and are capable of dealing with it consciously."

When I counted and snapped my fingers Lisa opened her eyes and looked around and stretched. Her face broke out into a huge smile and she laughed, almost hysterically.

I was concerned. "What do you remember Lisa?"

"Wow! I remember it all. It wasn't my fault. I was just a little girl." She was laughing and crying, tears streaming down her cheeks.

I offered her a tissue from my pocket. "Breathe and relax. You're okay, take all the time you need."

"Yes. I am. I'm all right. All these years I didn't know why I didn't want anyone to touch me yet I did want it, didn't want anything to do with sex but did want it."

I breathed easier; she was going to be all right. I didn't say anything, just waited for her to go on. I wanted it to come to her on her own.

"I'm not damaged goods, am I?"

She'd gotten there. "No Lisa. You're precious goods. You're beautiful and have a whole new life ahead of you."

"I feel free from, free from . . ." she repeated, grasping for words, "free from the evil Uncle Vincent did."

"Yes?" I waited.

"I want to hate him but it seems so long ago now. It just was; now it's like he has truly gone away. The memory of what he did to me is still there but the pain and shame have gone away."

Chapter 99

Hart and Lisa

I took a deep breath. "Do you feel okay?"

"Yeah. A little tired but really okay, in fact better than I've felt in years. Oh, thank you Hart. You've given me my life back."

"You're welcome, Lisa. Thank you for letting me help you."

I smiled tenderly at Hart. I was ecstatic that I had recovered the memories of my abuse and seemed to be over that particular part of my past. It amazed me that something I had repressed and feared for so long could be released so quickly.

I got up with Lisa and we embraced for a few seconds. The sexual tension was still there but now the barrier from Lisa's past abuse were gone. Before I could help myself I pressed against her. I stroked the small of her back and kissed the side of her neck. She looked up with eyes closed and lips pursed ready to be kissed. I was able to stop myself and pushed away.

Lisa opened her eyes and shook her head as if to say, "*What's wrong Hart? Don't you care for me?*" That was the problem; I cared too much for her.

"I need to leave. Let you rest. I'll be by tomorrow," I said as I walked to the door. I didn't want to take advantage of her current emotional state.

Damn, Lisa thought, *why didn't he stay? Now that I'm ready for him, he leaves?* Still it felt wonderful to be free of the nameless monster who had been haunting me all these years. I walked out to my lanai and looked out at the blue Pacific Ocean, powerful and vast. The sea breeze was strong today and I was glad to be free and alive.

I didn't look down and to the side of my property where Randy stood far outside my fence watching me as he jerked off. *Don't worry Lisa. I'm going to protect you,* he thought as his fist jerked furiously.

Chapter 100

Hart

That night I slid down, soaking myself in the claw-footed tub in my old home. I was sick about the possibility that Mr. Stallworth might be coming back to cause Lisa more grief, just when she had recovered from her childhood abuse. I felt that I should refer her to one of my colleagues to follow up for full recovery from her past abuse.

I began to think of Lisa, her warm sensuous body, and her breasts as I'd seen them the night we had almost made love. I couldn't and didn't want to get the vision out of my mind. My hand moved below the water seeking release.

PART SIX

Chapter 101

Randy

I'd followed Lisa in the weeks before and knew where and when the Hilo Arts Group met. I had gone to the building long before the meeting was to start. I had a half dozen other disguises that completely changed my appearance. This time I had dressed like a janitor. I wore a large black T-shirt that I had found for twenty-five cents in the thrift store on Bay Front. The old shirt even had "Phil's Janitor Service" and phone number "404 555-1550" printed in faded yellow paint across the back.

Finding a mop and bucket in a hall closet, I pretended to be mopping the floors as Lisa and the other members of the club gathered for the evening meeting. That's how I'd found out who her friends were. The club members made it easy for me. Members wore those "stick on" things with their names printed in large letters. No one seemed to notice the janitor and it was only that stupid shrink who even looked at me. I had been careful to not make any eye contact.

I had been extremely frustrated in my continued attempts at reaching Lisa. I followed her in the daytime and at night but had never been able to see anything except from a distance. I had started to follow Lisa's friends and was able to follow Diana successfully. I even got into Diana's bedroom and jerked-off in her bed and left my wet "calling card" for her. I took one of her pairs of panties. One night I had caught Diana using a dildo on herself and I joined her in silent orgasm as I watched outside her window. But none of this was what I really wanted. I fantasized that Diana was Lisa.

Chapter 102

Diana and Cheryl

Diana and Cheryl had scheduled one of their usual lunch dates. They had met years before in the Arts Group and had become friends. They seemed to hit it off, each meeting a need in the other. At times they would provide alibis for each other if their husbands asked where they were. It gave them both opportunities to get away from home for a socially acceptable reason. "I'm just going to visit my friend," each would say. And sometimes, like today, they actually did meet for lunch. Cheryl was already seated in the back of the Kaikodo restaurant when Diana came in. The hostess showed her to Cheryl's table. Both ladies were dressed in light sundresses and showing off their mani-pedis. Cheryl's were painted dark red with a white half moon, the white representing her coke. "Let's go to the Ladies Room," Diana said after the waitress had brought their wine and taken their lunch order. A few minutes later as they returned to their table, a bus boy seemed to be picking up Cheryl's wine glass.

"Hey, don't take that!" Cheryl called out. "We're not through." The bus boy took his hand from the wine glass, hunched his shoulders, and pushed his cart towards the kitchen.

"Can you believe that? The nerve," Diana said.

"Half the time you can't get any service and then this dullard is taking our glasses and we haven't even been served yet. This place is going downhill," Cheryl replied.

"Does this wine taste funny?" Cheryl asked as she sipped.

"No, it's fine," Diana said sipping hers.

They continued to eat in silence for a while.

"Diana, I'm scared," Cheryl said, breaking the silence.

"What's going on, Cheryl?" Diana asked.

"I don't know. I find myself looking around every time I go outside my penthouse. It's like I can feel someone watching me. Then I laugh at myself thinking how paranoid I've become," Cheryl laughed nervously.

"Hey, honey, no one's watching you."

"Sometimes I think about it, you know," Cheryl said.

"What?"

"Suicide."

"Well, knock that shit off. Okay? That's crazy talk."

Reluctantly Cheryl shook her head as if to clear away those negative thoughts, "but what we say to each other has to have meaning, for both of us. It has to."

"Well it does Cheryl, that's why you've got to stop talking about it. You're scaring me. Don't you know how that would affect me?"

"No, I hadn't thought of that. I guess you're right," Cheryl said shaking her head again.

"Dam straight I'm right."

Cheryl didn't always just use coke to get high. Sometimes she'd "borrow" one of Diana's hunks. She'd use him for sex to get high, for as long as she could until he became tired of her. Then she'd have to hunt for someone new. She knew she was using them; that's when she'd started thinking of suicide.

"Cheers!" Cheryl said, trying to change the painful topic of her failed life. Diana held out her refilled glass of wine and a "clink" sounded between them. They downed a few more glasses of wine as they talked about nothing.

Chapter 103

Cheryl

In the parking lot the women bid goodbye, hugged and air kissed.

Both Diana and Cheryl were old pros at drinking and knew how much they could drink and handle on the road. Diana got in her car and drove off.

Cheryl waited for the car to disappear, then walked back inside the building and entered the Ladies Room. She took a toilet stall inside and did what was helping her cope; she snorted another line of coke.

Doc, you would be proud of me. I'm taking a deep breath. The old fart. That's what he always says. Well I'm breathing now. God, I thought as I slumped back on the toilet seat. I closed my eyes and let the drug work.

Chapter 104

Cheryl

Cheryl remembered how she had gotten started "using" years ago. She had been in one of her bitchy moods at a small art gallery opening four or five years ago.

"Hey Cheryl," someone she didn't really know that well said to her. His name was Arthur something. She couldn't remember. He nodded and backed away into the alley behind the gallery, motioning for her to follow him.

Cheryl didn't have anything else to do that night and she was already slightly smashed by the free wine. She followed him into the alley. The door was open and let some light out into the muggy night. She could see the trashcans lined up on the other side of the ally. The moonlight reflected off of puddles in the cobble-stoned street. It was slightly romantic.

Cheryl had had a fight with her husband that night, one of thousands over the last few years. They seemed to be getting worse and more frequent and always ended the same with him calling her a "whore" and she calling him a "miserly bastard." The fights were always about the same things, sex and money. They had been married a long time and had grown further apart with each passing year. They now slept in separate bedrooms and didn't touch each other except when expected to in public. Cheryl longed to be held and touched the way her husband, Eric, had treated her when they were first married.

The fight that night had been more of the same. "Where are you going?" she asked him as he was heading out the rear door toward his garaged BMW. He was tall, nearly six feet, and distinguished with a full head of white hair. His paunch was beginning to show but he was still a dashing figure of a man.

"It's none of your business, Cheryl. Now get out of my way. I'm going to be late." He looked at his silver Rolex and brushed past her as she stood in his way to the door.

She felt his arm brush her breasts as he rushed past. The electricity was still there. "Well fuck you!" she shouted at his back. "I know where you're going, to your little whore."

"Fuck you too," he flung over his shoulder.

"You bastard. You give her your precious time and money. And after all these years I've given you. You don't even give me enough to pay the mortgage or buy groceries." But she was talking to empty space.

Tears had filled her eyes. She didn't know how much more she could take. She knew he didn't like her anymore.

Chapter 105

Cheryl and Coke

Over the years each time they would fight she turned to food and drink for comfort and the pounds had piled on. Her breasts bloomed; her waist and butt expanded so she had to get all new clothes. She preferred the loose-fitting muumuus. They were stylish and hid a multitude of sins. She knew he was disgusted with the sight of her body. He'd told her so, "You're disgusting Cheryl," he'd said once years ago the last time they had been naked together. She'd just finished giving him a blowjob and letting him fuck her tits holding them tight together so his penis would feel the friction. She'd done it for him and then she felt like the whore he called her. She went to her kitchen and got a gallon of Rocky Road from her sub-zero freezer, a bottle of wine, and retired to her bed to sulk, eat, and drink her sorrows away.

She was disgusted with herself, too. As the years passed, eating her comfort foods and drinking didn't seem to help with her suffering. She seemed to be enjoying the suffering. She needed something more.

As Cheryl had walked out the alley door from the gallery that night years ago, she thought she must know the man. He had called her "Honeybuns," which was a nickname few people knew and only those who were intimate with her, used. As she stepped out into the alley she felt arms come around her from the back. She regretted not having worn a bra but she had wanted to do something different. She gasped and opened her mouth to scream. It never came. The man behind her turned her around and she recognized him. She'd had a "one night stand" with him. She'd been lonely and desperate for some attention. She had bitterly regretted it afterwards. She had felt used and knew she had used him too. Tonight she just looked at him, relieved it was someone she knew.

"Hey, you don't need to be afraid. Just trying to help you feel better," he said, letting her go. He smiled knowingly.

"You scared me," she said shaking.

"It's okay. You look like you could use a lift."

"What? Is it that obvious?" she had begun to cry.

"It's okay baby," he had said not unkindly. "I've got something that will make you feel better." He had held out a small compact mirror with a pile of white powder on it. It had all happened so fast. He had taken out a little razor blade and divided the white powder into four white lines. He had handed her a rolled up dollar, and said, "Here, snort this."

He held out the mirror to her. Cheryl looked at it confused. "It's okay, it won't hurt you. Just snort it."

"I, I don't know how," she had stammered.

"It's easy. Just put one end of the rolled dollar at the end of a line, the other in your nose and suck in through your nostril as you push the dollar up the line. Use a finger to close the other nostril." He demonstrated, snorting one of the lines.

Cheryl leaned forward and took the mirror, holding it in her left hand. She could see her face and the night sky in the mirror. She snorted a line and felt the rush immediately.

"God, I feel wonderful. Is that coke?"

"Yeah, it's pretty good stuff," Arthur replied. He took the mirror and "did" another line himself.

Cheryl took the mirror back and did the last line. She was floating. She couldn't believe anything could make her feel so good so quickly. Nothing the Doctors had given her over the years had ever done anything like this for her.

She had tried pot when some of her "friends" had suggested it. It hadn't done anything for her. She didn't smoke and didn't want to "do drugs."

Her fear and depression were instantly gone. She had felt like she was twenty-five again and had become aroused.

Taking Arthur by the hand she had said, "God, that stuff is great. I want to fuck. Let's go to your place."

Chapter 106

Cheryl

After beginning her "habit" all those years ago, it had quickly escalated to snorting as often as she could get some from Arthur, sometimes two times a week, and usually involved her giving him sex as well as money. She started to hoard what little money Eric gave her and went into her own savings to pay for the drugs. She didn't mind. She looked forward to it. She was hooked and besides the coke had taken care of her weight problem. In fact the coke took all her problems away, at least for a while, and then she had to have her next fix.

Back in the toilet stall at the restaurant, Cheryl thought, *and Dr. Albertino wants me to give all this up. Don't think so Doc.* Though part of her wanted to quit, she justified her continued use by telling herself she couldn't stop. That was why she'd gone to therapy after all.

The music in the ladies room was great and so was the air conditioning whooshing from grills overhead. Her senses seemed extremely heightened. She felt so powerful, nothing could bother her; she could do anything. There was too much alcohol mixing with the coke. She put her stash back in her purse and walked out, floating, to the outside doors.

She was distracted when she got into her car and forgot to "buckle up." She started her CD playing classical piano, feeling in control of her fear. As she drove, the bright and beautiful Hawaiian surroundings became distorted. She got goose bumps on her arms as she gripped the steering wheel more tightly.

Randy had watched her from behind the restaurant as Cheryl drove off. Cheryl wasn't just paranoid. It had been so easy to put the ground up "shrooms" in Cheryl's wine, but they had come back before he could get to Diana's. He hoped he'd gotten rid of one of Lisa's friends.

Chapter 107

Cheryl

Cheryl had lost it. The mixture of booze, shrooms, and drugs were making her hallucinate. She was also driving faster than she realized and it was evident to other drivers that her vehicle was swerving over the centerline. Twice horns jolted her back to her side of the road.

Panicked, it took her full attention to stay on the road and when her vehicle hit a slick patch of oil and water she suddenly veered into the oncoming lane of traffic. A minivan was speeding towards her honking but too close to avoid a collision. Cheryl's car sideswiped the midsection of the van, causing both vehicles to ricochet out of control.

The minivan turned 180 degrees and tipped on edge before settling down on the far side of the road. Other cars were honking and trying to avoid hitting the two cars. There were cars in both directions screeching to a stop; some had been following too closely and plowed into the ones in front causing more wrecks and pandemonium. People were screaming and all traffic had come to a halt.

Cheryl's head was stuffed into the deployed airbag. She was unconscious from the impact and all the drugs but she was still alive. Her car had never really stopped and was sliding towards the steep drop off on the Makai side of the road. The car continued to slide over 20 feet to the one spot where there wasn't any guardrail. It slipped over the side and started to tumble over and over down the side of the hill, until finally coming to a standstill, upside down on the side of the roadway below.

The vehicle now looked like a squashed sardine can. A few minutes later the car burst into a huge fireball with a loud whoosh and burned fiercely for a long time. Nobody could survive a crash like that.

Fortunately for Cheryl, without her seat belt being fastened, she had been thrown clear and was 20 yards away when the car exploded in flames.

Chapter 108

Cheryl

Cheryl woke up in bed in the Hilo Hospital. Her head hurt; she was terribly thirsty and wondered when the nurse would respond to her repeated pressing of the call button. Finally the nurse came and brought her some crushed ice and told her to sip it slowly. Cheryl had been coming in and out of a coma for the last twenty-four hours when Dr. Green came in to check her.

"Cheryl, you're one lucky lady," he said as he finished making an entry in her chart. "You're an exception to the rule. If you'd been wearing your seat belt you'd be in the morgue now. Of course it didn't hurt that you were so stoned and liquored up that your body was so limp. Not even any broken bones, just a concussion and some bruises."

"Thanks for the update. It's nice to be alive," Cheryl said with as much sarcasm as she could muster.

"It's official then. You're definitely back with us. Oh, and the police want to talk to you as soon as you're up to it."

Lisa and Diana and even Dr. Albertino came to see her during visiting hours that evening. Her husband didn't make it in, but he had had his secretary send some flowers.

"Throw those damn orchids away. Will you Lisa?"

"These? But they're so beautiful."

"They're from that thing that calls himself my husband."

"How did it happen?" Hart asked.

"I don't know. I guess I just had too much to drink and too much coke," she admitted. "Lucky me. Was anybody else hurt?"

"One guy had a broken leg. But that was it except for two totaled cars and several with serious dents," Hart said.

They talked on until the nurse chased them out at the end of visiting hours. They had taken pictures to commemorate her survival of the wreck.

Now if I could just get out of the wreck of my life, she thought as they walked out.

The blood analysis the hospital had done as a routine procedure showed very high levels of alcohol and cocaine which they had expected and unexpectedly, high levels of a psychedelic hallucinogen.

Chapter 109

Hart and Lisa Affirm Life

I had picked Lisa up to take her to visit Cheryl in the hospital. We drove back to Lisa's home in silence and she invited me in for coffee. We went to the couch in her living room and sat holding each other looking out at the ocean. White caps were just visible in the moonlight on the dark water. I embraced Lisa and we kissed. I held her silently for a few minutes, wanting to touch her and wondering if it would be okay. Lisa was shaking with anticipation, and hoped that her desire wouldn't scare Hart off.

She reached for Hart and hugged him and kissed him deeply and passionately. Cheryl's brush with death in the accident had shocked Lisa. Both wanted to affirm that they were alive.

We got up from the couch, walked to the bedroom, shedding clothes as we went. I threw back the bed covers and sank into my fresh soft white sheets. This time we didn't stop with just petting and caressing. Hart was over me bending down to kiss me, as I lay naked below him. I opened my legs and grabbed him with my hand, pulling him down towards me.

Hart entered me and I arched my pelvis to meet his thrust. My whole body was alive and I was wet and ready but there was a brief stab of pain.

He rested on his hands to take his weight off of me. I pulled him close and held him until he softened and slipped out of me. It was the first time we had had full intercourse and my first time ever and my first orgasm. We'd been so excited and hurried that neither of us had thought of birth control. Seeing some blood on the sheet between my legs, he asked if it had been too painful.

"No. Silly. The pain only lasted a second. At least you know I was a virgin," I laughed. "God, now I knew what it's all about. That's what an orgasm is. My God it was wonderful and . . ." I was at a loss for words to describe the beauty and power of my orgasm.

"I love you," he said. I started crying, tears running down my cheeks silently.

"What's wrong?" he asked.

"Nothing's wrong, silly. Everything's right. Thank you for loving me. I love you too."

"Oh," he said.

After that first night of lovemaking, he began staying at my place. He told me that he marveled at how different and better this lovemaking with me was from the sex that he had had with his two ex-wives.

Chapter 110

Hart Makes a Connection

We were having breakfast the next Sunday morning. It was a beautiful clear and not too windy day and we were out on Lisa's lanai.

"What do you say we do some shooting today?" I asked.

"That would be fun. It's a great day. We haven't been out to Laupahoehoe Point in a while.

"We talked about it at the last Club meeting."

"Okay, let me just finish cleaning up the kitchen. I don't like to leave dirty dishes in the sink." Lisa got up and picked up their plates and I brought in the cups.

"Here, let me do it."

"No. It's my kitchen. You just sit there and admire me."

"That's not hard, but it's getting that way," I said as my penis began to tent my pants."

Lisa looked, "Keep that thing inside."

"I'll put it inside you," I said getting up to grab Lisa.

"No, stop." She protested, laughing. "We'll never make it out of here." She pushed him playfully away.

It was when she opened the closet door in the kitchen that I made the connection. I saw a mop bucket and something snapped in my mind.

"What's that?"

"What?" Lisa said, thinking I was making some sexual innuendo.

"That bucket."

"Oh. That's just the mop bucket."

"That's it," I said, sitting down at the kitchen table.

"What?" Lisa said, sitting down beside him.

"That bucket reminded me. It was at the Club meeting several weeks ago. Do you remember seeing the janitor mopping the floor?"

"Vaguely."

"Think back. Can you get a picture of him in your mind?"

"No."

"Well I can. He was wearing an old black T-shirt that had something about a janitor service. It was printed in yellow letters. I didn't think anything about it at the time. Now I can't believe I didn't see it."

"See what?"

"The phone number. I don't remember what it was but the area code was wrong for Hawaii. It wasn't 808."

"But what does it mean?"

"I don't know but something isn't right. There's never been a janitor at that building when the club meets."

"No. There hasn't."

"Too many things have been happening: The FBI investigating an anthrax letter and coming here looking for Paul Stallworth, asking me if he's dangerous. Dr. Cho called and told me that Stallworth was released and was probably coming to Hilo. Cheryl's blood analysis showing high levels of psychedelic hallucinogens."

"Wait a minute Hart. You never told me that creep was released."

"I didn't want to scare you."

"I can't believe you didn't tell me. That jerk who broke into my house is back here on the Big Island? And you didn't tell me! You bastard!"

I tired to ignore Lisa's anger. "Well it looks that way. Oh, and there was that bus boy Cheryl and Diana saw at lunch the day of Cheryl's accident," Hart said, still trying to put the pieces together in his mind and avoid Lisa's anger.

"Why didn't you tell me?" Lisa asked again, more hurt than angry.

"Please forgive me Lisa. I should have told you but I just couldn't."

"Couldn't? What? You think I can't take care of that creep?" she said, her anger mounting again.

"No it's not that. I just want to take care of you. I was wrong. Please forgive me, honey. I'll never keep anything from you ever again." I was afraid I'd irretrievably damaged our relationship.

"You'd better not buster," she said, letting go of some of her anger.

It was the closest we had ever come to having a fight.

Chapter 111

Hart and the FBI

I tried to contact Special Agent Richardson at the local number the Agent had given me but was told that Agent Richardson had returned to Honolulu. That afternoon when I finally reached him on Oahu, the Agent seemed rushed.

"What's up Dr. Albertino?"

"You remember that Stallworth guy you were looking for?"

"Yeah?"

"I think I may have seen him."

"Yeah."

"So. Aren't you interested in catching him?"

"We've had some other things come up. I've been assigned to another case."

"What other case? I thought Stallworth was high on your list, terroristic threatening and all?"

"I shouldn't tell you but you'll read it in the paper tomorrow anyway. There was another anthrax letter sent and this time it was the real thing. So Stallworth isn't our top priority now."

"So you're not interested in Stallworth anymore?"

"Oh, we're still interested, and we'll send someone over to talk to him if the locals arrest him."

"That's all?" I said, trying to hide my disappointment.

"Yeah, the powder in the first letter was just baby powder. We're busting our chops on this real one."

"So what should I do? Just forget it?"

"No. No. Just call the local cops and let them know. You've got their names? I've got them around here somewhere but I'll have to look for them."

"That's okay Agent Richardson, I've got the names. I'll give them a call."

I called detective Oshiro, who took the information down over the phone.

"Okay, we'll check it out. But I wouldn't get your hopes up that we'll catch this guy. You've got to admit that seeing a janitor that you hadn't seen before isn't much to go on and you can't even give me a description. But give me a call if you see anything else."

"Yeah. Okay," I replied resignedly and hung up.

Chapter 112

Hart and Lisa Plan a Trap

That evening over a late dinner on Lisa's lanai I told her about my frustrations with Agent Richardson and Detective Oshiro.

"But they're right," I said. "Without more evidence there's not much they can do."

"What can we do?" Lisa asked. "This is just too creepy."

I was somewhat despondent. I didn't know what to do and I was supposed to be able to fix things.

"Maybe we could set a trap for him?" I said as I looked up at Lisa.

"How?"

"I don't know. I'm thinking."

"What do we know about Stallworth?" It was a rhetorical question.

"We know he was the pervert who was stalking me."

"Yes. And he must be frustrated. He can't get close to you now that your house is surrounded by the fence and you have two dogs patrolling."

We sat in silence, slowly sipping wine.

I didn't know how much to share with Lisa. I didn't want to scare her but I wanted to be honest with her.

"What?" she said, looking at me.

"Well, most stalkers follow the same patterns over and over again. So he's trying to get to you and we also know he's stalked others. He's probably been watching and following you for days or even weeks."

"You mean stalking me. Say it Hart. I'm not afraid of the word. It's happened to me before in high school, remember, I told you about it."

"Yeah okay, stalking you, and finding out your habits and who your friends are, especially female friends. He may be stalking them as a substitute for not being able to get to you.

"And remember Diana told Cheryl that someone had left some semen on her bed and stolen one of her best pair of panties?"

"What a creep. We've got to warn Cheryl and Diana. Why do men do things like that Hart?"

"Not all men do," I said somewhat defensively. "I can explain it to you but I'll give you the short version. The vast majority of them were sexually abused as children and are repeating the patterns they were taught. They almost always have very low self-esteem, which they try to cover up with bravado, but are really very insecure. They want love and attention, like we all do; only they haven't learned how to get it in socially acceptable ways. They seek it through stalking and often fantasize that the person they're watching wants them."

"Well, I never wanted him."

"I didn't say you did. You asked me why stalkers did it."

"Can you quite acting like a shrink, you doofus?"

I was silent.

"So what's your plan, Hart?"

"We know he is probably following, stalking, you and your friends and that he's been pretty good at doing it without being recognized. He's probably been able to overhear your conversations."

"The creep," Lisa said, shivering and not just from the cool ocean breeze.

"We could set a date for you and Diana to have a lunch and talk about plans. Maybe plans for a time and place where Stallworth would be able to see you? Maybe at Diana's house?"

"Use me as bait! You don't really mean that?"

"It wouldn't be dangerous. Stallworth hasn't done any 'hands on' assaults, only stalking and breaking and entering. And I'd be with you. I'd hide and capture him on camera and then we'd have the evidence the police need to take action."

"Only stalking! It still freaks me out."

"I didn't say it to Agent Richardson as I didn't want to go 'on record' but Stallworth really isn't that dangerous. He has no history of violence and has never escalated beyond stalking, breaking and entering, and masturbating."

"What about Cheryl's accident? And breaking into my home? And don't we have to tell her too?"

"We don't know that he had anything to do with the accident and Cheryl is still recuperating."

"Well what about the toxicology report that show the psychedelic hallucinogens?"

"Okay, let's think about it and then see what Diana thinks," Hart said.

"Are we going to tell the police?"

"I don't think so," I said. "They'd tell us not to do it and we'd be back to square one. This guy isn't going to quit until he's caught."

"Well I want him caught. My God, I couldn't believe you were willing to use me as bait, but the more I think about it, the more I like the idea. I mean, I am bait already. He's stalking me isn't he? Whether I want him to or not?"

"Yeah."

"Well let's make a plan and catch the bastard!" Lisa was almost shouting.

"Okay, but cool down."

"Cool down. Cool down. I can't believe you'd say that but then you aren't the one he's been stalking."

"I'm sorry. You're right. Let's do this."

Chapter 113

Randy Listens

Randy had been sitting well beyond the fence and downwind so that the dogs wouldn't get his sent. He had what was supposed to be a very good parabolic microphone he'd purchased from Radio Shack. He was able to pick up most of their conversation. *That bastard,* Randy thought, *using Lisa that way. Don't worry Lisa, I'll protect you and get you away from him. I'll come take you away.*

Chapter 114

The Plot Thickens

Lisa and I had lunch with Diana the next day and explained our plan. Lisa was surprised at how quickly Diana accepted it. I, on the other hand, knowing Diana's sexual history, wasn't surprised. I had some professional reservations about using a patient but rationalized them away by telling myself that I was only using Diana's house and wasn't really involving her, and besides, she was involved already. I could rationalize as well as any of my patients.

We made plans for Lisa and Diana to have lunch at the same restaurant where Diana and Cheryl had seen the bus boy. At the lunch they would talk about Diana planning a trip to Honolulu. Diana would ask Lisa if she would "house sit" for her as Diana's husband would be off on a trip to the mainland and she didn't want to leave the house empty while she went to Honolulu.

Lisa and Diana had their lunch the next day and Diana was pretty sure she saw the same bus boy hovering near enough to hear their conversations.

They're so dumb, Randy thought as he cleared off their table, *what, do they think I'm a retard?* He was busy making his own plans. He'd get to see his beloved Lisa. He'd take care of Hart and his camera too.

"Have a good trip," Diana said and practically pushed her husband out of the house. Lisa and Hart would have plenty of time to photograph Stallworth in the act of stalking Lisa or breaking and entering if nothing else.

Diana was to be back up and had her cell phone. She was to wait in the house next to hers. It belonged to an elderly widow, Mrs. Kanaka, who was eager to help with the plan. If things got out of control Diana was to call 911.

Chapter 115

The Trap Is Set

Lisa and I had been waiting in my car. When we saw Diana's husband leave we walked up to Diana's front door. We went in and reviewed our plans. Now all we had to do was wait for dark. I sprayed myself with "Off" and found a hiding place in some bushes outside, some distance from the bedroom window. I had my camera and flash attachment ready and set the zoom to focus a couple yards from the bedroom window. I also set the camera to shoot in bursts of three, one-second apart with each push of the shutter button.

Lisa turned off all the lights in the house except for the bedroom and positioned herself so that she was silhouetted in the light. She even took her blouse and bra off. That hadn't been part of the plan. But she was so pissed. She was determined to give the creep a good show that would startle him long enough so that Hart could shoot him stalking her.

Chapter 116

Randy Freezes

I had my own plans. I had a baseball bat. I'd find the Doc and knock him out and then I'd be able to see my beloved. I crept silently around the back of the house, and finding the Doc squatting in some bushes, I walked silently up to his hiding place with the bat held high, ready to strike. I had to get just a few steps closer. When I crossed past the open bedroom window, my breath was sucked out of me when I saw Lisa.

She's so beautiful, I thought as I looked at Lisa through the open window. I froze, staring at her naked breasts. It had been so long since I had last seen them. I swung the bat. I had intended to hit Hart on the head but missed and hit his left forearm. I didn't hear Hart's scream of pain. I walked towards the window and my beloved, unzipped my pants in a frenzy; rushed closer toward the window and pulled out my stiff dick. My plan to find Hart and take care of him first was forgotten.

There was a bright flash from the camera. I turned; there was another flash. I ran and there was a third flash.

In the first flash, Randy had been facing the open lighted window, his body only partially blocking the view of one of Lisa's breasts. In the second he had turned to face the camera with his dick in his hand. The third flash caught him running away. All the shots were taken from ground level.

"Call the cops," I shouted to Diana.

"Did you get him?" Lisa shouted, coming to the window. In the excitement she had not bothered to cover herself. Hart couldn't fault Stallworth for freezing.

"Yeah, I got him."

"You're hurt. He hit you. We'll get you, you crazy sick pervert!" she shouted in rage at the empty black night.

"No, I'm alright," I winched in sudden pain as I tried to use my left arm to push myself up off the ground. I'd had to take the shots holding the camera with just my right hand. I'd been lucky to get the shots I had.

"Diana, come help me. Hart's hurt."

Chapter 117

After

We all gathered in Diana's house to wait for the police. Lisa had gotten dressed. While we were waiting I used Diana's computer to print up the three pictures. I cradled my left arm against my body.

"Here Doc. Take these," Diana said, handing me some pain pills and a glass of water.

"I think I need a drink," Lisa said, as she poured a shot of Jim Beam.

"Me too," said Mrs. Kanaka.

Detectives Oshiro and Barton were on duty that night and they showed up about twenty minutes later.

"Okay, Dr. Albertino," Oshiro said. "This is all the evidence we need and these are good clear pictures."

The detectives seemed to spend much more time looking at the picture that showed Lisa's breast than the others.

"Diana, if you and Mrs. Kanaka come down to the station we can get your statements written up. Lisa, you'd better take Dr. Albertino to the ER to have that arm looked at. We'll get your statements later."

They were all pleased to go, especially Mrs. Kanaka. This was the most excitement she'd had in years.

"Did you see him?" she asked of no one in particular. "I don't think I've ever seen a dick that size."

Lisa, Hart, and Diana laughed, the tension draining away but we were all still buzzed by the adrenalin rush from the events of the evening.

Chapter 118

Hart Recuperates

After the others had left, Lisa and I hugged and kissed and I wanted to make love to her right there, yet cooler heads had prevailed. Lisa drove Hart to the Hilo ER.

After Hart was checked out of the ER, I drove carefully home. That night was a long quiet one in my house. I held Hart's hand and watched him sleep.

Chapter 119

Allusive Randy

At last the craziness was over, at least for several years, Lisa hoped. She felt relieved and happier than she could ever remember.

After a few days of slow and painful recovery, Hart seemed to be able to move and eat somewhat normally. The nights, and for that matter the mornings and afternoons, were filled with lovemaking as often as we could. It was somewhat awkward with Hart's arm in a cast, yet we managed.

It had been two days before Hart got to the police station to give his statement. Lisa had given her statement the day before.

"You haven't caught him yet?" I asked Officer Oshiro.

"No. Even with the photos you took. As you said he's pretty good at changing his appearance. But we'll get him."

"Any other developments?" I asked.

"We found the bat he used on you. Fortunately it was a metal one and he left a good set of prints. Turns out he's a guy named Randy Parson, Jr."

"But I saw him at the State Hospital and he had identification as Paul Stallworth."

"He was using Stallworth's name, SSN, and birth date, but the guy Stallworth is a mental patient in the Cleveland State Hospital."

"You're sure?" I asked, realizing how dumb the question sounded as soon as I asked it.

"Yeah," Oshiro chuckled. "He had us all fooled. Randy Parson was a patient there also and escaped several years ago."

"Is there anything more I can do to help?"

"No, Dr. Albertino. You've done enough and we don't want you getting hurt again. You should have told us what you were doing, you know," Oshiro said in a scolding voice.

"Yeah. Right. Where are you looking now?"

"We've got a BOLO (be on look out) out on him and, of course, his photo."

"How about staking out Ms. Havenhurst's house? There's only one way anyone can get there and that is by the road in front of her place. The land falls off too steeply for anyone to come up from behind."

"We've been doing that each night but so far no luck."

"We know he's obsessed with her. He's got to be trying to get to her," I said.

Chapter 120

The Shutter Clicks

The days dragged on and each night Lisa and I could see the unmarked car and the officers watching her house.

"He's certainly not stupid," I said in exasperation. "If we can spot the police I'm sure this Randy Parson guy can, too."

"What?" Lisa said. "What was the name?"

"Randy Parson."

"Hart you bastard!" Lisa hissed.

"Why are you getting so upset?"

"You never told me his name. That's the same guy who was stalking me in high school. I can't believe he's followed me here. Why didn't you tell me his name?"

"You never asked," I replied. "You'd told me about some boy stalking you back then but you never told me his name."

Lisa fumed in silence for a few minutes.

"How was I supposed to know it was the same guy? And I just found out myself. Anyway, it is the same guy and we have to deal with it."

Lisa fumed some more, glaring at Hart, though she was really mad at Randy coming back into her life.

"Well, he is really good at disguise," Lisa replied. "He didn't look at all like the kid I knew back then; even when I saw him in court this last time in Hilo I didn't recognize him."

"Maybe if I watch with the police and take my camera, I can spot something they might not notice," I said.

"You think they'll let you?"

"Won't hurt to ask."

That night Hart walked up to the police car, camera in hand. Fortunately, Officer Oshiro was alone on the stakeout that night.

"Do you mind if I sit with you?"

"I shouldn't let you, but hop in. I could use the company."

At my own expense I had had a light pole installed on the road right outside Lisa's house. I had had to pull some strings and ask for some favors to get it in the same day.

I sat with Officer Oshiro that night and several more nights. Anyone who walked or rode by in any kind of vehicle or bike, I would take their picture when they were in the bright light from the special pole. There was never anyone Oshiro or I recognized or who looked out of place.

After the fourth night of not seeing anyone suspicious, I was getting frustrated. During the day I had printed up the pictures I'd taken the last four nights. On each night there had been a person peddling by on a bike. But it was never the same person. That in itself struck me as strange.

Lisa and I were studying the pictures laid out on her dining room table.

"Why would a different person be peddling by each night?" Lisa asked.

I studied the pictures some more, looking closely at the people's faces. I was about to quit for the day when I noticed the yellow ribbon decal on the fender in one of the pictures.

"Lisa. Look at this."

"What?" Lisa asked, looking at the picture.

"See the yellow ribbon decal," I said as I rapidly placed the pictures of the other bike-riders side-by-side on the table.

"That's it!" I exclaimed excitedly. "Look at the bike in each picture."

"They're all the same with the yellow ribbon decals."

"Yeah. The person is different but the bike is the same one. How could I have missed it?"

The next night at Hart's request, Officer Oshiro brought an extra officer with him and made sure that Hart understood that he would have to stay in the car. Based on Hart's suspicion of the same bike with different people, they planned to stop the bike whoever was on it.

At about the same time as on previous nights, the bike was peddled down the road and into the light.

Randy had kept hoping that eventually they would get tired of staking out Lisa's house. This night he was surprised when the policeman got out and told him to stop. He tried to peddle away but there was another cop on the road in front of him. He skidded to a stop and tried to run into the trees on the Mauka side of the road. After a brief chase, Officer Oshiro tackled him and quickly had him in handcuffs. Randy was crying incoherently about how he had to save Lisa.

It wasn't until the police had him back in a cell and had washed off all of his theatrical make up, that they clearly recognized him as the man who had been impersonating Paul Stallworth for so long.

When I heard the news, I couldn't wait to tell Lisa. I had really been wrong in my estimate of Randy's dangerousness. It could have been much worse. Both Lisa and I felt that Paul or Randy wouldn't be able to bother us again for a long time. Randy didn't have to act crazy this time because he already was, and in addition to the assault and stalking charges, he was still wanted in Ohio for his escape.

Chapter 121

Hart and Lisa

It was another wonderful Sunday morning. This time after our post-coital bliss, I didn't pick up the paper. I got out of the bed and walked over to Lisa's side, got down on my knees and took her hand. I glanced again at her beautiful breasts and then locked my eyes with hers.

"You'd better look up here buster," Lisa said playfully.

"Lisa, will you marry me?"

Tears were again flowing down Lisa's cheeks. She took my hand to her lips and kissed it. "Of course I will. You think I'd let you go. Now get in here," she said, opening her arms to me.

But first I reached under the bed where I had placed the tiny box containing the ring. I opened it and held it out to Lisa.

Lisa stared wide-eyed. Nestled deep in the purple velvet rested the most beautiful engagement ring she had ever seen.

"It was my great grandmother's," I said. "It's been passed down since then by the women in the family, and since there weren't any more girls, it came to me."

Lisa was speechless.

"It's not a very big diamond, just a little over a half karat."

"The gold filigree is stunning. I've never seen anything like it," Lisa said as I slipped the ring on her left hand ring finger. It was a perfect fit.

In the days and nights after I had proposed to Lisa, she couldn't get enough of me and often alternated between tears and laughter. By now, being a sagacious psychologist, I knew, without asking, that the tears were from joy.

The wedding took place two months later. We were married with a few of our friends as guests. Diana and Cheryl served as the bridesmaids and both cried throughout the ceremony, tears of joy for Hart. Cheryl had had to get special permission from the court to let her leave her residential drug treatment. *Everyone wants to be loved and to live happily every after*, Hart thought.

I was on good enough terms with Alison that we decide to invite her to the wedding. I had told Lisa all about my past with Alison and Peggy Sue. I was determined to have a close and honest relationship with Lisa.

Although now in the active stage of AIDS, Alison accepted the invitation. She was truly happy for Hart and Lisa, and wished that she had been the one to make him happy. She knew that Hart was "clean" as she had insisted on blood tests as part of the divorce, only she'd had her results falsified, as she didn't want Hart to know.

Alison came to the wedding in a cream colored dress trimmed in gold and was with another woman. They hugged the bride and groom and wished them well. Alison made them a gift of a small apartment in Manhattan so that Lisa would have a place to stay in New York for the opening, that Alison was sure was going to happen, of Lisa's photographic exhibits.

Lisa invited Sally Rafael, her friend from high school, to be her head bridesmaid. Sally gladly accepted and was excited at the prospect of seeing her old friend again.

Hart invited Dr. Cho and his family and asked Dr. Cho to be his best man, which Dr. Cho delightedly accepted. It would be a good reunion.

Lisa and I had also decided to ask Dr. Longfellow, Marge now. Dr. Longfellow and her husband were happy to attend. It would be like a second honeymoon in Hawai'i for them. They'd been married 39 years and Hart wanted to know the secret of their success. Marge had told him that she and her husband had both actively sought to keep their relationship fresh and exciting. They continued to seek out new intellectual pursuits and to share them. Most of all they still liked each other's company and didn't take each other for granted. Dr. Longfellow and her husband practiced the art of love, making dates and fantasizing together, acting out in their minds, and various areas of their house, fantasies of outrageous sex, so they didn't have to act it out in real life. They had fun playing like kids.

The wedding was in Queen Lili'uokalani Park and Hart looked very striking in his rented tux. Lisa was beautiful in her white wedding gown, which was satin trimmed with off-white seashells. Her pink garter belt was high on her thigh. The many pleats in the fabric flowed from her narrow waist over her curvaceous hips. She looked like a bride from Vogue.

"You're beautiful Lisa," I whispered. I wondered if, and hoped, that this marriage would last longer than my prior two. I knew the research statistics; after the first marriage each subsequent one had less and less chance of lasting.

This marriage seemed to be different, or so I hoped. I felt more committed this time and I certainly knew Lisa in depth and our relationship was based in love, not just sex.

"I wish my mother could have been here for this," Lisa whispered to me as we stood waiting for the ceremony to start. "I can't believe all this, Hart, it's like a storybook and we're the story."

It was almost too much to believe; it was like they were two new people. Lisa certainly wasn't the shy withdrawn young woman who had moved to the Big Island years before. Hart seemed more alive and appeared 10 years younger. He wasn't the harried psychologist. He was a man in love with a wonderful woman. Each considered the other to be the most important part of their lives.

Chapter 122

The Wedding

We had arranged for an ecumenical minister to do the ceremony. He was slender and appeared very serious and somber in his black robes, holding the Bible with both hands as he stood in front of Hart and Lisa.

The bridal music was being played by two violinists and a flautist all dressed in brilliant white, tuxes on the men and a full-length gown on the seated woman. The music was ethereal and floated over the small gathering. They played from memory without the need for sheet music. The bows moved in unison on the strings of the violins and the woman pursed her lips as she blew and moved her elegant fingers over the keys of the flute. When the music stopped, the minister started.

"Dearly beloved . . ." and soon it was over. We exchanged rings and I lifted her veil and kissed my bride for the first time. The kiss was long and the crowd began to cheer and clap.

Lisa whispered in my ear, "I'm pregnant Hart."

I was speechless. No one in the crowd had heard or knew. It was our secret. I was finally going to have the child I had always wanted. Lisa took my hand, and with hers on top of mine, she briefly placed it on her abdomen and rubbed for a second.

"God, I love you Lisa."

"Me too," she whispered back.

The reception, held at the Hilo Hawaiian Hotel, was a joyous event and Lisa and I couldn't wait to get off on our honeymoon on Maui.

Chapter 123

Return to Hilo

At the end of the formal two-week honeymoon, both Lisa and I realized we were more than ready to get back home to Hilo to start our new life together.

In the evening, on the last night of the honeymoon, we had a sumptuous room-service dinner out on our lanai and watched the sun settle into the sea. Just another glorious day's end in paradise, golden reddish clouds in the distance, a few white-capped waves, and the sound of the surf breaking gently on the sandy shore.

We returned to Hilo; I sold my house and moved into Lisa's ocean-view home. We were making a home for our family. I so wanted to believe in happy endings. Lisa was busy taking care of herself, the baby to be, and me.

I started seeing patients again because I loved doing therapy; helping others. I had chosen clinical psychology after I got out of the military. I knew it was a sedentary profession and came to understand the loneliness. It was my way of healing myself and I wanted to spend the rest of my life helping others. Most of the time I did short term therapy, not necessarily because I wanted to, but because it turned out that way.

For the first twenty plus several years of my practice, I had no problems letting go of other people's problems and suffering at the end of my day. However, as the years wore on I found myself more and more dragged down emotionally by their misery. The nature of the business of the "talking cure" seemed mechanical at times, dissecting the hour into 45 to 50 minute segments and listening to other people's problems, one after another all day, day after day, sometimes helping but often feeling powerless. Still, it was the source of my life and being, to share their pain, to connect with them in an intimacy that most people don't experience. I would offer some hope, guidance and suggestions of ways they may learn to cope more effectively and to enjoy their lives more fully.

Chapter 124

Diana

It was Diana's first therapy session since Cheryl's accident. She wasn't dressed as provocatively as she usually was.

"I don't know what happened, Doc. Since I saw Cheryl in the hospital, I just haven't been the same."

"What do you mean?" I asked.

"I haven't sucked a single cock. I don't know what happened. I just feel so empty."

I waited silently.

"I had a talk with my husband. Don't worry, I didn't 'confess all.' I told him it wasn't working and that I wanted a divorce."

"How did he take that?"

"He started to cry, the poor guy. I told him it wasn't his fault. 'It was me.' I couldn't go on hurting him even if he didn't know it. He would have found out sometime. But I didn't stop for him. You should be proud of me Doc, I did it for me."

"Are you sure, Diana?"

"Yeah, I'm sure. It's crazy I know. I have another reason now though. My last checkup I showed positive for HIV. I'm not a mean person and I don't want to pass that along."

"I'm so sorry for your HIV status. But if that is motivation for you to change, use it. And there are now more effective treatments. And no, it's not crazy. It's the first healthy step you've taken since I've known you. I am proud of you."

"Yeah it is. Thanks to you, Doc."

"Oh, it wasn't me Diana. You're the one who made the decision and you're the one who has to live your life."

"I couldn't have done it without your help, Doc."

"Give yourself credit Diana. It's you, not me." I remembered Dr. Longfellow saying the same thing to me all those years ago. "All I did was make some suggestions."

"Okay. I won't fight with you about it, but thanks again."

"You're welcome Diana. What are you going to do now?"

"I've talked to an attorney. Warren and I are being reasonable. He doesn't want the divorce. He wants to try marriage counseling."

"What about that?"

"Like I said, it's too late for me. I never really loved Warren; I was just using him. Since we don't have any children and aren't fighting anything, we can probably be divorced in six months."

"Then what will you do?"

"Oh, you don't need to remind me. I know I'm not out of the woods. I want to see you at least weekly and I'm starting to do some of those coping strategies you kept after me to try."

"Wow. You are making progress."

"Do you think there's hope for me Doc?"

"Yes I do Diana."

Chapter 125

Cheryl

After the accident and near-death experience when Cheryl got out of the hospital she went to the dug court. As an alternative to prison she was given the choice of intensive drug therapy and probation for five years or jail. Cheryl had gone from the court directly to a residential drug rehab program. She was now out on a special pass for a treatment session with me to facilitate her return to intensive outpatient treatment.

"How's it going?" I asked.

"Like shit," Cheryl replied.

"That bad?"

"Not really, Doc. They keep me busy with developing my interests in photography, taking computer classes and exercise. All the things you wanted me to do."

"Good."

"Yeah, I'm so busy with all the activities and twice-daily group therapy sessions, that I hardly notice the urges."

"Really?"

"No. I'm through lying, to you and to myself. I still get the urge to use, and it would be easy to get some, but I don't."

"What's the difference, Cheryl?"

"I don't really know, Doc. I guess I reached what they call bottom. I just said 'enough,' I'm not going to go on living this way. I'd thought of suicide you know."

"I know."

"How'd you know? I never told you."

"I am a shrink, Cheryl."

"Like I could forget that. Where do we go from here, Doc?"

"You're due to be released from residential treatment in a few weeks, and then we will do intensive outpatient treatment for a few weeks, you'll attend NA meetings, and continue all the things you're learning in treatment now."

"It's almost like I don't want to leave the residential program. They even have me leading some of the groups for the newbies. It feels great."

"That's normal. You can continue doing all those things and you won't have to leave that phase of treatment until you're ready."

"But I'm scared, Doc. What if I slip?"

"It's good you're scared. I'd think you were lying to me again if you said you weren't. If you slip, you'll get back on the wagon. You've got lots of help now."

"I'm still scared."

"That's why you have the complete structure of all of your time. Have you found anything to really fill the void, to give your life meaning?"

"Yeah, I think I have. Three things. First, I'm really enjoying helping some of the new members. I may even go back to school and get my drug-counseling certificate. Two, I'm finding I really have a passion and some talent for digital photography."

"What's the third one Cheryl?"

"I'm kind of embarrassed. But you'll be proud to know I even gave myself an orgasm," Cheryl said smiling. "I'm learning how to love myself."

"Congratulations."

"Thanks, Doc."

"Thank you, Cheryl, for letting me be a part of your life and thank you for doing the hard work of being responsible and making changes in your life. It's the intense bond in psychotherapy that builds a base for change that is deeper than what you may have with anyone else. The stuff from your past will keep coming up to haunt you but now you have tools to deal with it."

"Oh, I forgot there's a fourth thing. I'm really gaining a passion for running. I get what they mean by a 'runner's high.' I may even try for a marathon."

"Great. But there is one huge area we haven't finished yet."

"I know. Eric sent me the divorce papers. I just got them a few days ago. Love wars," she laughed.

"How do you feel about that? Love wars," I went on not waiting for her to answer, "aren't ever over, some end in an uneasy truce. Some wars end with a peace offering and some in complete victory. Love wars are nothing at all compared to the drug use you have to keep fighting."

"It was about time. I should have done it a long time ago. I think we'll both be better off divorced. My attorney will make sure I get a fair deal."

"I think you're going to make it Cheryl."

"Yeah, me too, Doc."

Chapter 126

Lisa and Hart

I loved to caress Lisa's belly, as she grew bigger. Her breasts got fuller and when they hurt she would ask me to massage them. Unlike many women, Lisa wasn't ashamed of her growing size and rather reveled in the knowledge that she was carrying life, a child for her and me.

In the evenings I would rub oil on her belly and legs. Often when I kissed her belly she opened her legs wider giving me more access, holding my head as I licked her sex. Soon her clit would be on fire and it wouldn't take her long to climax.

The pregnancy seemed to give her a voracious sexual appetite and I was happy to oblige her. I was in heaven. My other wives had enjoyed sex, but it was just sex, not love. Lisa really enjoyed sex and love and it gave me immense satisfaction to be able to give pleasure and love to Lisa. I had found love for the first time.

That had really been all Randy had been after in his own distorted way. In fact, that is what Cheryl, Diana, and even Alison and Sue had also wanted.

Lisa was becoming as prolific in her painting and photography as she was in her sexual needs. It seemed like she had an unlimited source of creative juices. She certainly got wet enough when she climaxed and that seemed to carry over to her photography. We made plans to eventually open our own gallery.

Lisa and I lived from day to glorious day, happy to be alive and together and waited for the birth of our baby. We played the baby name game, "Lisa Joy" if it were a girl. We'd call her Joy. That was Lisa's favorite aunt's name. If it were a boy we couldn't decide. I didn't want a Hart, Jr. I thought of one of my old ancestors from Italy, Alberto. "Alberto Albertino." That sounded okay. We'd call him Al. Lisa had kept her maiden name for her artwork but for their friends she was happily Lisa Albertino.

Some days I took long walks alone in the park. Our days had become predictable. *Was this the beginning of the end? The end comes when we quit learning new things about each other.* The child was one new thing. *Was I unconsciously beginning to itch? Was it the start of an inevitable decline? Lisa didn't really need me anymore.* I needed to be needed. I'd "saved" Lisa from Randy and freed her from her sexual fears. Now what would I do? *Crazy thoughts*, I told myself and turned to go home to Lisa.

The reality was always different than the fantasy. Most people didn't live happily ever after; one could only try. *I have met the enemy and he is me,* I thought sadly, then smiled as I saw Lisa waving in the distance, waiting for me.

Thank God, I've gotten all that kinky sex behind me. It just doesn't interest me anymore. I'm determined to talk to Lisa about my concerns; I truly love her so much, I thought as I walked back to receive a warm hug of greeting from my bride, my wife, my partner.

Once we face our fears, we defeat them and then when we think of our friends we realize we're not all alone in the dark, I thought as I hurried to hug Lisa. I remembered what Dr. Longfellow had told me so long ago, "We all have choices to make; to choose to do something that others will label as heroic, or do nothing or run away and be judged a coward. But the really important decision, the decision that really takes courage, is to love or not to love, and to love means to share, all of yourself with the one you love and hope they love you back."

The End

Look for more Psychosexual Thrillers from Dr. Pollard in the future.